Praise for *I Piped, That She Might Dance*

Revealing, sensitively written and eminently readable. It is an imagined autobiography of Angus MacKay, piper to Queen Victoria, but it is well-informed and thoroughly researched and convincing. Besides piping, it provides insights into the social life of the time, from croft to palace, as well as into the treatment of mental illness. Iain MacDonald is to be warmly congratulated.

John Purser, author of *Scotland's Music*, researcher at Sabhal Mòr Ostaig

A sympathetic view of a driven and complex man ... Above all, a tale told with verve, flair, a fine eye for detail, and a sensitive depiction of the ultimate tragedy of the central character.

James Beaton, former librarian at the National Piping Centre

I loved this book ... It empathetically captures the triumphs and tribulations of MacKay's life – from Raasay croft, via Balmoral and Buckingham Palace, and ultimately to the asylum. It is true to the facts, deeply researched and easy to read. Victorian life is described with pathos, humour and colour. A deservedly positive light is shone on MacKay's lasting contribution to the music of the Highland Bagpipe, especially the classical Pìobaireachd. Iain MacDonald is to be congratulated. MacKay might have written this himself.

Jack Taylor, former president of the Pìobaireachd Society

The fascinating story of a controversial, flawed, but musically talented Scottish Gael who put the notes of the Highland bagpipe on the page.

Ellen Beard, editor of *100 Òran le Rob Donn MacAoidh*

MacDonald has fleshed out the narrative of arguably the most interesting man in piping history, and certainly the most influential piper to date.

Nick Hudson, *pipes|drums*

I Piped, That She Might Dance

IAIN MACDONALD

Contents

Foreword

Rescuing Angus Mackay

This narrative by my good friend, Iain MacDonald, provides an account of the life of an early nineteenth-century Hebridean who has long deserved to be brought to our attention. Enough has always been known about Angus MacKay (1812-1859) to allow his name to be quoted in the relevant cultural and historical contexts, but rarely has this gone beyond the name, and the name of his family. The inquisitive mind – and especially in our world of Highland piping – wishes to know more about this figure; however, even the most prominent research on him has attacked, rather than celebrated, Angus MacKay's reputation. This has appealed to a media-driven response which has invited mockery of what was being represented as the narrow and complacent cultural bastion of Highland piping. Our author deserves the heartfelt thanks of the piping community for rescuing Angus MacKay by means of this scrupulously researched and insightful reconstruction of an "autobiography," one that proves beyond doubt the value of historical fiction. The life of this prodigy is carefully charted and followed to its tragic outcome, thereby sparing Angus MacKay from what seemed to be the condescension of history.

The music of the MacKay family lies at the heart of Scotland's piping tradition. The circumstances of this world are taken for granted and, for the most part, only minimally understood. Standard accounts dedicated to exploring Highland history generally open with a disclaimer pleading a lack of source materials, or are not overly-inclined to try and further search them out. As a piper interested in piping history, my move to Sabhal Mòr Ostaig on Skye in 2007 brought me near to the home of the MacKays on the adjacent Raasay, an island I had never before visited. Here was the chance to re-engage with the MacKays of Raasay, which I duly did together with my colleague, Dr. Decker Forrest. We believed that we could fill out a bare reference to the family's origins in the annals of piping with what might still be to hand in the traditions and landscape of the island.

The old roofless church of Kilmoluaig on Raasay has a stone and memorial plaque in the Mackay family's burial lair. Where better to begin delving into MacKay history? A brief text in both Gaelic and English records a key moment in the received history of the Great Highland Bagpipe and its music. The English text reads:

This plaque commemorates John Mackay of Raasay (1767-1848), the last great piper to have had lessons from the MacCrimmons. He was the best player, composer and teacher of his day, and through his expert pupils – John Bàn Mackenzie, Angus Macpherson, Donald Cameron and his own four sons – the playing of the great music was carried forward faithfully to all the top pipers of the present time.

There is a certain modesty in this account of John, father of Angus MacKay, that prompts the reader to sense something of the oral tradition sustained through the centuries. According to the islanders, John Mackay's home was at *Oighre* or Eyre, at the south end of Raasay, and this was where he raised a family of nine children, of whom his four sons – Donald, Roderick, Angus, and John – became notable pipers. Descendants of the MacKays in Raasay – and especially Rebecca MacKay of Osgaig and her husband – have generously guided us to the standing remains of *Tobht' Taigh a' Phìobaire* or The Piper's House;

the word *tobhta* telling us that the house is now roofless and uninhabited. A savage clearance of Raasay began after 1846 when the long-standing proprietors, the MacLeods of Raasay, sold the island and emigrated to Australia. "Everything went with the people," the tradition bearers would say, but it is our good fortune that the MacKays and the Raasay Heritage Trust are still able to place before us so much of Hebridean memory and identity.

Iain's research and interpretation adds further stones to the cairn commemorating this remarkable family and young Angus. He reimagines the environment of music and song in The Piper's House where John MacKay and his wife, Margaret MacLean – *Mairearad nighean Aonghais* – nourished a large family and taught their four sons how to pipe. He explores Angus's mind in a worthy literary exercise, and builds his responses to his contemporary world of dramatic change, from horse-power and sail to steamships and railways; and he finally portrays the piper himself as harbinger of change, moving from an oral tradition to his creation of staff notation on the printed page.

This book stands also as a record of Iain's own intense dedication to and passion for his subject. Meeting first in the National Piping Centre in 2008, I was struck by the quiet calm and modesty of a highly important contributor to our cultural world. Reflecting on this after some years in the *Gàidhealtachd*, I am attributing a comment to him which might recall his South Uist forebears if asked what was his business: *O uèill, tha mi greis air ceòl is canntaireachd.* A masterly understatement, of course, which cannot be so neatly rendered in English without a prior knowledge of the word *Canntaireachd*: Oh well, I've been a while at music and chanting!

Professor Hugh Cheape
Sabhal Mòr Ostaig
Oilthigh na Gàidhealtachd agus nan Eilean
An Lùnastal 2019

Author's Note

My introduction to Angus MacKay came when I was a spirited young piper at summer camp in Saskatchewan. One of the sessions offered was The History of Piping, which unsurprisingly was a summary of the current knowledge and understanding of the history of Highland bagpipes and famous pipers. Most of this would have been material taken from Army School of Piping courses, old volumes of *Piping Times*, and introductions from music collections, such as *The Kilberry Book of Cèol Mòr*.

Angus MacKay was referred to as the great, early genius of piping, and most notable as the first piper to the sovereign in Britain. We in the class were told how he became insane, and then died by drowning while trying to escape from an asylum. This thumbnail sketch of a life is all I knew until the mid-1970s, when I purchased a reprint of MacKay's *A Collection of Ancient Pìobireachd or Highland Pipe Music*. Reading and playing the music transcribed by Angus, I began to get a sense of the immense knowledge represented by this collection.

In the late 1970s, I was living in Paisley and taking piping lessons from the great Pipe Major Donald MacLeod. Donald often commented on the genius of Angus MacKay and the authority of his manuscripts, and it was about this time that *The MacCrimmon Legend: The Madness of Angus MacKay* was published by Alistair Campsie. Campsie was a journalist, an author, and a piper. He did a thorough examination of all the original materials pertaining to Angus MacKay, and concluded that MacKay was a sinner whose drinking and syphilis made him insane, and that both the music he wrote and the MacCrimmon history he celebrated were the products of a diseased mind. Campsie claimed this had put pipers on the wrong path for generations. Of course, this book was loved by the press. There were threats of lawsuits and many denounced Campsie for his views. I borrowed the book from the Paisley Public Library, and although the research appeared to be legitimate, the conclusions did not. The material was presented in an aggressive, almost spiteful tone. Many pipers dismissed his work on that basis alone.

Donald MacLeod had what he called a "wee piping room" in his house. In the room was a small bookshelf that held a variety of piping objects: old chanters, reed-making tools, collections of music, reeds, and other bits and pieces. When there was a lull in the chat, or while waiting for Donald to set up a cassette tape, I would sometimes inquire about the objects. One of the items was the broken bottom of a very old practice chanter. Donald told me that it was given to him by a descendant of Angus MacKay. The donor had thought that Donald, being a piper of the same order as Angus, should have the relic. We discussed the chanter and Angus MacKay; each of us tried the chanter in our hands and felt the worn grooves of the finger holes.

Donald MacLeod died suddenly in June 1982, and the following summer I returned to Cardonald to visit Mrs. MacLeod. She asked me to accompany her to the piping room as she had questions about some of Donald's things. One of them was the chanter. I told her the story of it as Donald told me, and she was amazed. Her first inclination had been to throw it away because it was just a broken old bit, but she hadn't, sure Donald must have kept it for a reason. She asked me to take the chanter and look after it, both as a keepsake of Donald, and also because I was the only one who knew the story behind it. I had the chanter for a long time. Every now and again I would take it out and finger tunes on it. I considered trying to repair it, but that never seemed quite right.

Years later, at Glasgow's Piping Live! festival in 2008, I attended a lecture by Hugh Cheape on the contributions of the MacKay family to piping. Professor Cheape had previously made a similar presentation at the Piobaireachd Society conference and was in the midst of preparing articles for publication about the house of John MacKay of Raasay. Professor Cheape's very real, human, and empathetic view of Angus MacKay's life and legacy is what started me on the journey to give Angus a voice.

I approached Professor Cheape after the lecture, disclosing that I had in my possession what was thought to be Angus MacKay's practice chanter. After Hugh's jaw was retrieved from the floor, we hatched a plan which returned the chanter to Scotland the following summer. I donated it to The National Museum of Scotland, in memory of Donald and Winnie MacLeod.

I tried several times to write about Angus MacKay, and what I hoped to achieve was to tell his story in a way that was respectful to the known facts, but also more real and interesting than much of what has been written about him. Anyone who has struggled with mental illness, or who has experienced close friends or family dealing with it, understands the toll it can have on all aspects of life. They will also understand that such illness does not diminish the value of the person. The dehumanizing descriptions of mental illness – and the casual dismissal of people with mental illness – is an unfortunate feature of much of the literature concerning Angus MacKay. What I felt strongly at Professor Cheape's lecture in the basement of The National Piping Centre was this: while Angus MacKay's struggles with mental illness must have been tragic for him and his family, they should not frame our view of his life, or diminish the value of his contributions to the music.

This novel is an attempt to let Angus MacKay tell his own story, focusing on the extraordinary life experiences and abilities of an icon who has undoubtedly been crucial to shaping the piping world as we know it today.

Iain MacDonald

A piobrachd will be understood by those to whom "The Battle of Prague," and similar pieces of that class of music, are familiar. It opens with a certain measure called the ùrlar, subject, or ground work of the piece, and by variations of this air, sometimes extending to great length, the piece is completed.

James Logan, The Scottish Gael, Volume II, 1831

Finally, he will rejoice if this volume is esteemed a suitable though humble contribution to the yet scanty stock of Highland literature ...

Angus MacKay, A Collection of Ancient Piobireachd, 1838

Deuchainn Ghleus

The Piper's House

Even now I see it when I close my eyes, that clear Hebridean sky, vast and flooded with morning light, no sound of screaming or fighting or slamming doors, just the sea breeze and the waves lapping at the Raasay shoreline.

A new day dawning at my father's house in Eyre.

Of course, the sun wasn't always shining; that's my mind playing tricks. Many a day would begin with me and my siblings out feeding the animals in the sleet and the rain, milking the cows with frozen fingers, arguing for the right to tend the fire, fixing breakfast with the wind whipping in where it could. Never will I forget that smell of porridge, peat, and cattle, nor the chill of the winter months in our bones. But aye, when I cast my thoughts back, to that other lifetime, that clear morning sky is always what first appears to me.

All of that is a long way from here, this plain cell in which I'm kept. A yellow light is growing around the edge of the shutters, heralding my own day, staving off the gloom just enough for me to write. I believe it's October. This must be one of my "lucid" moments.

In an hour or so a uniform will enter, an attendant. He'll open the shutters if I've not yet opened them; the younger attendant or the old one, I don't know. After all this time I have seen no established order. The younger one is mouse-like, twitchy, with sallow skin that is almost translucent. I think sometimes he needs free of this place more than I do. Whenever he comes in, he eyes me like I'm something wild, and if I move a muscle in his presence – even if just to yawn – he shrieks out for one of the guards in the corridor to come and pin me to the floorboards. The older one, him I remember from the last time I was here. He is a walking piece of driftwood, warped and twisted by the world. Gray hangs over him – everything about him lacks color – with eyes sunk so deep they are almost invisible. He acts as though my cell is devoid of all other life, paying more attention to the state of the floor and the furniture than to the human being for which it is all intended. I get the impression he will continue to tend this place long after I'm gone. Chan eil dragh orm.

Last week Dr. Hood informed me that this stay has now stretched for over a year. When he told me this I was not affected. It's strange, but nowadays it can take weeks and months before I'm able to properly react to what's around me, before I can absorb the meaning of things. Before I know what is a dream. I do not sleep, each day blends into the next – and the boredom! the pounding, relentless, maddening boredom! – all of it means that sometimes I can be disoriented, sometimes I find myself off my guard. I saw little reason to contest Hood, is what I'm saying. I stood to leave, and matter-of-factly he said the words, not even looking my way. Then I stared at him for a moment as he started writing his report, the pen scratching the paper, before I felt a hand on my shoulder, escorting me back to my cell. Now, a full week later, I understand what he said. A year is a long time. When I think of how I have filled my years before, how I packed life into them, aye, I realize that a year is a very long time indeed to spend in such a place. I have forgotten why freedom mattered to me.

But what does hell look like? There's the cot bed, this table, this chair, a wee bookshelf, a slop pail, a battered pewter candlestick I took from the London house. No candle. A patch of black mold is growing on the ceiling, always wet but never dripping. I suppose you could say the view from the window is agreeable on a good day, looking out over St. George's Fields, and I am fortunate to have a view of the sky, the only thing in my life that still changes. But it's hard not to notice how the scene is divided by the metal bars, and with the window glazing thin and partly missing, the chill in winter can rival any Raasay morning.

I am grateful that I was allowed paper and ink for my tunes, so at least I have something to distract me, take me away from my delusions, as they insist on calling them. It's still impossible for me to completely trust these claims of theirs, but when you're told you've gone mad enough times you begin to believe it. I will say that there are things rattling around in my head that confuse and frighten me, but that does not make them false. I know for a fact that others in Her Majesty's service would sooner have me in here than out there, and I am not so naïve as to think that they would not use their influence against me.

I say "the others" as though I am still one of them, though if the note Mary provided earlier this year is truly authentic, which by now I do believe it is, then after over a decade of service I have now been officially relieved of my duties as Her Majesty's piper. If it is true that Her Majesty has seen fit to do this, I hold nothing against her. Her safety is paramount, and she needs to ensure those around her are those she can trust. But to be removed from the royal household staff altogether, and locked up under these pretenses, here I sense something more malevolent at work, an evil that will endanger the Empire itself, something that places Her Majesty in even greater peril than–

No. These are the very suspicions they implore me not to dwell on. I will keep them at the back of my mind for when they are needed, but right now there is no use for them. Oighre. Aye, it will do me good to write about Eyre, and my long journey here, all these hundreds of miles away. That'll help me clear my thoughts. Perhaps one day I'll read these pages to my children, showing them the man I used to be. Or more likely they'll be scattered to the wind.

Ratharsair was a long time ago. I was born in 1812 to John Mackay and Margaret MacLean, and for this I'm thankful every day. My father was a good man, a true family man. More so than I have been. He was piper to John MacLeod, laird of Raasay, which to our family felt like a significant position, providing us with our land and home, our means to live. Our house was known as Taigh a' Phìobaire, or The Piper's House, and it was my mother who kept it in such fine order. She was kind, intelligent, protective of her children – to a fault, perhaps – and in every way the perfect match for my father. I really could not have asked for more from them.

That house was the center of our world. The roof was heavily thatched, and the walls made of thick island stone, a good sixteen paces in length. There was a central doorway with a window on each side, and the top of the outside wall was less than a man's height. It seems peculiar now, with the grand places I've played, but at the time seeing an adult crouching to get through the door was just the way of things. That door led directly into the lower end of the house where the cows were kept, while the higher end was where our family lived, with only a small partition between the two, just enough of a wall to keep the cows out of the kitchen. Cattle and people under the one roof! Now I'm writing it down here that seems strange to me as well, and yet it still smelled a damn sight better than this place. I remember there wasn't really the space for us bairns to be inside much until it came time to sleep or eat. Maybe I should be happy with my lot now. A cell all to myself …

My memories from the very early days are as shifty as they are from the past couple of years, but as an islander I've learnt how to stitch a tale together. For most of my life, the strongest connections I've formed with people have come through recounting our own unique stories, and whenever I was asked for mine, I'd always begin in the same place. It was the day I knew for certain that music would be the pursuit of my life. Ah, yes. Let's see how the pen remembers it.

I was about eight years old. It was springtime, and there were a couple of pipers staying at Taigh a' Phìobaire with us; there was always a flow of them coming and going from the island, keen to learn from my father. In my eyes and those of many others, he was the greatest piper in Scotland, and that was taking into consideration some very fine pipers indeed.

A watery light crept into the room. My brother John and I rose silently, carefully clambering over the sleeping bodies so as to get to our chores as early as we could. The hardened clay that made up the floor was ideal for moving without a sound, and already we knew our roles. I'd be taking the ashes outside; John would be collecting the eggs. It was important we got on Mother's good side, as the previous night we'd made the dreaded mistake of falling asleep before the adults had finished their conversation. All those who came to the island brought with them new tales, providing us with the scripts for the next day's play, and so if we drifted off too early, the only way to salvage the situation was if we persuaded Mother the next day to relay the best of the talk.

It hadn't been our fault, mind, us falling asleep. The evening before had been incredibly mild and clear, and while the adults began singing tunes, the older children had taken us wee ones up on the grassy hill nearby to play a game in the dying light, lying on our backs and finding the patterns of the stars. The lot of us made a full house: Donald, Mary, Margaret, Cursty, Katherine Òg, Roderick, John and me. Donald was 19 at this time and had recently left to become piper to MacDonald of Clanranald, and there was often much talk about who my sisters would marry, though at that stage they were still all with us. I was the youngest besides John. There was also Katherine Mòr, but I have no real memory of her. She died an infant and was not much spoken of on account of my mother, who grieved her deeply. But the rest of us, we'd spent the whole day taking the cows to the grazing and then, happily exhausted, we lay there listening to Cursty tell us about each of the constellations we spotted. According to her, she'd memorized all the Greek stories from the book at Raasay House, but she was a sharp thing, Cursty, and I now suspect she must have done some improvising from time to time. I vaguely recall she had my favorite – the huntsman Orion – battling with the Picts on one of his adventures, which now seems rather unlikely.

Around when we would normally all start wandering towards the house to join the adults by the fire – it was now just about pitch dark – Cursty made the bold claim she could point to each of the constellations with her eyes shut. Margaret decided to take her up on it.

"But we'll be blindfolding you," she said. "We know you can't be trusted."

"That's fine."

"And we'll be spinning you round," Margaret decided after a moment's thought, which we all roundly approved. "Someone go and fetch one of the lamps so we can tell if she's cheating."

Cursty did remarkably well, despite being so dizzy she could hardly stay on her feet. We all had a go for the next hour or so, but it was having fun playing this game that meant as soon as John and I got back inside the house and felt the warmth of the fire, sleep immediately overcame us. We hardly even stirred when Father shifted us over to our sleeping spots on the straw, but when morning came, we knew what to do.

By the time John had found all the eggs and I'd scooped up the ashes and spent wood to take to the ash heap, everyone was up and moving about. We found our mother in the byre end of the house, adding fresh hay. She looked quite tired, and just in case she was short on patience, I decided to let John take the lead.

"A mhàthair, we know we missed something worth hearing," he said, his voice squeaky and not yet broken.

Our mother didn't look at us. "Well, you should've stayed up then, shouldn't you?"

John persisted. "We've finished out morning chores, but we're not doing another thing until you tell us what it was."

"Oh, really?" At this, she raised her eyebrow, and a mischievous smile passed over her lips.

John looked to me for support, and I nodded. "Aye," he said.

"Well, I guess I'd better tell you then, hadn't I?" And here she pretended to mull over our request, as though it was something meriting serious consideration. "You know, I remember John Ban was talking a fair bit about a particular mouse on the mainland."

"A mouse?" I asked. Already I was on the alert. John Ban was one of the pipers staying with us to learn from Father. He was an older lad, closer to Donald's age than mine, and I always greatly looked forward to his stays, admiring him enormously for his wit and piping talents. That said, I knew how fond he was of spinning tales; more than once he'd fooled me by sending me off to find his glass chanter or his bottomless cup.

"A mouse, aye, everyone's talking about it over there," nodded my mother. "He said it tended to get more meal when not seen or heard, I think that was it. Not seen or heard, aye."

Seeing from our perplexed faces that she had said enough to keep us occupied for a while, she smiled and gave each of our manes a ruffle. "Now, I don't have much else for you to do today, but the two of you are looking like you could do with a wee haircut. How does that sound?"

Gun taing, we thought! This was all she needed to say to get us out of the way for the rest of the day. Even though we'd not got quite the gossip we were after, John and I bounded off to do what we loved best: roaming about the island. What adventures we'd have! One day we could be playing in the rugged hills around Dùn Cana, next we would be tracking ships along the coastline, and then crashing through the woodland the day after that. Sometimes – if we had our older siblings with us – we'd be allowed to tramp all day to the far end of the island and find somewhere to spend the night. Though in truth we knew nothing else, even as children we could tell that our home in Eyre was unlike anywhere on Earth, sat there high above the water with its stunning view of Skye. Everyone who came to stay with us would marvel; there was just no getting away from the magic of the place. From our house you could watch the mist come low on the mountains, eventually hiding the view altogether before it rose again, unveiling the color and beauty of the Cuillins on the far side of the water. Oh, I can almost reach out and touch them now, believe me.

So off we went. John took some oatcakes and cheese for lunch while I fetched one of our father's empty bottles to fill in a spring, and with that we knew we could be out until dark.

Over the years we fought many battles, the pair of us. We were at the Rout of Moy, leaping behind rocks and peat stacks, making musket sounds with sticks for rifles. We bowed our heads in silence at the death of MacCrimmon, who would return no more. In our minds, we were the Jacobite army on the march, a mighty Highland force to sweep all foes from the land. Jacobite sympathies were in the past on Raasay, but to tell the truth, it was a cherished and quite recent past. My father heard first-hand stories from those who were out in '45, and people still talked about the destruction of An Taigh Mòr and many other Raasay homes after the Jacobite's crushing loss at Culloden. Father himself also had some stories of his own to tell, having served in the armed forces to defend the Napoleonic threat from the continent. That spring morning, however, I decided that rather than a battle, it was best that we just go on a scouting mission to conserve our energy. John Ban was staying for just one more evening, and I didn't want us to make the same mistake as the night before.

"Government troops!" John whispered as we lay on our bellies at our vantage point, looking out at the boats on the water. It was choppy, and white spray flew every time a wave crashed into the rocks in the shallows.

"Come to take further revenge on the MacLeods for harboring Prince Charlie, no doubt," I replied gravely. "We should leave now, and warn them on our return."

"Or we could stand and fight?"

"No, brother," I said, smiling and staying his arm. "That's too many for us."

John looked put out by this. He gloomily put his finger through a hole in his sleeve and began picking at it.

"You know Mother will put a hole in you if you make that any worse, John."

"I'd like to see her try," John retorted, trying not to smile when he saw the amusement on my face. He stopped picking at it pretty soon though, I noticed.

It was the gloaming by the time we made it back to Taigh a' Phìobaire, and the singing had already begun. Island life came with ups and downs depending on the season and the state of the crops – even at eight years of age I had noticed it was becoming steadily more difficult to grow what we needed to see us through each year – but there was one constant in our family, and that was music. Father taught all my brothers tunes using canntaireachd, singing them to us and having us echo them back to him, offering us extra praise if we managed to throw in some improvisation of our own. He was crafty about it though, not giving us the same tunes, so we would all swap and inevitably this would result in scrapping between us about who had more and how they went. More than once, Roderick and I would get into it about how we thought a tune was to be played, and we'd end up wrestling in the long grass until Father came to prise us apart.

"It can be played either way, you idiots," he'd say, always laughing as he did so. "Now, you sing it his way, and you sing it his way, and we'll all decide which one we like best."

When John and I returned on this night, however, there was a concerted effort amongst us bairns to get along, as not only did we have the company of the pipers but some of our neighbors had also come by to spend the evening. With this in mind, we made like John Ban's mouse and kept quiet!

Everyone was crammed into the house and conversation was bubbling. Women perched on the narrow benches and stools, the men mostly stood, while us children were scattered around the floor like so many discarded dolls. Our table was spread with food and drink for all, and when the temperature dropped, the fire was banked with fresh peat, until everything was glowing orange and reeking wonderfully of smoke.

For a couple of hours everything was as it always was on nights like these: eating, laughing, listening to the fanciful tales that our neighbors had come by. But a little later on, I noticed that an unfamiliar quiet had broken out, as one-by-one, everyone hushed to listen to young John Ban. Usually on his final nights with us, he'd offer his thanks to my mother and father for their hospitality, but it soon enough became obvious he'd prepared something a little more special this time.

In his low resonant voice, set against the warm crackling of the fire, he had started singing a tune, and though the melody was of his own creation, as we listened to the words we recognized the beginning of "Ruidhle an t-sìthein," a tale of two farmers waylaid by fairies on the way home from the market. But the ever-sly John Ban had done some tweaking. He had shifted the story to follow a plot well-loved by all of us, the tale in which my father took a week coming home from a wedding on

Skye, after he and his friend Fionnlagh stopped to empty cups at every croft on the journey home.

As people realized they knew the story, the crowd's interest grew, until each new rhyming line, bringing my father into an even more precarious position than the last, drew howls from us all. My father was shaking his head with a wide smile, his eyes cast to the heavens. By the end, a neighbor had picked up the melody on the fiddle, and the rest of us joined in the singing. I'm sorry to say I can't remember all the lyrics, but there was one refrain it kept coming back to. I watched, utterly enraptured, as everyone in the house danced about together, shrieking and whooping in the firelight, the men swinging the women and children by the arms, yelling out in full voice:

> *Then MacKay stood up, emptied his cup*
> *And bade Fionnlagh goodbye,*
> *He kissed the bride and went outside*
> *And made to leave bonnie auld Skye,*
> *But he woke the next day wi' his heid in the hay*
> *And asked himself, "Where am I?"*
> *The fairies said "You're no in yer bed"*
> *Which told him his plan'd gone awry!*

It was brilliant, it really was. I cherish that moment, and can still see the mirth on everyone's faces as they sang. It was one of the first times I felt that strong sense of something deep and unifying, warmth we could feel even as children. The music, the stories, the songs: these were the shared wealth of our community, and still they remain the greatest wealth I know. They sustained us when nights were cold and food scarce, through the seasons that came and went like the tides, providing the rhythm that influenced everything on our island.

But now my guts are aching terribly. It's as though they're expanding beyond their size. I'm starting to wonder if this new medicine they give me is of any benefit at all. Iodide of Potassium, they call it. I don't understand what it's meant to do, or how it differs from the mercury. All I know is that the slop pail beckons, and then I will try and get a few minutes rest before the attendants arrive. The noises are growing louder already. The hospital is coming alive. Seems there's a rhythm in every place, even here at St Mary's, a constant drumming that must be fought or ignored. I just need rest. And a drink, though they've now even stopped allowing me that; just a mug of beer once in a while. I'll come back to this when I can. So long as I'm confined to this place, with no purpose or employment, what else am I meant to do?

Ùrlar

Raasay House

I realize that in writing all of this here, I had best keep my wits about me. One day soon Mary must be due another visit, and if she spies these pages, I imagine she will make the staff put a stop to it. I do not trust that she would want me to write down any of what is happening – what I suspect to be happening, she'd say – but if I'm careful and keep these sheets between my music, I'm sure no one will come across them. I can't have the staff finding these, though. There's no telling how far the enemy has infiltrated our nation.

She's changed, has Mary. She was a good woman once, a good mother. I imagine she continues to be a good mother, though I've not been permitted to see my children for an age. Jessie and Margaret will be asking after me, John too. The youngest one, Angus; I've no doubt he'd be a stranger.

Exactly when Mary was last here I could not say. Her last visit did not go well; I remember that much. I had been in bed for most of the previous few days. Under the weather, you might say. My thighs had scabbed over and swollen to such an agonizing size I felt they were ready to burst, not that I knew what might erupt from them, and from the moment I saw her I could tell that she was in one of her moods. As we walked slowly along one of the endless galleries linking the cells, she lamented first our finances and then our tattered reputation, each – as she bitterly pointed out – greatly worsened by my dismissal. The echo carried her voice Lord knows how far, and I knew everyone was listening. By the time we had walked around the garden we were cursing one another in full voice. All I can picture after that is a struggle and the faces of the men I took down, my fists flying and often landing on skin and bone, the tortured screams of Mary as they dragged me away. I woke the next morning restrained, my body bruised, my face swollen, my thighs oozing, here in my all too familiar cell.

It's the very same one I was discharged from the first time I was committed. I lay on my side in a straitjacket, half on the cot and half off, spitting out the blood that had pooled in my cheek overnight. When my head stopped spinning, I began calling out in Gaelic, screaming until my voice deserted me. In the end I gave up with sentences, resorting simply to list everything I had lost: my brothers, my father, my livelihood, my health, mo bhràithrean, m'athair, m'obair, mo shlàinte. Hours went by but no one came. It would have sounded like nonsense to them anyway. These people can barely understand my English, let alone Gaelic.

I regret my actions that day, but only because they lost me my garden privileges. I used to enjoy the garden. It's surprisingly large and well-kept, all things considered. Boredom never seemed to rear its head so high when I was out there. There's the courtyard where the linens are hung and dried; the small beds of flowers and vegetable patches amid trimmed grass; the smell of yeast being carried on the wind from the kitchen. Beer and bread are in constant production. It's a scent I once found delightful, now nauseating; it has mixed itself too completely with the abominable odors of vomit and shit that are overpowering in St Mary's. Yeast, vomit, and shit. I'd never have thought these would become the signature aromas of my life.

In my early days here, I would not speak to those I'd pass in the garden, lying on the grass or wandering around, unshaven and deformed and wild-eyed. Each and every one of them was in decrepit condition, and I admit I was frightened of what they might do. Recently, however – I mean before I was prohibited from going out there – there were instances when I would find myself inclined to offer a courteous nod, even a word of encouragement. It was clear that everyone had now learned who I was by then, where I had come from and who I'd represented, and so during those moments it almost felt like a civic duty, interacting with them in some way. I would bless them, commend them for doing well enough that they'd been allowed out into the garden, and tell them if they needed anything then they need only offer my name to the staff and the message would be passed on. Then I'd inform the guard on the way in how they seemed, if that inmate required extra attention that week or not, if the guards would perhaps be a little softer with him, which the guard would in turn report to the doctors.

But now Hood has refused my help, and has decided that until I show signs of improvement, I am not to be permitted into the garden any longer. What is the saying? "The world is but a great Bedlam, where those that are more mad, lock up those who are less.

I think before I attempt to recount my own story, I should go back to the start of my father's. His beginnings in life were not easy. He was an orphan and a herd boy for MacLeod, looking after the cattle and moving them as needed. Never did he mention how my grandparents died, only that the MacLeods took him in. I found out later from my mother that his family had been impoverished, with too many mouths to feed and too little income from a struggling croft. He was lifted from his family and brought to Raasay by Captain Malcolm MacLeod – the tacksman and eccentric old cousin of the laird – who even in those early years must have sensed a sharpness worth nurturing.

The MacLeods had ruled Raasay since the fifteenth century, and the laird's house was a focus for everyone there, in my father's day and in mine. It was the place that most visitors would head to first upon arrival, and was the source of many an islander's livelihood, be it working with the fish, cattle, oats, barley, or just the maintenance of the place. Generally speaking, if the big house was successful, the rest of the island would also prosper. The Scottish lairds are not merely landowners with Crown connections: they are chieftains who think themselves fathers to their people. MacLeod was no exception. In any case, with the thirteen children John MacLeod raised with his wife Flora, he was the birth father to more than his share of folk on Raasay as well!

Of these thirteen children, three were boys and ten were girls. My father, with him being what he was and them being destined for higher things, did not much socialize with them. Mostly they were stuck being schooled in Raasay House, the magnificent new structure that had replaced An Taigh Mòr. The boys had a tutor who provided regular teaching and discipline, while Flora MacLeod oversaw the education of the girls. While my father could only speak Gaelic and a little bit of English, the MacLeod children could read English, French, and Italian, and there was Gaelic both spoken and read. As well as this, the girls' education also involved a lot of music. They learned to play the pianoforte and sing, including many Gaelic songs. This was how fresh music was always finding its way to Raasay, either from new study books or simply brought in the memories of visitors who knew the latest trends in the drawing rooms of Edinburgh.

One day, when my father was seven years old and had just finished bringing in the cows with the other two herd boys, he told us he heard the voice of Captain MacLeod calling him in from the byre.

"With me, MacKay," he said, and without another word he turned and began striding towards his house, muttering away to himself as he always did. The three herd boys looked at one another, each assuming that my father was for it in some way.

"MacKay!" the captain bellowed, and at that my petrified father scurried after him.

He had to run to keep up, and by the time they'd arrived at the captain's house my father could hardly speak. He thought he knew what it was about. He'd heard the captain teaching pipes to a lad in the big house, and a few times had hidden close to the window to eavesdrop on the music. Inside, when the captain told him to sit down on the chair at the table, my father was almost in tears.

"But the mud," my father said, gesturing to his legs which were still splattered from his day in the fields. He didn't have any shoes, and the mud used to cake every one of his toes.

"Never mind the mud," the captain said, and he left and went into another room. My father heard him telling his housekeeper to make tea. When he came back, still muttering, he lifted the chair my father sat on off the ground as though my father wasn't in it, before planting it in the center of the room.

"I'm sorry, sir," my father said. "I didn't mean it."

The captain stopped muttering and looked at him. "Didn't mean what?"

"I … I listened to you at the big house. I hid in the bushes by the window." My father looked helplessly at the floor, sniffing.

The captain narrowed his eyes. "Yes, that is indeed why you're here, MacKay."

He then grumbled and again left the room, with my father now in utter despair. But a few minutes later, he returned with a feadan: the wee elder branch chanter used to learn the notes for the pipes. An older woman followed, carrying a tray laden with tea and buttered bread.

"You're here because you clearly have an ear for tunes, so I thought I'd spend my time teaching you rather than those dim-witted lads up there." Spilling most of it, the captain set his tea on the table and then put the feadan into my father's hands. "You have to handle it carefully, mind. They break easily and the reeds take time to make."

My father looked down at it, still struggling to understand that he wasn't in some sort of trouble.

"You've hardly been subtle about it, lad," the captain said, eyes widening. "I've heard you singing away with the herds, playing on that wee chanter you've made. And it's no wonder. You're a MacKay! There's music in your blood. Now let me show you what to do. Unless you want to go back to clearing the cow shit, of course …"

And so that's how my father told us he came to learn his first notes. It was not long before he'd been taught all there was to be taught by those on the island, and he was said to make a great impression when he played. MacLeod hospitality was renowned, and my father would often be called upon to entertain the laird's guests. Of course, he did like to remind my siblings and me at every opportunity of what he termed the greatest injustice, when he was deemed too young to perform for the writers James Boswell and Samuel Johnson, who famously visited the island in 1773. If he'd enjoyed a few drinks and we managed to hound him into it, we could get Father to recite by heart the passage Johnson wrote about his stay. Never have I met someone with a memory as impressive as my father's. This recital was made all the more hilarious given his loose grasp of English; hearing his unique pronunciation of such extravagant language was enough to make us near weep with laughter.

"Our reception exceeded our expectations," he'd begin, starting quiet and slow as the room hushed. "We found nothing but civility, elegance, and plenty. After the usual refreshments, and the usual conversation, the evening came upon us." Here he paused, and then sped up the tempo and crescendoed, encouraging the children to start clapping along. "The carpet was then rolled off the floor; the musician was called, and the whole company was invited to dance." Then he did a little jig, before seeking out my protesting mother and taking her up in a twirl, crying, "Nor did ever fairies trip with greater alacrity!" which was then the cue for everyone to leap up with them.

And so the passage ran on, something about the "mansions of pleasure" and full of other phrases we didn't fully understand, but still, not a little pride was taken from these writings on the island. My mother, though, she was always more eager to remind us of another of Johnson's observations from his time on Raasay, whenever me and my brothers were reenacting the night before a little too boisterously: "More gentleness of manners, or a more pleasing appearance of domestick society, is not found in the most polished countries." I suspect perhaps the locals were on their best behavior during the writers' stay.

But it was in that sort of atmosphere that Father grew up. I see now that had my father not been an orphan, but say had been born a MacLeod, he would never have learned music as a craft. Recently I have found myself doing this more: speculating on how this all came to pass, seeing the links that have made up the chain. Had Father been a MacLeod and not an orphan then he would have lived like the three boys, studying literature and mathematics and politics, and listening to the faint sound of his ten sisters singing from another wing of the house. As it was, though, being a low-born lad served him well. As time went on, so wonderfully did he entertain the guests at Raasay House that the MacLeods eventually arranged for him to travel to Gairloch for piping tuition with his distant MacKay relatives, and with the last of the MacCrimmons on Skye. This was hugely generous on their part. It was this that really allowed him to become the man he did, the man who would then shape my brothers and I into serious musicians as well.

I was a bairn myself when I started showing that same skill for the pipes, and in my own days as the most famous piper in Scotland, much was made of my piping lineage from the MacCrimmons through my father. I suppose it was offered as some sort of explanation. Even sitting here in this chair, this still frustrates me. Of course, it is a great point of pride to know I descend from such a line, but anyone who lifts a pipe and plays a good tune knows that lineage is but a thread or two to the past, and a few threads do not make a sturdy garment. My father and I were great pipers firstly because of the luck of our situation, and then because we worked at it our entire lives. Were I able-bodied and they allowed me pipes, I would be practicing now, and tomorrow, and the day after that. Perhaps through my father I inherited a sense for music, a natural inclination for it, but not squandering that gift, working diligently – that is real talent.

That will do for now, I think. Tomorrow I shall start my journey anew.

Journey from Skye, Summer 1823

The day we found out we were leaving Raasay is scored across my memory like a notch gouged into this desk. For a long time, my parents had been trying to hide from us the dismal state of the laird's health and the threat of emigration, though we had guessed as much, and were afraid. Mother's pained expression when she weighed our meager portions was not so well hidden; she and Father would bicker at night when they thought us asleep. We couldn't always make out the words exactly, but the fact they had started arguing at all was enough to alert us that the winds were changing. At the age of ten, I didn't fully comprehend why this might be, but now I know all too well: Britain was evolving. Railways, roads, harbors, the agricultural revolution and the Clearances, the structural improvements across the cities. One visiting piper had told us that Glasgow now had several thousand gas lights illuminating the city streets. We struggled to believe that. How would anyone be able to sleep if it was still light outside?

Father was 56 at the time, and Donald had come back to Raasay to take over most of the responsibilities as MacLeod's piper. To the family's relief, Donald had at last been awarded first prize at the Highland Society's pìobaireachd competition in Edinburgh, having been inexplicably denied the award the previous two years, despite being the finest performer on each occasion. He'd been a little gloomy during those years, to put it mildly! In his efforts to console, my father had reminded Donald that most of the judges had no piping ability or know-how anyway. They were "gentlemen" and "enthusiasts": these had been the essential requisites since the start of the competitions, but they had likely never picked up a set of pipes in their lives. They wouldn't have even heard of Taorluath or Crunluath, my father assured him, nor could they tell apart the different graces.

But still, it was undeniable that the pìobaireachd competitions were the highest reward in the piping world, and when Donald received the award in 1822 it at last put a smile on his face again, and showed the world the standard he had achieved. However, the income as laird's piper, be it Donald or Father, was simply not enough to pay the taxes required and have enough left over for the whole family on Raasay. To make matters worse, farming what was required to survive on the island was also getting harder; the overworked soil that had our neighbors concerned was yielding less and less each year. Our hearty meals of potatoes or oats that could nourish us throughout the day were increasingly being replaced by milk and what we could forage and hunt, which took yet more time and energy. I would not say that the bliss accompanying island life had vanished, though there was no denying that times were tough for us.

I remember sitting by myself in a den I had made in the bluff down the hill from our home. A warm, salted breeze was rustling the grass around me, and the few garlic flowers that had taken to my den were nodding their white heads. The night before there had been the most glorious sunset; the sky had been alive with pinks and purples painting the crinkled clouds, with all of it reflected on the glassy water, so still you could surely walk right across it. Though the sea was a little rougher today, I saw up above in the clearing sky that a similar sight was on the way tonight. To busy myself until then I was memorizing tunes, fingers soundlessly moving over the twig in my hands that was making do for a chanter, occasionally taking a break to chew on one of the flowers, letting the flavor tickle my tongue before biting into it.

"Angus? Are you down there?"

I recognized John's voice calling from up on the ridge. "Aye, what is it?"

"Athair wants you home."

"Look up, John! Can it not wait?"

"He just said to get you." John paused. "I think it's the laird."

When the two of us got back to the house and went inside the whole family was there. I saw that every child's eyes were rimmed with red. My mother was distracting herself, barely noticing John and me coming in. I thought perhaps she hadn't even seen us until she began dishing out cups of hot soup, thrusting one first into John's hands and then into mine, all the while saying nothing. I noticed her apron was covered in stains from the soup, as though she'd perhaps spilled a bowl on herself.

"James MacLeod is dead. A chuid de Phàrras dha." My father stared hard at the floor when he at last broke the silence. His hand kept moving to his scruffy beard, absent-mindedly rubbing his jawline. "Young John MacLeod will be taking over at the big house. Your mother and I have decided that Raasay is no longer the place for you bairns. We'll be away within the month."

His words hung in the air for a moment; though we'd almost expected as much they were still a shock to hear. Then all at once, each of us children began blurting out all of the questions that sprung into our minds, trying to fathom ways in which it might be possible for us to stay. Though it was all in desperation and we knew it.

"If these measures weren't necessary, we wouldn't be taking them," my father said, in a flat voice that did not suit him at all. "There is no changing of minds at this stage."

"And I'll be staying here," Donald said quietly. "I'm to be put up in the big house as Raasay's piper when the lot of you leave."

My father stared at him for a long moment, and eventually he exhaled and gave a slight nod. "Aye. Donald will be staying here. And Mary and Margaret shall be staying too. Mary has been promised to John MacKenzie, while Margaret shall be leaving for Badinoch, to marry Willie Robertson."

Hearing this, we really were all too stunned to say anything. Besides Donald being piper to MacDonald of Clanranald, we'd all rarely been separated by more than a few miles, and never for longer than a week or so. It sounded like we would be losing three of our siblings for a lot longer than that. I could tell from the expressions of Mary and Margaret that they'd known of this for a while.

"We're sorry that now is the time for telling you," my mother stepped in, at last holding some soup for herself. "But things will only get harder here if we stay."

"And what will we do? If not here, then where are we going to live?" Cursty asked.

This is when my father regained a semblance of his usual optimism. "Now, there is the right question, a Chiorstaidh. Though it may not seem like it now, our fortunes are on the rise. My friends at the Highland Society are not permitting me to leave Scotland. According to them your father is much too valuable, and I'm inclined to agree."

A few smiles managed to crack through the blotchy faces, and we listened as our father told us of the position that had been found for him – or rather, created for him – at Drummond Castle in Perthshire. He was to be piper to Lord Willoughby D'Eresby, who was allegedly obsessed with Highland culture, having formed a small but authentic Highland force to display for King George IV the year before. According to the exchanges he had had with my father, Baron Gwydir, as he was usually known, believed that a respected piper would make a natural addition to his estate. Our family had been forwarded a small sum to make the journey.

"Everything is going to work out fine, but there's a lot to get organized," Father warned. "For the next wee while, you'll just have to do as your mother and I tell you."

"And our first order is to eat!" declared my mother, snapping her fingers at John, who had been standing motionless, a vacant expression on his face. Looking at him, I couldn't help but feel pity for my wee brother, and I put my arm around him. Of all of us, he had enjoyed the fewest years on Raasay, and was probably of an age that he wouldn't remember much of it at all when he was older. As we began the process of packing up our lives over the next few weeks and saying our final goodbyes to Donald, Mary, and Margaret, I made sure to constantly whisper into John's ear tales of castles and lords, trying to convince him – and myself, to some degree – that though we were leaving behind all we knew, there was excitement and opportunity ahead.

The only real option we had available to us was that we would walk the distance to Drummond Castle, following the droving trails well-known to Highlanders for generations. There was little point in taking much more than ourselves because the house we were to be staying in within the castle grounds would be furnished and equipped with far more than anything we could bring. What ensued was the unsettling process of giving away and selling most of what we owned: tools and housewares and clothing, all of the things we had been taught to cherish and protect. Neighbors and relatives came to the house with empty cloth sacks and awkward expressions, and though many tried to give us something in return, unless it was food needing to be eaten then we had to refuse it. I remember standing at our door or looking out of the window, watching the bits and pieces of our existence being carried away, carried by the only faces I'd ever known. I realized then that what we were doing was permanent.

A couple of days before we were to leave, my father took myself, Donald, and John to Raasay House while he arranged some final business. We were to purchase two stout Highland ponies to help with the load, using some of the travel funds we had been given. Immediately upon seeing them at the stables of the big house, John and I fell in love with these proud little creatures. The first was sandy and the second a dappled black, like deep water. Each of them was standing very still, their tails occasionally swatting away a fly, their orb-like eyes following our movements curiously.

"Don't be shy, they're very friendly." The old man who was selling them to us smiled as he pulled on his pipe. "Why don't you lead them on a wee loop round that wall?" No doubt he and my father exchanged amused looks as John and I did so – me taking the rein of the lighter one, John the darker – each of us talking animatedly to our respective companion.

By the time we had returned from this short trip, the ponies had been named: Hercules and Orion. The others laughed as we announced this, but it was my father who enjoyed it most. Since announcing our departure he'd not been his usual self at all. His love for Raasay surpassed all of ours – the island and its people had given him everything he had – and I understand now that he likely took our leaving as a sign of failure on his part. He was a proud man. But he must have been glad to see John and me in good spirits at last, as his sense of humor finally shone through again. Without our noticing he had crept behind us, and then he picked us up in his arms.

"Here are those strange animals I was telling you about," he said between our squeals, displaying us for the old man. "Name your price."

The old man gave a raspy laugh. "Temperament and condition?"

"Ah, well, this one's a little stubborn," my father said, shaking me. "And to be honest, this one's a bit shaggy and not that clean." John squirmed as Father sniffed his hair. "On second thought, maybe we could just give you this one, or we could feed him to the fish before we go!"

As we meandered back home with the ponies, we had fallen into a steady pace. John was quiet, devoting all his attention to Hercules, still muttering inaudibly as he reached up to stroke his mane. To me it seemed these animals had made the prospect of our imminent departure more tangible, and I was beginning to think ahead to the journey and wonder what dangers might lie before us.

"Athair, will we be safe walking all this distance across the country?"

Father didn't answer immediately. He gave me a long look and put a hairy hand on my shoulder.

"You're worried, are you? Well, nothing in future is certain, Angus, but that's no evil thing. For every time something turns out worse than you expect, there'll be something turning out better. Trick is to celebrate those times."

Father laughed loudly when he looked down to see this had hardly reassured me.

"Don't worry, lad, our chances of making it to Crieff are good. There's a piper we know called Morrison. From Uist, remember?"

I shook my head.

"Well, you've met him, I think. He's the most relaxed man I know;

nothing fazes him at all. Sometimes he stops for a tune and a chat when he's moving the cattle. Once when the weather was foul, I asked him if he was worried about losing livestock on the crossings. You hear so many stories, don't you? He told me he wasn't. He said he lives life like it's a pìobaireachd, enjoying his play through the variations, not fretting about when he's getting back to the ground."

I pondered this for a moment. "What happened when he crossed that time?"

Father glanced at me, smiling. "Made it across fine, of course."

That night marked the final gathering at Taigh a' Phìobaire, with people coming from across Raasay to fill our nigh-empty house. We had prepared a large kettle of mutton stew using much of what was brought to us, and there was whisky and bannocks to go around. This alone was enough to ensure it was a fine send-off, as it was the first time we'd eaten our fill for some weeks. Before too long the songs and stories started, but I must confess that my recollections of the night are a little muddled. Roderick and Cursty sneaked me my first wee swig of whisky when no one was looking. It didn't taste quite like the nectar it does now, I'll tell you that! I just about spat it right onto the floor.

"Sgreamhail!" I said, struggling to believe that for my whole life people around me had been merrily sipping away at that.

"Aye, it is," laughed Roderick with a nod, taking it back and gulping another mouthful down before one of the adults decided he'd had enough. "But it'll grow on you if you stick with it!"

"And don't you be mentioning this to John," Cursty said, waggling a finger at me. "That boy just wants to do as you do."

"Agreed, not a word. But here's one more," Roderick said, sneakily handing me the bottle back. "It'll taste better this time, I promise …"

Soon enough the pipes came out. A few players took a turn around the fire, playing the last goodbyes to the house. Even us boys had a tune.

I could barely contain my excitement; everyone stopped to watch me when my turn came, this wee skelf of a lad blowing his heart out, without so much as a break. My father was the last to play. After hearing a few airs he decided to go for a reel, and after this the night really took off, everyone clapping and singing until their throats ran dry. Needless to say, I can't remember much from my father's playing after all that whisky, only being lifted up and thrown around and reeling until the early morning.

And what a morning it was … I was certainly glad to have a day of rest and final preparations before the journey began. I couldn't understand how some folk were able to get up and go about their business so briskly after such a night. Still, when I poked my head up at seeing the sun streaming in, a good number of people were still snoring and tucked into corners, sharing a last few hours together. For a long time, everyone lay there, watching the smoke from the evening's embers curling to the roof.

That day we cleared everything out while my father made sure the boat he'd arranged to take us the next morning would be clear to come in, and then we said our final farewells and watched the stragglers head off. Though emotions were still lying just beneath the surface, something did seem to have shifted. I think as we readied ourselves for one final sleep, we were all simply relieved to have at long last reached the moment that had been on our minds for so long.

Porridge and tea. I'll never forget my final bowl and mug in Taigh a' Phìobaire when I next woke up. They tasted exactly the same as any other morning, and that was all I wanted. I did a final wee walk around the house, running my hands over the rough stone walls I'd slept between, smelling the scent of my family in the air, seeing their impression in the land. They were coming with me, of course, but it felt like I was saying goodbye to a part of them, and a part of me too. I was ready, though. Placing our utensils in the last bundle to go, we helped our parents strap up the well-cleaned peat creels to the sides of Hercules and Orion.

The walk to the western shore was short and bright, and we found a cattle boat waiting to take us to Sconser on Skye. Though the droving season had not yet begun, a few of them were still available to take travelers. I was glad to be leaving on such a beautiful morning, and the effect of the warm sun, the sparkling waters and the gorgeous view, all of them filled me with a strange joy. It was a worthy final glimpse of the island, and I reckon the clear Hebridean sky that's fixed in my mind is taken from that very morning. After all of my fantasizing about going off on an adventure with Orion, here it was coming true!

What they don't tell you about adventures is that there's an awful lot of walking involved; seems you need to trudge some hard miles before anything exciting happens. Once we'd made it to Skye, we turned south and headed toward Broadford. What started as a fine day gradually clouded and darkened, and by late afternoon we were walking in a steady rain. This is the tale of Scotland: one or two fine days typically spells a rotten week. The rain soaked us through, and everyone's feet were wet and aching. That first day we must have walked about ten hours. We didn't say too much to one another, everyone occupied with the sound of feet and hooves squelching in the mud; the sight of the changing landscape; our own tumbling thoughts. It was dusk by the time we arrived at the inn at Kylerhea, where mercifully there was a room available for us and a small stable for the ponies. There were a few people about the inn, and a ceilidh going on in the main room, but for once I was not interested in the music, as after our first full day spent walking, it was the smell of roasted meat and potatoes and that was captivating me most of all.

After heading to our room and washing we raced back down again, hanging up our soaking clothes by the hearth and looking around for where to get a bowl. Once they'd been secured, us children all squirreled away into a shady corner, listening to the rain lashing down outside and savoring every morsel. As always, we proceeded to lick our dishes when we were done, until with just a flash of her eyes our mother told us to be a little more discreet. We weren't in Taigh a' Phìobaire now! Bellies full, we were then sent upstairs again to rest, while our parents stayed down for ale and tobacco with the other guests.

"I'm off to give this to Orion," I whispered to John when we got back to the room, showing him a large red apple I took from under my shirt.

"Where did that come from?"

"Innkeeper," I grinned. "Let's wait until everyone's asleep and we can give half to Hercules too."

With just the one bed in the room, we children spread out on the floor. John and I shared a mat and some blankets, and we had every intention of carrying out our covert mission with the apple when Mother wasn't paying attention, but as soon as we lay down the day caught up with us and neither of us could stand up again. Between dreams I heard my father laughing downstairs on the main floor, someone entertaining with a song about a Highland cow and its assets. I have no idea how I remember this, but part way through that song, those assembled joined for the chorus and sang these words:

> Bheir mi ho air m'urrainn ho,
> Bheir mi ho air m'urrainn fhèin,
> Bheir mi ho air m'urrainn ho,
> Thogainn fonn 's gun ceannaichinn sprèidh.

And that was the last I heard that night.

Next day we knew was the crossing from Kylerhea to Glenelg on the mainland. Most of us had never been further than Skye, so this felt like a significant moment. And a bit terrifying as well.

Waking up at the inn, I looked around at the unfamiliar room and it took me a moment to remember where I was. Almost every day of my life I had wakened to the same walls, my family lying in the same places around me. But now everything was different; it felt like everyone was in the wrong spot. I saw my mother was up already, tucking things away into bags. She gently began to stir the sleepier and stiffer among us into action, though after a couple of failed attempts she recruited my father, who started giving Roderick and Katherine Òg slightly more forceful encouragement with his boot. Seems their slow rise made us late, as after a hurried meal we reloaded the ponies and started running to the pier, struggling to navigate the ponies, which were still getting used to us just as we were getting used to them.

I was a little nervous about the crossing, but not nearly so much as John. Despite the day ahead of us he had barely touched his breakfast at all. I was last in the party but I saw up ahead that he had stopped moving, and Mother was standing by him, trying to coax him on.

"I heard the inn keeper tell you and Father last night the water was going to be fast today," John said to her when I caught up, "and that two cows drowned last week."

My mother rolled her eyes. "You've a pair of ears on you, John, I'll give you that. Listen, you're a smart lad to be fearful of the water, but I promise you, today it'll be fine. The drovers know how to keep their cows safe, and we'll look after you and the ponies."

Reluctantly, John let her take his hand, though by the time the pier came into view, we saw that the ponies were only just getting led on to the ferry. We slowed to a walk. When we did get to the crossing, there were a few cattle, and it looked as though they were waiting for more to arrive.

"That water's fast," John groaned. The mainland wasn't far at all, but I could see in the ripples what he meant.

"It'll be alright," I said, staring across the water. I don't know what I was expecting – something foreign and unfamiliar, I suppose – but the mainland really didn't look that different from Skye, with the hills looking hazy behind a fine mist that I'd seen a thousand times before.

"Are you sure they can swim that?" John asked weakly.

"Aye, they can!" my father called, walking back to find out where we'd got to. "I promise, I've seen this often, they know they just need to swim hard. But if you're really worried, we could always tie a bairn to each cow for the ride across, and you can just yell to us if anything looks wrong." He winked and took John's other hand. "That'll give your mother and me more room on the ferry. And wouldn't we then be looking at the only cattle in Scotland with màsan behind and on top?"

"Enough of that rough speaking, John MacKay!" my mother scolded, cuffing him behind the ears as she tried not to laugh. "You're not draining cups with the drovers now!"

We hung around a few minutes more, waiting for the last cattle to arrive. It was low tide, and my father used the time to explain in detail to John exactly how the cattle got across the water.

"Look at what they're doing," he said, pointing to the drovers. "See they're tying a rope around each animal, looping it around the neck and just under the jaw. Once each rope is tied to the tail of the beast in front, they'll lead a few cattle into the water, and the lead animal will be guided across, with the whole line following." John's brows were furrowed as he tried to picture what was being said, tracking the movements of my father's hands. "They'll take them in wee groups and then they'll hitch them on the Glenelg side until the whole herd is across. These men here, they've done it a hundred times, with thousands of cows! It'll be fine. Still time to catch a lift, though. Just say the word and I'll strap you up!"

Unbeknownst to us, our mother had been standing close behind, and we turned when we heard her clear her throat. "Go and see to Hercules, John. I'm going to work out how much I have to pay these men to leave your father behind."

When we got out on the water, we could tell from the angle of the ferry and the swirling eddies that the current beneath us was very strong. Our parents kept a watchful eye out, making sure everyone was holding on to something and that we didn't stand too close to the ferry's edges, while we in turn looked out for the cattle. The animals seemed to know what they were doing – they kicked up no fuss about getting led into the water – but it was odd seeing them splashing and swimming away, with the rain falling down around their large heads. The only animals I was really used to seeing in the water besides fish were the seals and porpoises that would move around the coasts, so it was a surprise to see how fast the cattle were.

Safely to the shore, so began our journey across the mainland. It was still early morning so there was no lingering, and immediately we began again on the road toward Shiel Bridge. Any excitement we'd felt at the crossing soon wore very thin. Always on those droving trails you had to focus on where to put your feet, and I think we all felt we were seeing more of the ground than the world around us. Either the trails were sodden and slippery or else they were wildly overgrown and jungle-like, with weeds and nettles and ferns you were forced to wade through. The sticks John and I would use for our swords would come in handy then.

Over the next few days, wearing clothes barely dry from the day before and often struggling to find somewhere to take us for the night, there was little that could stoke a laugh in us. At first, we would take turns riding the ponies, but eventually we agreed that John and Katherine Òg should be the ones riding, as he was struggling to keep up and she'd hurt her ankle on a loose stone. It had swollen up and turned a dark purple, which we all found quite fascinating. To those we passed on the road we must have fit the part of weary travelers perfectly. Father passed the time by singing tunes and making us guess the names, teaching us a couple of new ones he'd been saving for the trip. In the glens, Mother made us point out all of the trees we passed: oaks, beeches, pines, larches, rowans, birches, elms, sycamores … Many more trees than we were used to, but there was only so much singing and tree-spotting that was going to keep five bairns in high spirits while trudging in the rain.

When efforts to wrest a tune from us were met with groans and silence, our father – who was as much a teacher as he was a piper and looked to make a lesson out of anything – started offering something of the history of the places we passed through. Somewhere just before Kilchumein we were walking side-by-side, and he told me of the Battle of Glen Shiel and the Little Rising of 1719, when the Spaniards had come all the way to the Highlands.

Breathing slightly heavily, I asked him why they would do that. "That's a long way to travel, isn't it?"

"Believe it or not, they were trying to encourage Jacobite sympathies," my father said. "They had their own cunning reasons for doing so, however. Being opposed to Britain, they wanted to destabilize the House of Hanover. By the time the fighting drew to a close here, they'd stopped sending troops, and it was the Highlanders who were shot down in their droves."

After a moment's thought, I spoke again. "Why do so many people we know remember those Jacobite days with such fondness? Surely it's now impossible to go back to Stewart kings, yet that's what so many seem to want."

Now it was Father's turn to pause. "You know, it's not easy to answer that, lad. This is an argument that concerns more than just the folk of today, like you and me and those families you're mentioning. It's mixed with the religions and loyalties and betrayals of centuries' worth of people on this island, nobles and peasants alike. I'd wager the Stewart kings gave those families untold grief in times gone by, just out of memory." He glanced at me, seeing if I was still listening. "Being part of two nations is complicated, Angus, and you'll see that more and more now we're moving inland. Perhaps it's as simple as that. Sometimes what's best for the British is not best for the Scottish, and sometimes what's best for the Scottish is downright bad for the British. No wonder Scotland's history has been filled with conflict and hard choices. But I suppose for those sympathizing with the Jacobites, sometimes following a path you know well – even one that's not perfect – feels easier than taking a new path, doesn't it? Or making a new path. I don't know. Too much talk of paths. What's true is that change is never easy, and we've been walking too long!"

I've always remembered Father's words here; they left me with much to ponder, and I can't say I'm much closer to finding the answers. Perhaps if I'd been a little older, I would have known what to say to get Father to share more of his thoughts, but he'd already changed the subject to the state of his boots, and I wasn't able to get more out of him that day.

When at last the sun did grace us again, it did so in the right place. In the early morning we had left an inn at Kilchumein in a misty drizzle, but by the time we had started on the rocky Corrieyairack Pass it had cleared and turned into a fine summer's day, with swelling white clouds drifting above us. It was so clear that the hills in the distance could be easily seen; we could see the dark shadows cast by the clouds sweeping across them. The Corrieyairack Pass is many miles long, cutting through the great highland peaks. Compared to the treacherous trails we were used to it was a pleasure to be walking on the stones of a military road, built by General Wade. This was a man we had heard much about from my father throughout the journey. As we jumped over a peat-blackened spring and started up on a steep incline, Roderick teased my sisters, trying to convince them that the general himself was responsible for laying every stone on all of his roads.

"And he single-handedly built the Tummel Bridge," Roderick assured them.

"Don't listen to a word that boy says!" my mother shouted from the rear of the company.

"Good advice," said my father, walking by my side. This boulder-laden incline seemed to be part of the highest peak we'd walked that day, and his forehead glistened with sweat. "You can listen to me instead! Nearly two hundred years ago, the army of James Graham, Marquess of Montrose, was walking on very road you're on now."

"Here we go," Cursty sighed.

"Here we go, indeed! Now, hard to believe in this heat, but back then there was a terrible winter storm raging here," my father continued. "The sky was dark, the ground was frozen. The Earl of Argyll and his Campbells were approaching from the south, and they thought no one would be mad enough, brave enough – stupid enough, even! – to lead their forces through Corrieyairack in such weather. Wrong! The great Montrose took his Highland and Irish soldiers through the pass, the snow driving down, already ten inches deep, and the bitter winds slicing the men to their core. But lo and behold ... it worked! The Campbells couldn't believe it! They'd never dreamed an army could make the crossing, and what followed was a resounding victory for old James Graham." My father's voice hushed, as though he was in church. "But the part of the story people don't much talk about is the ghost army that still marches to this day."

None of us said anything. The shadow of a cloud that had been racing towards us from up the hill now reached us, as if our father had planned the pause, and we felt the cold air on our skin. We were so high up, the cloud almost seemed to be at arm's length.

"They say at night when the winds pick up," my father went on, "Montrose's army marches again through the pass. You can hear the clanking of metal and the pounding of feet. The whispering of prayers. And there's something else …"

The hairs on my arms were standing on end at this point. Without meaning to we had slowed almost to a halt, and looking around, all of us children were waiting with bated breath.

"The sound of … pipes!"

Just then, a blood-curdling noise sounded behind us, and the lot of us screamed in fright. We'd been too caught up in the story to notice that our mother had made a hand reed with grass between her thumbs and blown it to make a loud screech. She and my father started roaring with laughter; they must have been planning it all day. Looking back, though I do think they enjoyed this more than any of us children appreciated, I sense that the joke was also a defense against the unease they both felt. They were superstitious, and I'm not sure they would have let us travel through the Pass if it was close to getting dark. As we came down the hill on the other side, we all made ourselves a hand reed as well.

"Even ghosts like a good tune now and again," Father said when he saw me looking at him.

The next days were the longest of the journey as we left the west of Scotland and made our way through Dalwhinnie, Dalnaspidal, Tummel Bridge and Aberfeldy. Hills turned to valleys, and the closer we got to our destination the less we stopped to rest. It seemed as though money and food were in short supply; by the end, we were sharing more plates than not. Though it was nearly dark, Crieff was busy with people and cattle when at last we reached it, three weeks after leaving Raasay. We passed straight through and continued to the Drummond estate, where we arrived exhausted, hungry, filthy – and sick of the road.

A tall old man greeted us at the gate which loomed over our heads, the gate being almost twice the size of him. He held a bright lantern. Smiling and politely asking my parents about the journey in a strange Gaelic, he led us up the drive for what seemed like forever, before we veered off towards the wee cottage that we were to be staying in. Through the towering oaks that lined our way, I thought I could see the black outline of the castle on the top of the hill. I know now that the cottage was very basic, but I remember marveling when we got there a couple of minutes later. It seemed like a palace compared to Taigh a' Phìobaire.

From the window we saw my father and the man leading the ponies to the stables. From then on, those fine ponies became part of the estate, though it wasn't long before we were too big for riding them.

I turned to look at the fireplace built into the wall. I noticed there was no hole in this roof; the smoke was going up a chimney like it did in Raasay House. And there was proper furniture! To start with, we sat down at an actual table to eat the food the old man's wife had left us. It was a sort of broth that had more flavors than anything I could remember eating, though truth be told, I would have eaten anything at that point. After that we washed with warm water and then gladly went to bed when our mother asked us to, which is when John and I found to our excitement that we had a small room to ourselves.

Warm, well-fed, and lying on an exquisite bed of my own: these were simple pleasures I'd rarely experienced, and certainly not all at once. For the first few days, as we were left to familiarize ourselves with the estate and Crieff, these luxuries were all we needed to melt away the aches and pains of the journey. Father's work began quite soon after arrival. Arrangements were made for his clothing, and he spent much time getting his pipes in particularly good order: setting the sound, refining the fit of the joints, settling the reeds after their time in transit, re-adapting them to the new atmosphere. We could tell from his demeanor that he was taking his new position seriously, even if he was aware that he was being employed not because Baron Gwydir really desired a piper, but simply to prevent him from emigrating. Still, it turned out to be a good thing for us all, as it meant we could remain in the country, and Father's joy in being able to support his family once more was plain to see.

Dithis

Piper to Lady Gwydir, 1823

And so my childhood began for a second time. It certainly took some getting used to. I had assumed that our decorum around the residents of Drummond Castle would simply have to mirror how we behaved around the MacLeods at Raasay House, but soon enough we learned that we were in the company of a different sort of privilege altogether. I suspect it even caught our parents by surprise. Over the previous month or so they'd told us a hundred things that we ought to do and ought not to do, but essentially it boiled down to one simple rule: act as though you are more sophisticated than you are.

That said, some things were easy to adjust to. The house was incomparably better; the food was more varied and abundant; to us Crieff's market seemed vibrant and exotic. In their own way, our new surroundings were of an equal beauty to Raasay, with woodlands and glittering lochs and rolling hills to climb. And the gardens; the gardens of the estate were unlike anything we'd ever seen. They were terraced with more stone than was needed for several houses, and the parterre – one of many new words for me – was pristine, full of plants that seemed from a different world. Arriving in summer helped, no doubt, seeing it all in full bloom, the sky staying light long into the evening before fading into a starry tapestry.

Being situated more centrally in Scotland we were occasionally able to visit some places that had featured so often in our stories – the majestic castles of Stirling and Edinburgh, of course, perched dramatically on their respective crags – but mostly we were kept too busy to go much further from the grounds than Crieff. I'll never forget the number of butterflies that were in the grounds when we first arrived. Every day we'd see dozens of these black and red ones – red admirals, my mother called them, though it was preferable around Drummond Castle to call them by their Latin name, Vanessa Atalanta – sunning on unfamiliar flowers, all fluttering up and swirling about if any of us disturbed them. Aside from getting used to the odd Latin intermission, we also had to adjust our ears to the nasal sounds of the English language, so different from our sweet Gaelic. We learned new ways of saying the same things. "Tìoraidh" became "cheerio" when taking leave, our 'r's unrolled, and soon enough the new placement of our tongues when speaking became the norm for us.

My siblings and I were given jobs around the castle. Cursty and Katherine Òg were taken into the vast mansion to work as maidservants and kitchen girls, polishing dishes and laundering and the like. Meanwhile, John and Roderick were put to use by Tom, the gangly man who had met us at the gate on our first night and who ran the stables. This was a delight to John, working every day with the animals, though he was dismayed that I wouldn't be the one joining him. As it turned out, I had been put forward by my father for something quite different.

"Piper to *who?*" I asked, standing still while my mother cleaned the dirt from my fingernails. She'd never done this quite so thoroughly before, so I was eyeing her with suspicion.

"Sarah Drummond. Or Miss Drummond of Perth. Or Lady Gwydir, if you like," my father laughed behind me. He was eating his breakfast at the table.

"The baron's wife?" I said over my shoulder. It had struck me as strange that no one had mentioned what I was to be doing, but I had assumed this was because something was yet to be found for me. "You mean the lady that owns this estate?"

My father nodded, stretching his arms above his head and speaking through his yawn. "The descendent of a very noble family indeed."

"Oh, leave the boy be," my mother said, though she couldn't help but smirk when she saw the nervousness on my face. "You'll be fine, Angus. She just decided yesterday that if Baron Gwydir's to have his own piper, why shouldn't she? Just call her 'm'lady' when she speaks to you and keep your answers short. You're a good enough player that you won't struggle in that respect."

"Well, I'm not so sure," said my father. "She does already have a tune named after her by the Perthshire fiddlers. She might not be that easily pleased."

"I still can't tell if you're making fun or not," I said warily, before we heard a soft knock on the door.

"Not joking, lad," Mother said. She pinched my cheek. "That'll be for you. She just wants to say hello today. Best behavior."

When I opened the door, I found a servant girl standing there, apparently waiting to escort me to Lady Drummond's parlor, where she was expecting me. I looked back to my parents, who shrugged and ushered me out, already thinking about the next thing they had to do. Accepting that this was to happen whether I wished it or not, I started walking. I suppose this was why my parents had delayed in telling me; I'd not the time to play it through in my head or come up with protests. It was a warm, overcast morning, the world a shadowless gray. The air smelled of wet leaves after a night of heavy summer rain, and a few fat drops still fell from the trees.

"Your parents didn't tell you that the lady was to see you this morning?" the ginger-haired girl asked after a minute. She was pretty, a few years older than me.

"They did not," I replied. "Didn't want to scare me, I reckon. All I know is that the lady owns the estate."

The girl smiled. "I'll fill you in."

I learned the girl was called Anna and was the daughter of one of the cooks. We spoke in English and her accent was unusual to me, so I had to listen carefully to understand, occasionally asking her to repeat herself as we approached the castle. She said Lady Gwydir was born, raised, and educated in Scotland, growing to womanhood with a strong character and many talents. By the tone of her voice, I could tell that Anna admired her greatly. She said the lady was very beautiful and inherited both fortune and estates. In 1807 she married Peter Burrell, the eldest son of Baron Gwydir, who was an English peer. Peter Burrell was broke, but had many connections, political aspirations, and though I wasn't meant to tell anyone this, a huge desire for wealth.

"I think it's fair to say he enjoys life in her keep," Anna remarked. "Not a bad dowry, this place. They are well settled here now, with four children of their own."

I didn't answer as just then the castle came into view, and though I'd now been there for over a week, it still captured my attention. At five floors and with a garret on top, the keep was the tallest building I'd ever seen, built of thick gray stone, towering even above the mansion beside it and my memories of Raasay House. It looked as though it grew out of the rocky hill on which it was perched, with one half of it seeming to be supported by the rough, unhewn stone. It was this side we had to head to, through a huge archway, as the entrance to the keep was up a flight of external stone steps, taking you into the first floor. The scale of the buildings and the grounds was truly startling to me, and I'd spent many hours already discussing with John just how one family could live here.

"So, what is she actually like?" I eventually asked as we made our way up to the entrance, our shoes slapping off the giant paved steps.

Anna paused for a moment, and looked over her shoulder to make sure nobody was within earshot. "In truth, she can be a bit haughty to ordinary folk, but I think she likes young people. If you do what she asks of you, you'll know she's pleased."

After taking me inside and then up a dark stairway, me trying not to stare at the size of the fireplaces or the height of the ceilings, Anna left me at the entrance to an even grander room, where she said she'd wait. I stepped inside. So captivated was I by the array of deer antlers mounted to the wall that I didn't even notice the figure sat on an armchair near one of the many tall and narrow windows. It was Lady Gwydir. She sat with her hands clasped on her lap, still as one of the statues in the gardens. She must have been watching me for almost a minute.

"How do you like them?"

I spun around. "M'lady," was all I managed to stutter.

"The deer," she prompted, nodding to the wall. She was indeed very beautiful, the angle of her eyebrows giving her a critical look. She wore a plain dark dress with matching shoes, with a lace cap just covering the top of her head.

"They're … they're very nice, m'lady."

"Really? I think they're ghastly," she murmured. Her voice was deep and slow, with an almost ironic edge, as though she was articulating herself even more so than she normally did. She shook her head and then fixed her eyes with mine, giving me a look that pierced straight through me. I made sure not to look away, and thought I saw a small smile flicker. "Young Master MacKay," she said, "come closer so I can have a look at you. I've heard some good things, and my husband is certainly pleased with your father." She paused as I stepped towards her. "It's only I'm not sure how much I really need a piper."

"Aye, m'lady."

"My, you're still very young, aren't you? How old are you?"

"Eleven, m'lady."

"Mm. And do you think your playing would be able to fill a hall this size?"

I looked around. "Certainly, m'lady."

She cocked her head. "It's too small? You would prefer bigger?"

I wasn't sure how to respond to this, and felt panic swell in my chest. "If it pleased, m'lady?" I looked around, wondering how much bigger a room could possibly get.

"And what would you play for me on a day like today?"

"Well … it would depend on what you thought the occasion needed, m'lady. Happy, sad, fast or slow. The pìobaireachds are lovely but it's a lot of fun to play for the dancing," I ventured. "Though anything would sound fine with high ceilings like these, m'lady."

Here, to my relief she gave what sounded like a snort of approval. "Very good, very good. Perhaps in time you'll prove yourself a braw laddie, MacKay. Yes, perhaps we'll find enough for you to do." She clapped her hands and stood up. "Now, I have another engagement, so I shall keep this brief. I need you to be ready when called upon, always presentable, and able to take on whatever I ask of you."

I nodded. "Of course, m'lady."

"It won't all be piping."

"Aye, m'lady."

Once again, she gave me that piercing look, and muttered something to herself that I couldn't quite make out, before frowning. "What was your last meal?"

"Porridge, m'lady."

"Are you hungry?"

I nodded.

Lady Gwydir narrowed her eyes.

"Aye, m'lady."

Again, a smile seemed to flicker on her lips – over time I learned to recognize that this was the most the lady would do to betray her pleasure – and she beckoned to the door. "Very well then, MacKay. Away with Anna and see the cooks. Tell them I said you're too gaunt right now, and must be well fed before I can have you play for me. But with a bit of meat on those island bones we'll make use of you yet, I'm sure."

And that was that. That morning I took home a bundle of new clothes for daily use, and I was measured for Highland garb to wear for all my piping duties. From then on, the cooks and maidservants of the castle kitchen took me as their special charge, feeding me and tidying my appearance for life at Drummond Castle. All of a sudden, I'd become a piper just like my father.

I would say that this first employment as a piper led to some of the happiest and most carefree times of my life. When I look back on those days, it feels impossible to attach them to the same person sitting here scribbling away in this madhouse.

At first, I would only be given small jobs: welcoming visitors to the castle, sometimes playing for an hour in the gardens as background for an afternoon spent reading by Lady Gwydir or her friends. Her reputation as a formidable lady was indeed justified, and I saw many servants shrink under her icy stare. Though I perhaps didn't notice it at the time; during the initial weeks and months I must have been little more than a novelty; piping certainly wasn't revered on the estate to the extent it had been on Raasay. Yet as I continued to fulfill my duties as best I could, I saw that Lady Gwydir gradually began investing time and money into my education. She started engaging me in more complex conversation, testing me by bringing up matters I had little or no knowledge of. It was arranged that every day at lunch I would sit with Anna who would help me refine my English, both in speaking and reading. Often – if their own work schedules allowed – my siblings joined me for these lessons, and as a group we would huddle in the servants' quarters or in the grounds, going around the circle pronouncing odd new words and phrases. My sisters were much quicker in picking up proper English than the boys. I myself owe Anna a great debt for her patience; her lessons have been of benefit to me almost every day since they began. After just a few months, I felt able to converse appropriately with people of any class, and perhaps even more useful for my future employment, I became able to identify the class of people by their attire and demeanor.

With so much to fill my time, the months really did fly by. Any major piping responsibilities were still the charge of my father. I didn't see much of him as he catered for Baron Gwydir, who I suspect didn't have the faintest idea who I was until about six months into my employment. The main difference in my life was that I now had the time, duty, and resources to practice to my heart's content. As a family, we no longer had to spend days worrying about where our next meal was coming from, and Lady Gwydir always demanded new and more exciting music. My father was happy to oblige in teaching me. When the weather was fair, we could take lessons outdoors on the estate, playing pipes or just singing on woodland walks. When it was rainy or too cold, chanters by the fire was the way of it, which brought back warm memories of tunes in Taigh a' Phìobaire. All of this contributed to creating the perfect environment for me to improve as a piper and a musician generally. I would not have reached the heights I did had fate not led our family to this place, with me at that age.

The happiest of all developments was that my new role called for me to have my own bagpipes. On Raasay, we had shared the one set, but now we had enough resources to allow for us to each have our own. I remember it was Hogmanay of our first year at Drummond Castle that I received mine; I'd had to make do with playing the old Raasay ones for the first six months of living there, but when I laid my eyes on that new set, mo chridhe! Mo ghràidh! They were beautifully made, with foreign, deep-colored timber mounted with bone and ivory, and decorated like the columns of the great buildings in Edinburgh that my father had started taking me to on his trips to the capital.

I had to wait an age as my father carefully re-tied the bridles on the drone reeds, ensuring a complete balance, and also adjusted my chanter reed to allow for an easier blow on such a chilly night. For much of the previous few days my brothers and I had been out in the frost gathering firewood and leaving it to dry in the stables, as Baron Gwydir had requested that just before midnight a huge blaze was to be lit in the castle courtyard to see in the coming year. Lady Gwydir had told me the day before that there was to be a ceilidh, and the best part was that I was expected to play a few tunes for dancing.

"The year'll be over by the time you're done," I muttered, shifting my weight from foot to foot, holding the wee mug of ale that I'd been allowed for the special occasion.

"Just you be patient, lad. Not many young players are so lucky to have their first pipes made by Donald MacDonald of Skye, or set to perfection by John MacKay of Raasay."

"I'm grateful, Father," I said, trying to keep my voice level. "It's just been ages since we had a proper ceilidh, and I want to test the sound out beforehand."

"Oh, aye, it's been a while," my father nodded without looking at me. "They might know how to make those nice soft beds here, but they don't know how to dance like they did in Raasay, that's for sure. Right, these are ready for a tune, I expect."

My face lighting up, I sprang towards him and reached out for what was already my most cherished possession, but mo chreach, Father waved me away with his hands! Before playing, he liked to recite a favorite verse from the bard Duncan Ban MacIntyre. I think that evening he spoke as slowly as he could just to annoy me that wee bit more. I'll see if I can remember it here:

> *Proud Pipe of polished joints and bone-mounted tops,*
> *Of hardwood that comes from Jamaica, the best that grows there,*
> *Lathe-turned round and straight, ring-mounted with ivory;*
> *With mouth-piece and chanter, just right with sweeter temper.*

I suppose it wasn't the worst reason to delay. It's strange, but seems it's easier to appreciate a good bit of poetry when you're locked in a cell with nowt to distract you.

I played for a bit of the dancing inside Drummond Castle after the fire that Hogmanay, and I was certain Lady Gwydir was pleased with what she heard. She muttered something about my being rewarded when I passed her on my way back towards my family, but she was much too busy to speak to me for long. I didn't mind. I felt like I was walking on air, so thrilled that the dancers enjoyed the tunes and that my parents were happy with my performance.

"He's inherited my knack for getting them going, hasn't he, mo ghràidh?" Father asked my mother with a wink.

"I was actually thinking Angus was a bit better," Mother replied without hesitation, before taking a sip from her glass to mask her smile.

It was a week later when I fully understood how impressed Lady Gwydir had been with my piping. It had really started to snow by then, and Anna and I were in the servants' quarters, warming our feet by the fire and having bread and warm milk. Instead of helping me with English as she was meant to be doing, Anna had spent the whole time winding me up, telling me that the lady would be awaiting me at the mansion after lunch and that I should expect the worst.

"Can you please just tell me what it's about?" I tried again.

"I'm telling the truth!" Anna protested through a huge mouthful of bread. "She told me she no longer requires your services anymore."

"You're not funny."

"Honestly!" Anna said, finally managing to swallow. "She said she never wanted to hear the sound of bagpipes ever again. Something about it sounding like a dying goat."

I sighed, and gave up. Thanking the cooks on the way out, I made my way across the snowy courtyard, the paths of gray slush made by all the staff on their various trips visible against the stark white. Immediately my teeth started chattering from the cold. When I went through the door built into the mansion's main turret, I found Lady Gwydir standing and lecturing two of her maidservants in the hall. I quickly smoothed my hair and made sure I brushed off any snow or crumbs of food before she saw me. Bidding her maidservants leave, by the time I reached her the two of us were alone.

"M'lady."

"MacKay. Why have I summoned you?"

Though by this stage I knew to expect sudden questions from her, this did not mean I had learned how best to answer them. "Anna … No, I don't know, m'lady."

Lady Gwydir's face was blank. "Good. Follow."

She led me to the end of the hallway and up the stairs. I still had not yet managed to find my bearings in this building; every corner seemed to lead on to an identical corridor lined with identical portraits, all with giant gilded frames. The lady walked briskly, and I hurried close after her, so close that when she stopped abruptly in front of one of the many tall doors, I nearly ran straight into her.

"Steady, MacKay. I'll need you on your feet for this."

She opened the door and motioned that I step inside ahead of her.

I did so and found myself standing in the middle of a library, the likes of which I'd never even known existed. It was stunning – exactly the sort of room you would expect to find in such a place. The air smelled of leather and something else, almost spiced, like one of those fancy venison pies I'd seen the lords spread with jelly at banquets. The rug on the floor was thick, a deep red with embroidered golden flowers, and I felt my feet sink into it. Casting my eyes around the enormous mahogany shelves, holding volume upon volume, all in seemingly perfect condition, I wondered what on earth I was doing here. For some reason, I thought she was going to ask me to do something ridiculous, like count how many books she had or some other such tedious task. Even the walls themselves held shelves, and the books were lined nearly up to the ceilings, well beyond a man's reach.

I must have made some sort of sound, because Lady Gwydir silenced me with a flick of her wrist. She was still stood in the doorway. "Anna tells me you can now read English adequately, so I have decided that I will be lending you my library twice a week. Most of these books will be of no interest to you, but there is a section over here," she led me to the shelves nearest the window, "that I would like you to make a start upon." She ran her fingers over some of the spines, before selecting one and handing it to me.

I read the title. "*A Collection of Ancient Martial Music of Caledonia Called Pìobaireachd*, by Donald MacDonald." I had heard mention of this book, famous for being the first of its kind; never had I seen it, however, having been taught all of the tunes it held orally, through canntaireachd.

"Indeed," Lady Gwydir said. "I know that having learned from your father there is no doubt you shall be a fine player all your life. Already you are a fine player. But you are of an age when it is not too late for you to turn your hand to other things, like he did," she tapped the book. "Now, perhaps you will not take to writing music, but some musicians I have spoken to believe you would have the potential if you tried. If there was a way for me to nurture that potential, remiss would I be to not at least provide the resources. It's up to you to make the most of this opportunity, though."

I didn't know what to say. Eventually, I managed to mumble my thanks, though my voice sounded thin and far away.

She nodded and made to leave the room, and automatically I began to follow.

"No, no, MacKay," she said, suddenly stern. "Do you think I'd walk all the way here just to tell you that?" She pointed to a chair, and then closed the door behind her. I stood still, not knowing exactly what to do, before I heard her voice ringing from the other side of the door. "Your time starts now!"

What an honor this was. I will try my best to describe the ways in which this helped me, but it's impossible to adequately put into words how significant Lady Gwydir's gesture was. I certainly took to the task; Lady Gwydir needn't have worried about that. She had a large collection of music books and I read them voraciously, teaching myself the complexities of written music. As a result my grasp of the language drastically improved, and the many tunes I knew by heart from my father I could now imagine exactly how they would look if they were written down. To make this a reality, I learned to write notes and make study charts for myself, not just for pipes but for fiddle and pianoforte as well, and as it turned out the image of these scores made memorizing tunes far easier. I found that writing was also a useful way to remember small differences between similar pieces, in a way singing the canntaireachd could not. I wasn't permitted to bring Anna or any of my siblings into the library, so any words I didn't recognize I had to write down and take home to ask my sisters. Sometimes I'd write out entire passages from books I knew John would enjoy, and he'd sit up reading them by candlelight before we'd discuss them in depth in the morning.

I was surprised at that time to find that father wasn't entirely pleased at this development in my life. He learned all his tunes by singing, and he taught that way also. I thought that it was perhaps simply because he had never been exposed to writing the tunes scientifically that he did not value the written score, but when I said as much, I was swiftly given a lecture. Apparently, a young noble girl called Eliza – he'd mentioned her before, speaking of her charm and intellect – had first introduced him to these methods when he was in his mid-twenties, and he was quick to tell me that he hadn't thought the practice useful then either! Eliza was an orphaned niece of MacLeod's who stayed at Raasay House. All I really knew of what became of her was that she had moved to India, where she married her pick of the English gentlemen there, and that during our time at Drummond Castle, she commissioned a set of pipes to be sent to my father from those distant shores. It seemed that she and my father had been quite fond of one another. In truth, it was not the finest set of pipes on the Drummond estate; they were very tough to reed to our satisfaction. Still, my father composed a lovely pìobaireachd for her in gratitude.

Another reason for Father's disapproval of my new situation– and I've only now just realized this – may have been that Lady Gwydir did not consult him when she decided I was to undertake this extra study. Aye, I imagine that must have rubbed my parents the wrong way. Were the lady not our benefactor, I'm sure more would have been made of it. But I don't want it to seem like my parents were bitter or ungrateful. My father was undoubtedly proud of my ability and my obvious knack for notation and composition – and make no mistake, I had a knack for it – but I don't think he thought it a good use of my talents to spend so much time being lost in whatever I was writing, even if it was his own settings of tunes. Still, there was a lot to learn in MacDonald's settings too, and I studied his writing methods, even if I continued to play the tunes as father wanted to hear them.

Despite Father's misgivings, as a musician I benefited greatly, and my first real breakthrough in music – at least as I saw it – came just a couple of years after arriving at Drummond Castle. I think it was in 1825. Thanks in no small way to Lady Gwydir's benevolence, in this year I was presented a Highland Society prize of five shillings for my written music, and so began my grand designs for publishing a collection of pìobaireachd with the MacKay name on it one day. My family was delighted when I was awarded this prize, as was Lady Gwydir, though I could tell Father would have preferred I had been rewarded for my playing, as Donald had been. For this reason, when it came to the next year's prizes, that was chief among my goals.

Arriving in Edinburgh the following year, something felt different from our previous trips. I loved the feel of this city more than any I'd been to, with its winding cobbled streets and its daunting castle overlooking the whole historic town, and of course, how close it was to the sea. But when I walked past the columns and through the doors of the Theatre Royal on Princes Street, my nerves were blinding me to it all. The awards seemed to be more of an occasion than I had noticed previously. In the foyer, I felt that other pipers were looking at me, and I noticed them nodding their heads towards us, talking in hushed voices. Following my previous success, it seemed my name had started to spread a little throughout the year, although this more than likely had something to do with my family. I had the sense that pipers were expecting all John MacKay's sons to be great pipers and I was used to people watching me as I played, but it was a peculiar sensation, feeling eyes linger on you just for walking into a room. Particularly when you're still just a lad. All of this meant I was undoubtedly the most apprehensive I'd ever been before playing.

"You're looking a wee bit pale," John said, clearly suppressing a grin. "Seems like everyone's turned up just to listen to you."

"Give me peace, John," I snapped, before I burst into shaky laughter. I tried to focus on the magnificent ceiling, the adorned cornices. To no avail. "Think I'm going to be sick."

Our father returned from greeting a big group of pipers, many of whom we recognized from visiting us on Raasay. He rubbed his hands together. "Ready?"

"No," I said.

"Well, too late to back out now, so you might as well just tell those nerves to falbh 's tarraing!"

John's peal of laughter at this drew a few scathing glances from our distinguished company, and my father put his hands on each of our shoulders. "Better go get settled in," he winked. "Before they kick us out."

In truth, I didn't think much of my performance on that day. When I bowed and headed off the stage, my hands still trembling slightly, silently I was cursing myself. I'd played "MacKintosh's Lament" and felt I'd pushed the first variation a bit faster than Father would have liked. He had been listening from the side of the stage and seemed happy enough, however, brushing off my worries.

"The tune was fine and played with feeling, lad. And remember, the judges know as much of pìobaireachd as I know of making whisky, which is little."

The reels and the Highland dances that interspersed the performances then took my mind off things, which made it even more of a shock to find out I'd been awarded fourth prize at the end of the event. This was a bit of a sensation given I was barely thirteen, and how many seasoned performers had been playing that day, and I got louder applause than the three pipers who finished above me. I was sure that part of the advantage I had was that the tune I played had such a beautiful song at its heart.

Even the most cloth-eared laird could be moved by a melody so soulful and, if I might say, played on such a well-prepared pipe.

I was presented with a handsome Highland pistol to wear when piping, and I remember thinking it the perfect prize at the time. Unfortunately, so did John, and he decided to pilfer it whenever I was distracted. In my heart, though, I knew I was a better player than I'd demonstrated that day, and in the coach back to Perth, this notion was eating slowly through my mind like an insect would a leaf, though I knew I ought to feel pride.

Lament for the Union, 1835

I grew to manhood at Drummond Castle. In many ways my years there shaped me more than my eleven spent on Raasay. Not only was my day-to-day language forever changed – or at least very much divided between English and Gaelic – but with Lady Gwydir's patronage I became a better musician than I ever would have had we remained at Taigh a' Phìobaire. Of course, I like to suppose I never lost the island flair when it came to performing, be it piping or singing or dancing, but there is little doubt the time I spent with my nose in books changed me as a musician.

Lady Gwydir never outgrew her affection for a good tune, but as she got a wee bit older, I became increasingly aware that my duties were dwindling. Her ladyship entertained less and had fewer occasions to call on me, and she and the baron were spending more time away from Perthshire at their other properties. When I first arrived, I could expect to play each afternoon that the weather was fine, and even indoors at times, though I would often be placed a room or two away so that Lady Gwydir could socialize with the sound of pipes in the background. Now, however, the rhythm of life I had established in my early years at Drummond Castle had all but faded. I was only really summoned whenever the guests took a fancy for music, or to provide a special welcome to a visitor at the castle.

Every now and then – and these were my favorite duties – I would still be requested to wander in the gardens, playing tunes at a distance from folk walking through the central gardens. In those times, I was able to really lose myself in the tunes, and focus fully on the sound of the instrument, all while taking in the richness of sight and smell in the gardens. Occasionally, I was called on to ascend the keep tower, and play there on the battlements as visitors arrived at the castle entrance below. Playing in such a location, all sounds disappear except the pipes, and when you stop, there is a profound calm that reigns where the music once was. I'd hear the peal of the bells ringing over in Crieff, or possibly carriage wheels on the roads to and from Drummond Castle, perhaps the sound of cattle far off. To be up there now, breathing that crisp air, feeling the wind reddening my cheeks, aye, that would do me a world of good.

My weekly sessions in the library were never altered: two hours on Tuesday and Thursday afternoons, no more, no less. The rest of my time was spent practicing or writing or sorting my pipes, perhaps heading out of the estate with one or the other of my brothers on some errand. We were much too big to ride Orion and Hercules any longer, but I'd still make the trip to the stables every so often with as many treats as I could carry. It was a nice enough routine overall, but when my twentieth year passed, and then another, and then another, having read every relevant text in the library several times over and having very little to challenge myself musically, something began to take root in my mind. Admittedly, I hadn't really recognized what this something was yet, but with hindsight it's obvious: I was already thinking about leaving Drummond Castle. Though I knew Lady Gwydir would have me as long as I wished to stay, the place had become stifling.

It wasn't just me. As we grew to adulthood, my siblings dispersed. Cursty and Kathy Òg took husbands and started their own families in different parts of the Highlands, while Roderick and Donald were now both moving around Scotland, taking whichever piping position presented itself. This left just John and me with my parents, and they were not getting any younger. Father was approaching his seventh decade and more than once had mentioned his desire to return to the islands, where he and my mother could live simply and see out their days. Piping for Baron Gwydir had been profitable in many ways and had provided our family with a security we'd never known before, but they both missed the peace and community of life by the sea. Not that Crieff was a hive of industry, mind, but these things are all relative. Part of the challenge would be affording the move and paying for accommodation in a new place, but father had thought that through, and I reckoned that plans might be already underway, despite not being told as much.

So, these were the things that were roiling around in my head as we arrived in Edinburgh in July 1835 for the Highland Society competition. The esteem of these triennial competitions had grown among pipers, and while some – including my father – felt that improvisation and artistry were being sacrificed to a rigid formalization of the scores, the competitions had become important for pipers wanting to make their living or at least a name in the piping world. Having no serious piping expertise, the judges needed a fair playing field for assessing the competitors, and so anyone who played the music they had written in front of them most accurately stood the best chance.

As my father, brother John, and I stood outside the Theatre Royal, the sky was murky but the air mild, we greeted all of the faces that had become so familiar to us over the years. The pipers gathered were all trying to make their way as full-time musicians, but many were really just household staff who occasionally picked up a set of pipes.

We weren't all that different, but our knowledge of the instrument allowed us to ply trade in things other pipers might need and couldn't make themselves. In those days, piping equipment was almost impossible to come by if you didn't know someone who could make it, and that was one thing we were able to do. Since we'd struck up a friendship with Tom – the gamekeeper on the estate – we now had the advantage of an expert leatherworker giving us a hand. Normally Tom would be repairing equipment, boots, bridles, saddles, harnesses, and the like, but when he turned his mind to pipes you could always tell by the quality craftmanship when a bag had been stitched by him. I remember watching him turn tanned wedder sheepskin into a beautiful pipe bag. He had a simple form that we made for him from cloth, and he'd lay that on the hide to cut the shape of the bag, then use furniture glue on the edges to hold them together, before adding an overlap piece with more glue. Once that dried, he'd use a fine awl to make thread holes through the seam, and then sit at the saddler's bench and stitch, needles going both directions at once, using the largest thread he could. We told Tom what the bag needed to be, and he taught us how to make it so. For his troubles, he took a share of the extra money we made selling to pipers on days like these, days when we were getting more requests than we could handle.

I hadn't been particularly talkative throughout that day, though, being too wrapped up in what I was going to play. I'd opted to go with "Lament for the Union," and was humming it through, my fingers moving behind my back. In previous years I'd come close, but this year I had set myself a straightforward task. I was there to win the prize pipe, as Donald and now Roderick had by this time, Roderick winning in 1832. I'd heard the prize pipe described so often in poems and songs with such seductive language that it'd become somewhat mythical. As my father was in attendance that year – and given my suspicions, who knew if he would be making that trip again – it felt this was an opportunity that had to be taken.

"You'll want to go make sure they have your name in the list," I heard my father say, before feeling his hand on my shoulder. I glanced at him.

His hair and beard were now more gray than brown, and his voice was a bit more cracked than it used to be. "Try to get on late."

"Last to play, first to win?" I asked.

"Absolutely," he nodded. "The fewer pipers between you and the prize giving, the more likely you'll be in it."

"Right, I'll see what I can manage," I replied, before adding, "I wouldn't want to be first on playing 'Lament for the Harp Tree.'"

After John and I had got our places on the list, Father headed inside to find his friends, leaving us to have a quiet conversation with a couple of other pipers. They were after a sale of drone reeds, and were lucky to catch us just before we'd sold out.

"You'll not find any with a richer sound than these," I assured them as I handed over the goods.

"I'd say mine would be at least as good," said a voice just behind us. "We learned from the same man!"

Without turning, I recognized at once who it was. "Not another John in my life," I grinned.

Approaching me was my dearest of friends, John Ban Mackenzie, still undoubtedly one of the most gifted pipers in the country. He was the very one who had made such an impression when staying with us on Raasay. Arguably, John Ban was one of the finest students my father ever taught – outside my brothers and me, of course! Our connection had since grown during our many Society meetings and piping events together. He had won prize pipe in 1823 and come second to Donald the year before, and on top of this, he had cultivated a reputation for being one of the first men you'd turn to if you were needing repairs to pipes or a new instrument altogether. A master with his lathe, he was. I'll admit it, if John Ban was there to sell reeds then I'd probably choose his over mine!

"Great to see you, Angus," he said. Before I knew it, he'd dropped his case and was embracing me. He was a bear of a man, and I felt the air being squeezed from my lungs. "Your father here?"

"Aye, he's around. Not lost that grip yet, then," I croaked. "How've you been, old friend?"

"Aye, doing grand. And here's wee John!"

"And here's big John, hullo!" my brother laughed, giving him a punch on the shoulder. "Let me finish this sale and I'll be right with you."

I turned to John Ban and we walked away from the crowd for a bit of peace. "So, family alright, then?"

"Getting by, getting by. But listen, you'll recall my reamer problem?"

"How could I forget?" Last time we'd met, John Ban had complained to me for nearly an hour over several bottles of wine about not having a reamer that gave him the sound he wanted from his chanter. To be honest, it had seemed good enough to me when he demonstrated, but I could see it was driving him mad.

"I've finally worked it out," he now said. "Wait till you see this." He started rummaging around in his case, and then brandished something metal.

It took me a moment to realize what it was. "Is that—"

"Aye, a bayonet!" John Ban declared, "Or at least it was. I was able to grind it down into a perfect chanter reamer, and what a sound, let me tell you."

He spent the next few minutes explaining exactly how he'd made this discovery, removing the blade from a musket he allegedly had lying around. Very appropriate for a devout man such as John Ban to be turning swords into ploughshares, I thought, or in his case, bayonets into reamers.

"If you're playing a great lament, lad," he said to me with a slightly deranged look in his eye, "what better tool for chanter making, tell me, what's more appropriate, than a deliverer of death?"

"I'm just glad you're happy," I told him. We talked for a while longer, and it felt good to take my mind off of my upcoming performance. When eventually we made our way inside, I noticed that I was actually looking forward to the simple act of playing music for my friends, something I'd lost sight of a little in recent years. Perhaps I'd been obsessing over the competitions to distract myself from my true feelings about my future, but whether this was true or not, I certainly felt more relaxed than I had been in a while.

And how did this change in me affect the outcome when I took to the stage? I need only put into words the smile that is stretching across my face right now. It was one of the best days of my life. I began with a few tuning notes, but the pipes were rock solid and ready, and so I launched into nearly thirty minutes of music. I think the floor could've fallen away in the hall and I might not have noticed, so lost was I in it, so buried in the detail of that performance. This tune is not so much a test of memory as of concentration, and its multiple variations washed over me like waves on a shore. I remember it perfectly even now: each variation has a small number of theme notes, often returning to A – the note of the piper, as it was known in pìobaireachd notation – and the slightest lapse of focus, or a trifling thought about your drone steadiness, and you can kiss goodbye to it. I remember in other years sometimes noticing wee things in the audience while I was playing – a particularly well-turned-out lady, or someone being served tea, or folk leaving at the back – but this time, I finished my tune almost with some surprise that there were still people in the room, or judges listening, because they'd been lost to me for close to half an hour.

When I finished, it seemed as though I'd just been plunged back into the room from up in the clouds. My shirt was soaked with sweat under the tunic and plaid, and my bonnet was soggy also. A long piece in a full room on a summer's day is a challenge to both the piper and the pipe, and it seemed we'd both held up well. Though I was only 22, I'd been playing pipes for a long time, and never had I had such a satisfied feeling after a performance. I knew I'd played superbly; I'd just expressed something that for a long while I'd been desperate to express in that lament. It was time for me to leave Drummond Castle. Not only that, I also knew that wherever I went, I was ready to do it alone.

It was no shock to anyone that day when I was awarded the prize pipe, though my competitors all played well. It was a stunning instrument I won, with an inscribed silver shield fixed to the chanter stock. To add to the celebrations, John Ban won the gold medal for previous winners, while my brother John was awarded a pair of Highland pistols for fourth prize. At last, he'd got his hands on some pistols of his own! I recall he was also well to the fore in the dancing that day, and received great adulation for his energetic performance of the Gillie Callum, to the merriment of all in attendance.

John Ban, John, my father and I all drank among friends for a long time in the Assembly Rooms, with much dancing carried on late into the evening. Eventually, the manager Murray escorted us from the premises, kind enough to hold our pipes so we could retrieve them the following day. From here, Father and John Ban called it a night, but John and I, I remember we lustily sang some songs from Raasay as we stumbled from pillar to pillar around Edinburgh. We might have attracted the attention of some ladies of pleasure for the first time, apparently fascinating them with talk of reeds and chanters, before waking up in a strange bed with less money than we'd had the night before. From then on, this became a vice of mine, though I don't think it was much to John's liking.

Simply put, with that performance of "Lament for the Union" I'd established myself as one of the most talented pipers alive, and at an incredibly young age, no less. You hear of some people who describe a certain melancholy when they attain their wildest dreams early on in life;

they describe a sort of hollow victory that leaves them feeling rudderless afterwards. I must say that winning the prize pipe did not leave me feeling hollow at all. Sure, I'd achieved something that I'd wanted to achieve for years and now that desire was sated, but to me that void was filled as soon as it appeared. It was made plain by the sheer volume of people expressing interest in my services – perhaps a dozen individuals afterwards were making enquiries as they shook my hand – that I'd opened the door to many new opportunities. I listened to all of them intently, and my eyes were shining at the thought of going out to forge a life for myself in this world.

But first, I had to vomit. That next morning heralded the most crippling bottle-ache of my life. After such a heavenly and indulgent day, it was only right that I was in for a hellish return journey. Many times, we had to stop the carriage so John or I could throw our guts up in a ditch, Father looking on smugly.

"You alright down there?" he called out of the window to me as I was crouched on my haunches, head in hands. "Oi, did you hear me, Angus? O' prize piper? I actually had quite a good sleep if you're wondering."

I had too much respect for my father to tell him where to go, and in any case, I couldn't turn my head without another wave of nausea swelling inside me. I felt my heart beating in my temples. I would have happily forsaken my grand plans if it meant being free of that feeling. Eventually, I managed to purge myself of everything it was possible to purge, and when at last we arrived back at the estate I fell into my bed for many, many hours.

I gave Lady Gwydir notice of my decision the following day. She understood. She actually went so far as to tell me that she was surprised she'd hung on to me for so long. I let her know as best I could how much I appreciated everything she had done for me, how I would never have got to where I was without her, and she responded with her customary half smile.

"You're quite right, MacKay," she said. "Now that you mention it, you do owe me a rather sizeable debt. Though I must say I have heard some fine music out of the bargain, so I'm willing to call it even. So, you must tell me where it is you are headed. Where on this earth are there gardens greener than my own?"

This was the question. I wasn't sure exactly where I would go, and so to whet the appetite, I began with some short stints of a few weeks and months at various castles and estates around the country, places I knew I could work while deciding on a long-term plan. About a month after winning the prize pipe, I printed and distributed a prospectus announcing my intention to publish a book of music, seeking subscriptions from the members and benefactors at the Highland Society. It was actually as a result of this that my decision about where to go turned out to be rather easy.

One of the people who got in touch with me was Walter Campbell of Islay, who was a Member of Parliament for Argyll, and laird of the island. We met in Edinburgh, where he talked animatedly about Highland culture, and explained that a piper on Islay would be a wonderful addition to the history of piping in that part of the world. To hear a man of high station hold Gaelic culture in such esteem in the modern world of politics and industry was certainly refreshing. Also present was the laird's son, John Francis Campbell, often called Young John of Islay, who was a lover of Gaelic culture as well, despite having been educated at the best English schools. He was only fourteen at the time, but as all who had been schooled so intensely from such a young age, he spoke in a voice that seemed learned beyond his days. He seemed to be quite taken by me; I think all his time spent in the south had led him to think of a big, kilted piper like me in full Highland costume as something of a fantasy!

His father went on to speak of how important he thought it was to preserve the music and stories that were at risk of being lost to the changing landscape of the West Highlands, and needless to say, he was enthusiastic about the prospect that I might come to Islay. I remember thinking how strange it was after this conversation that I had attained such a status that a laird would meet me with his son and shake my hand and request my help. As a lad, I'd certainly never had anything resembling such an encounter with the laird's family on Raasay.

Just before we were to part ways, the laird took hold of my arm and told me an anecdote I'd heard before from my father, about how John Campbell – also known as John Piper – had brought his father's manuscript of pìobaireachd to the Highland Society in 1818 for their consideration. John Piper had been the son of Colin Mor – a formidable player – and grandson of Donald Campbell, who had learned music from the revered MacCrimmons just as my own father had. Also, John Piper had been a relative of the laird Walter Campbell, and tutor to Young John. Lord, it's a miracle I can still navigate these Scottish naming patterns; I'd like to see any other patient at Bedlam manage it! In the end, to the scandal of players everywhere, the Society rejected John Piper's collection, alleging it was useless for pipers, purely because it was written in Gaelic and they couldn't understand its importance. I could tell that the laird and Young John remained livid about this, and they mentioned that the original manuscript was still kept in Islay House. It was quite plain that they mentioned this because they knew I'd be eager to use it as a source for my own collection, as it would undoubtedly make an excellent addition to the tunes I had from my father. And, well, they were not mistaken!

I wrote to the laird accepting his proposal, and arrangements were made. My enthusiasm to spread my wings never wavered, and within a week or so I was packing my things at Drummond Castle, this time for good. Suddenly, I found myself embroiled in a series of long and difficult goodbyes. My hands are doing that bastard thing again – not going where I'm telling them to – so I won't recall them all in detail here. Most notably there was of course Lady Gwydir, Tom and Anna, the cooks who had fed me so many meals, and Orion my noble steed, who was still kicking. Over those last couple of days, I bade so many farewells, offered such a quantity of gratitude, made such a number promises to see others again soon that my face ached.

Waking up in the cottage on my last morning, I received word my carriage was waiting for me at the gate. The driver had already collected my bags before I'd risen. The rain soon eased, giving me a window to walk down the driveway without getting soaked, and my family quietly gathered outside for our final goodbyes. Hugging each of them, I made sure to drink in every detail of their faces, every line on their skin, every smell, every strand of hair. I'd never been without at least some of my family for any significant period of time, and I already missed them. The last person I reached was John, who was soon to leave himself to become piper to The Right Honorable Sir Robert Gordon in Aberdeenshire.

"I'll be thinking of you, wee brother," I said, feeling his arms wrapped tightly around my greatcoat. Over his shoulder I saw the blackbirds and sparrows picking at unseen insects, dancing between the pinecones that my brothers and I were once so fond of throwing at one another's heads in our younger days.

"Wee brother? You know I'm taller than you," John replied, his voice little more than a whisper. "But aye, so will I. Good luck. Don't do anything I wouldn't do."

"Lord, hardly narrows it down, does it?"

He laughed as we separated. "Maybe not. Just keep up the music, Angus. A bit more practice and I think you might be able to make something of it one day."

"Aye, I'll try my best," I smiled, my lip quivering. "Well, until we meet again."

I left and didn't look back for fear of letting them see my tears. I knew I was on the right path though; I could feel it more with every step.

Piper to Campbell of Islay, 1837

The cottage I was given was on the east side of the main street in the village of Bridgend, a ten-minute stroll from Islay House. Yet another magnificent home, was Islay House. You eventually grow accustomed to them as a piper – can't afford them, right enough. Mine was a decent enough lodging by my own standards; the laird received me well. It was about the size of Taigh a'Phìobaire, but without having to compete with a legion of siblings and cows I felt I had more than enough space. There was a small fireplace in the front room, a decent-sized bed that kept me off the cold floor, and I was a stone's throw away from the salty waters of Loch Indaal. It was plenty for me.

I was soon enough charmed by the entire island. At that time, Islay must have had a population of about 15,000 people, so any apprehension I'd had about my sudden solitude turned out to be unfounded. The ports of Ellen, Charlotte, and Wemyss had all just recently been established to cater for this huge number of Ìlich. Often in the house alone I'd still find myself about to turn and ask John what he was thinking for his supper, or my mother if she needed me to run out for anything, but in general it was a thriving place, and I was actually having to get used to more human contact than I'd ever had before!

The laird and Young John were at the heart of most of it. Young John was athletic and clever, and unlike many of his peers, he saw Gaelic not as a barbarous language of the uneducated but as a treasure that needed to be protected. Despite his age, he and I soon became fast friends, and I could have said the same about many good people on the island. It felt as though my standing as piper put me somewhere between the classes: quite an odd position to be in though not at all unpleasant.

I remember spending the first of many late nights drinking at a tavern with the laird's staff, sat at a table, smoking and sampling some of the finest whiskies the island had. It seemed that everyone wanted to introduce themselves to me. I think we were on to the Laphroaig: a nice, peaty dram which didn't half put hairs on your chest. The innkeeper had been over explaining in detail why Islay whisky was so excellent. Apparently, before successive lairds had encouraged the development of the island's distilleries, every man and his dog had been concocting their own spirits to avoid the taxes, so they'd had plenty of practice. The result now was that the whisky was in cheap supply for all, and I agreed with him when he claimed it was some of the best in the world.

Sitting there, I felt a strange excitement at hearing snippets of conversation cutting through the hubbub. Everyone in the place was speaking Gaelic, and it felt as though I'd known them all for much longer than a couple of days. I'd started the evening with a man called Donald MacMhuirich, one of the laird's advisors and Young John's personal charge, though a large group had now formed around us. I'd briefly met MacMhuirich in Edinburgh where he had been a member of the laird's party. The crowd was listening intently as he went off on one of his frantic rants; MacMhuirich, with his wild mane of curly grey hair, was clearly just as enthusiastic about the heritage of the Gaels and the plans for the island's future as the Campbells seemed to be. And I'm sure he wouldn't mind me mentioning, he also wasn't shy of a drink!

"And Angus here," he slurred, slapping my shoulder, "Angus, you lot should've heard him in Edinburgh, I'm serious, he's going to remind us all what music is, he's going to write something that's …" He trailed off, before looking sadly at the glass in his hand. "It's empty," he mumbled.

I laughed, motioning to the bar for the decanter. We drank a while more, and every minute or so I caught the eye of one of the barmaids, a raven-haired beauty with eyes like pearls. She was clearly curious about this new feature on the island, one who seemed so well-connected with Islay House, and that strange rash – the infuriatingly itchy one that had been showing up terribly on my genitals the last few weeks, and which took all my strength not to claw at with my fingernails – had finally seemed to clear up. When a messenger arrived and whispered something into MacMhuirich's ear, I – feeling courageous following my skinful – was about to stand and speak to her. Yet before I could, I felt MacMhuirich's hand on my arm.

"Angus," he said, his words slightly more distinct than they had been before, "we've got to go."

The alcohol on his breath was enough to make my eyes water. "What do you mean?"

"It means Young John has called us and we're off to the big house."

"But it's after eight o'clock!" I protested. "And we're blind drunk! Or at least, you're blind drunk!"

"Oh, don't worry about that." MacMhuirich's chair groaned under the weight of his burly frame as he stood up. 'John'll probably have had a few as well. Believe me, you'll be glad to answer this summons."

The twinkle in MacMhuirich's eye was starting to stir my curiosity. "What is it?"

"A surprise, good piper, a surprise."

I glanced once more towards the barmaid, and MacMhuirich caught wind of my intentions and hiccupped with laughter.

"Oh, ceart! On Islay for one minute and already you're trying to rid the lassies of their dresses! Fear not, if that's what you're worried about then I can put you at ease. We'll have you back within the hour, I swear it. Trust me, this here'll be going on a long while yet."

Reluctantly, we said our goodbyes and I allowed MacMhuirich to lead me outside and along the road to Islay House. The golden moon was nearly full and the stars were bright, but without a lantern it wasn't quite light enough for us to make our way without stumbling every now and then. Nothing to do with the drink, I'm sure. I admired the silhouette of the castle as we arrived, glowing in the moonlight. Young John met us at the back door.

"I could smell the both of you before I could see you," he laughed. "Settling in, then, are we, MacKay?"

"Aye, I reckon I could get used to this place, Master Campbell," I replied.

"Glad to hear it. I'm sure MacMhuirich will tell me everything you get up to tomorrow. Now, in you come."

I was taken up into the house, away from the ground floor servants' hall and through the hall where I would usually play for the laird. Eventually we passed through a door, and I found myself in a gentleman's study. The light came from three candles on the mantle and a lamp on the huge desk by the window, giving the room a cozy feel. Many papers were stacked on a table, and so too the desk, where the sheets were arrayed in some sort of haphazard order.

"Welcome to your writing room," Young John announced to me. "I was going to show it to you tomorrow, but I couldn't wait."

For a moment, all I could do was laugh. "You're serious?"

"Of course! We need conditions to be favorable for your grand collection! Now, take a peek at what's there on the desk. I was just having one final read before passing it over to you."

I stood for a moment, shaking my head at the grinning Young John, before I duly obliged. Though I felt I already knew what it was, I read the title page with increasing excitement. "*Colin Campbell's Instrumental Book*! The one presented by John Campbell to the Highland Society in 1816, but the Society deemed it unworthy of a prize."

"The very same," Young John nodded.

"'Pretentious Society bastards' my father called them," I said, and then started when I realized what I'd just said in such company. The alcohol was still doing its work, though thankfully, it did not seem that Young John cared.

"My father thought the same, and right they were!" he said. "Just because the Society gentlemen couldn't understand a word of Gaelic, they decided it was useless to their cause. As though they'd know better than true pipers like you and your father!"

"And that was in spite of one of the competitors offering to translate!" I said.

"The laird thought you'd be able add the tunes to the collection you're compiling," MacMhuirich added from the back of the room.

"I'd be honored, absolutely honored," I said. Adjusting my eyes to the formation of the letters, I started to sing the lines on the page under my breath, and the first tune – "Clan donail Raoch" – took shape. I'd always longed to study these pages. Of course, after speaking to the laird in Edinburgh I'd known I would be exposed to some fine manuscripts on Islay, but to be given my own writing room in Islay House was more than I could have hoped.

Just then I noticed something else leaning against the desk, something polished and wooden. "What's this?"

"Ah, he's eagle-eyed!" MacMhuirich exclaimed. "That's your other reward."

I looked quizzically towards Young John, who had picked it up. I saw it was an empty frame, and Young John was holding it up to his face and looking through it towards me.

"I hope you know how to stand still for a few hours," he laughed. "As piper to the Laird of Islay, my father has commissioned Alexander Johnston to come and paint your portrait."

I was incredulous. "A portrait? Of me? But I'm just a lad from Raasay. Where on earth would it hang?"

"You're more than that now, MacKay," Young John nodded, comically raising his eyebrows at me through the frame. "We'll get you fitted for some good Campbell tartan for it. Right, it's high time you two got back to the tavern. I can smell MacMhuirich pickling in the corner."

Personally, I'd have happily made a start on the manuscript there and then, but I had to make do with heading up the road, back to the women and the whiskies and the singing … Ah, well.

That night was typical of my time on Islay. I was treated in a way that, to me, felt like royalty. Many pipers were employed about the country, but none of those men had employers with a real interest and enthusiasm for the music and culture of the Gael. Here was no gamekeeping, no table serving, no barn work for me. The post on Islay was privileged, and I was able to put all my energy efforts into playing, studying, and writing music.

On an average day, it was as soon as I woke that I could dedicate my time fully to writing. I'd usually wash and then head straight to the big house and up to my room, eating my bread and cheese along the way. Once there, sitting at that big desk would take up my first few daylight hours: poring over manuscripts, solving problems, making corrections, memorizing new tunes, sorting the collection. I always hated being disturbed during these mornings. If someone knocked and I knew it wasn't urgent I'd hold my breath and pretend not to be there. After all, I had many more tunes to notate, and I was enjoying the new challenges that came with the addition of the Campbell manuscripts. Also, my work was late enough as it was, with the Highland Societies nudging me to complete it; they were at that point in the process of assigning me someone to help present the work to the gentlemen and nobility that would be the chief subscribers.

The Campbell manuscripts at Islay House proved useful sources. I enjoyed comparing the settings across the collections and noticing if there were any differences between them, working out which worked best, and how they compared with the versions I'd learned from Father. They were written in canntaireachd. The challenges sometimes lay in finding the timing and precise pitches of notes – no wonder there were always so many versions of the same tune if each one called for different timings! – but I used my knowledge of playing the tunes to determine how they should be written. To the experienced piper, any manuscript serves as but a rough guide to finding the music anyway. Still, the Campbell manuscript was a great piece of work, and represented a deep knowledge of the music. I was pleased that I could put many of these pieces in front of pipers, by way of musical notation.

I spent most mornings immersed in music, noting passages and trying them on the chanter, and then adjusting until I was happy with the result. The house and my room were large enough that I could work without drawing the ire of anyone else, regardless of the hour. Practicing would take up much of the rest of the day, stopping perhaps for lunch and a walk down to Bowmore to see the old cross and round church. I'd say my favorite place to walk to was Finlaggan, to the ruins at that eerie spot which once marked the center of the lordship of the isles, that nigh-forgotten empire. You could feel history steeped in the earth there, but this was a fair jaunt away, so I'd only be going on trips like this if there wasn't performing to do, which often there was. The laird took every opportunity to organize events at which a tune would go down well. When the sun set, for me it was either back to the cottage for more practice or reading or – if I could manage to set it all aside for the night – on to the tavern.

Oh, there were a few late nights spent searching for the bottom of the cup! Perhaps there were one or two mornings I had to take off as well that I'm forgetting about. During these nights it's fair to say I met my fair share of the lassies of Islay. It seemed that being the laird's piper opened many doors, and not a few skirts, and there's hardly an outbuilding on that island that doesn't have a few secrets of mine to tell!

In short, life was good: a succession of joyful habits. Time moved quickly, the way it always seems to when this is so. That blustery winter, my parents wrote informing me that they'd moved to Skye. This was superb news. They were easier to reach, and I knew they'd be content there, if a little exposed to the elements. They were equally glad to hear all of my goings-on, and that I was well-provisioned, well-paid, well-liked, and well-connected. My father was particularly delighted to hear that my link to the Campbells was proving invaluable in obtaining subscriptions for the book. Knowing I was already capable of writing tunes on the great stave from my time at Drummond Castle, in his letters my father told me that he was glad that the man best equipped to present all of this immensely undervalued music was being given the opportunity. I was surprised: perhaps he'd come round to writing as a means of learning music after all, once he realized it meant his own tunes would be eternalized!

A Collection of Ancient Piobaireachd, 1837

My hopes were too high for this collection. I know this now. In truth, I don't wish to spend too much time reliving how it came to see the light of day; my cot has never looked so welcoming. After weighing me on the scales, Dr. Hood informed me this morning that unless my incontinence passes, it's likely I will be moved to the basement. The smell, apparently. It's too much for the attendants. I've pointed out that most of what comes out of me seems to be blood rather than shit, but apparently that matters not. Even the old one that surely has breathed in this air for too long to know the difference, even he complains. So, I will forgive myself for not dwelling on this episode with the publication too long, but to tell an honest tale I must include the bad with the good. The strange thing is, though the form in which the book ended up does remain among my chief regrets, I'm still not really sure what I might have done differently.

I had set myself an arduous task. There were many challenges to writing music best suited for performance, and previous collections had fallen short. I wanted the tunes in mine not only to reflect something of my father's creative style of playing, but also to simplify the overly ornate methods used to write music in the past. To me, all that just seemed like clatter, and modern pipers needed to have a clear path ahead. There would be no six months at MacCrimmon for the piper in the modern world. The players I'd grown up with near Drummond Castle had to work for a living, and a collection like this would hopefully preserve the best settings of the tunes, while meaning people no longer had to rely on memorizing them by singing canntaireachd. The day would come, I thought, when all pipers would read notes from a page, and it would be best for all if there was a common language of writing. This is how I aimed to help maintain something of Gaelic culture; I firmly believed it was a worthy cause. This I still believe.

But aye, what went wrong can be summed up with a name: James Logan. Even writing it here makes my skin crawl; it's all I can do not to scratch it out. I first met Logan in Edinburgh while there with the laird and Young John in the autumn of 1837. It was the first official meeting I was given regarding my collection of pìobaireachd. Back when I was informed that the Highland Society of London were interested in backing me, it was made clear that while I was the expert in pipe music, I was not permitted to personally present work to the subscribers. The Society therefore would have some say over the content and presentation, to – as they phrased it – "guarantee the success of the publication."

In truth, there was some relief in this for me at first. Being a native Gaelic speaker, I knew I might be looked down upon by those likely to afford the book, and even if this was inherently unjust, I wanted to be sure of the book's success as much as anyone else. The man allocated to help me in this regard was James Logan, a published author of several books and a man well-versed in the affairs of the Highland Society. He appeared to be the best candidate to help, and – still naïve to the character of the man – I was pleased to hear he had expressed his desire to do so.

That day we were to be introduced. I had wanted Logan to come to Islay so that I could show him all that I had done and explain exactly what I was seeking to accomplish through the collection, but for one reason or another he never was able to make the journey. This surprised me, as from what I'd heard of him – a member of the Club of True Highlanders in London – I'd have assumed he would jump at the opportunity to make that trip, and experience such a vibrant part of the country. But he was a busy man, it seemed. Instead, we were meeting in the grand dining room of the Charlotte Hotel on George Street in the New Town, and I had brought what little I could to make my demonstrations. The laird and Young John had traveled with me the day before, and having been unable to sleep in the carriage at all, I was still feeling the effects of the journey. The east coast of Scotland is invariably brighter than the west, and with the sun streaming through the tall windows and directly on to me, my skin felt hot beneath my shirt, waistcoat, and jacket. I loosened my cravat as much as I felt I could get away with.

Glancing around at the rest of the clientele, sitting there eating and drinking wine from tiny glasses beneath the chandeliers, I felt more than a wee bit awkward. At the table it was just the laird, Young John and me, and while to onlookers it was plain to see that the older and the younger man belonged in such an establishment, I – despite donning my finest attire – evidently did not. Though I'd been so near to it for most of my life, in reality I knew nothing of how to properly conduct myself in the upper echelons of society, and whenever I happened to find myself in a position like this without the excuse of piping, I could tell that people knew it to look at me.

The table was laden with an array of foods I had seen before, though never had the opportunity to try. Along with cheese and bread, meat was one of my staples, but I could not identify this meat on my plate for the life of me. Venison, perhaps? It was covered in a rich dark sauce, sat beside potatoes whipped until they were like fluffy clouds, and green beans covered in butter and onions. I had no idea how I'd manage to eat it without getting the gravy all over the table or my best clothes, so I subtly set to watching the other diners. They managed it very delicately, but still I felt too out of place to try. I felt myself turning red and took another gulp of my wine.

"Not quite right for your palate, then, MacKay?" Young John was eyeing me amusedly, glancing at my plate.

"Aye, a wee bit fancy for me, Master Campbell," I said. "I'm not too hungry anyway. In any case, sir," I cleared my throat in an attempt to wrest the laird's attention away from the paper he was reading, "is Mr. Logan definitely coming?"

The laird glanced at me, then back to his article. "Of course. Why do you ask?"

"Well …" I looked at my pocket watch, "it's only he's twenty minutes late."

The laird laughed, folding up the sheets and putting them down. "Time does not govern the affairs of the Highland Society quite so strictly as it seems to elsewhere, you'll soon learn. He'll be here."

I tried to relax, sitting back in my chair and crossing my legs in an attempt not to look as conspicuous as I felt. "Understood. May I ask, what is it that he's written then? Mr. Logan?"

"Hm, *The Scottish Gael* is likely his most recognized work, and I hear he is working on a travel diary of his journey to North America," the laird replied. "That should be published around the same time as your collection, if all goes to plan."

I'd heard of *The Scottish Gael*: it had sold well around the country the past few years. "Quite a trip, North America."

"Oh, aye. Sees himself as a bit of an adventurer, doesn't he, John?"

Young John nodded, and I thought I could see him roll his eyes. They explained to me that Logan's father had been a merchant in Aberdeen, and that James had grown up to be a scholar of Scottish clans and their histories, having written books on the topic with McIan, a well-known painter that even I'd heard of. McIan's romantic depictions of clan dress and tartans drew a fair amount of attention in Edinburgh sitting rooms. Logan was very well connected to both the publishing trade and the most likely subscribers, having sold many editions of his own works, and he would know how to present the work in a manner agreeable to a Society audience.

Perhaps another ten or so minutes later, the man himself arrived. He walked through the door with a smile on his face, greeting and nodding to many people he passed on the way to our table. He wasn't at all what I had expected an adventurer to look like: small, hair close-cut at the sides and balding on top, with a smart suit over a bright tartan waistcoat. When he came to us at last, we rose and all shook his hand – without any mention of his late coming, I noticed – and introductions were made. It all seemed perfectly reasonable, and before long we set to talking about the book.

"Perhaps it will be best if I run through what I'm envisioning," I suggested, and Logan nodded in consent. I hadn't prepared my speech as such, though I'd described the collection to so many people and had been working on it so intensely that the words rolled off my tongue. I told him I saw the work as a bridge to the new age. I was interested in preserving old, significant tunes in a manner befitting them, and when I said this,

I was encouraged to see Logan nodding enthusiastically. I rambled on a few minutes more, and ended by stressing that many fine tunes were still being written even now – not least by my father – and so I was adamant that some of these should be part of the tradition if the book was to have any modern worth, as it would illustrate how Highland music was continuing to develop.

The laird interjected here. "The tunes of Angus's father are fit to stand with many great tunes of the past, I will vouch for that."

"Much obliged, sir," I said, wiping away the sweat that had formed on my brow. "He would be glad to hear that. Mr. Logan?"

"Well, I have to say that all sounds terrific," Logan said, having not quite swallowed the mouthful he had been chewing. He rubbed his lips with a napkin. "Now, your father wrote a tune named after King George III, did he not?"

"Aye, he did."

"Yes, I thought so. Something like that would fit in very nicely, I think." Logan took a sip of his tea and put it down. "Though, of course, we must be careful that each tune we add bears significance for the wider audience. We cannot merely add tunes just because they are in fashion with current pipers. You'll understand, we have to make sure that the tunes we include attract suitable subscriptions."

I felt that with this statement, the first seed of doubt was planted in my mind. I hadn't expected Logan to have much of an opinion on what tunes were to be included; I'd anticipated that he would simply be involved in the latter stages as we polished the book's presentation. After all, I was the expert, as the Society had been swift in assuring me. "How do you mean, sir?"

Well, I won't bore myself with the vacuity of his replies; I soon enough learned exactly what Logan meant. As became clear over the following months, the man intended to aid me in overcoming the difficulty I faced in not having the respect of the nobility was the man who actually showed me the least respect of all. Needless to say, he had strong opinions on which tunes should be included in the book, and the fact that I needed his influence for the publication forced me to buckle to many of his demands. The quality of the music had to bow to class and society whims. I'd seen this pattern before. His main motivation for selecting one tune over the other was not anything to do with musical merit, no: it was simply that a tune might somehow raise the profile of clans or chiefs whose histories he'd wanted to delve into within other sections of the book. The music was to fit the writing, and not the other way around. And of course, he was more than happy to include tunes that were named for folk of high station, such as the one for King George III, which would cast him in a favorable light in his preferred circles.

Without putting too fine a point on it, the man was a braying ass. During our meetings – always in Edinburgh – he had a way of never directly saying what it was he desired, though he was very good at telling me why my own wishes weren't feasible. He had a way of taking long pauses before he answered, which he no doubt thought colored him as pensive, but which in reality showed a man preparing himself for the luxury of listening to his own voice. There, there it is, I can feel that same fury that accompanied me on my return trips to Islay bubbling once more! I soon discovered that his actual knowledge of the Highlands was doubtful, and that he knew staggeringly little of music, Gaelic culture, or in truth, publishing. As the laird continually reminded me, I had to remember that Logan's redeeming quality was an important one: he was able to write in a way that pleased the noblemen and gentlemen of the Society. And yet, for one reason or another that did not go far in redeeming him in my mind. I'd already seen enough Society-pleasing at the piping competitions, and this was just more of the same.

But what could I do? It was my first collection, and I had always known I would have to compromise if it should ever be published, even if I hadn't realized quite the extent of the compromise that would be asked of me. So, I carried on working, in the same fashion as before. In fact, I set to work with an even fiercer intensity, as I knew that if it was necessary for these great tunes – and some of them, not so great – to be featured alongside Logan's self-indulgent musings, the very least I could do for players was to ensure the presentation and accuracy of the music was as close to perfect as I could manage.

I lost friends during these months; I have little doubt of that. Many on Islay started to regard me as gloomy, someone who could barely make it through a conversation without complaining about his book. I was certainly leaving my cottage less, and most nights I slept just three or four hours at the most, which led to impatience and irritability during the days. Instead of socializing I mostly took to writing letters to my parents and my brothers explaining my woes, as it was them who would best understand me. For the first time, I was beginning to miss them dearly. I would write to them of my dread for the publication date, how even when I would leave the cottage on a bright day with things to do, off to pipe at Islay House for an hour or to go drinking with friends, still my worry about the collection hung over me. No matter what I did I couldn't escape it, and before long I'd feel compelled to make my excuses wherever I was, to go and lock myself in the writing room for the rest of the day, staring at the same sheets, if only to know that at least I was doing … Well, that at least I was doing something.

It was a trying time, but as my brother John assured me in his replies, whether I approached this task with angst or affection, the deadline would surely come, and so it may as well be affection. I wasn't quite able to heed his words at the time, but sure enough, the time did arrive for me to send the manuscript away. That was a peculiar feeling. It was not quite as though a weight had been lifted. More as though the process had shrunk me down to a lesser weight. I don't know. Perhaps last night's injection has not entirely worn off yet.

A couple of months after the deadline I was summoned to Islay House, where the laird and Young John were awaiting me in the writing room. It was a warm and windless summer's day, and as I made the familiar walk from my cottage, I saw that everything had been covered in a light morning dew, the grass soaking my boots while smoke from a distant bonfire rose in a vertical plume against the sky. I knew today was the day. There was a terrible knot in my chest, tainting the scenery around me. To add to my anxiety, I hadn't been permitted to see the proofs before the book had gone to print; Logan had sent the manuscript to be engraved without my consultation. I had sent him numerous entreaties not to do this but it was little surprise to me by this stage when I received no reply.

I passed a few acquaintances on the way to the writing room, but it seemed that everyone knew where I was going and why, and so our conversations were brusque. When I at last came to the writing room and entered, Young John was standing at the desk, while the laird stood by the window, looking outwards over the sparkling, daisy-covered lawn. I can still remember the musty smell of that room; I think I must have adopted that scent during the previous few months. All I was really paying attention to, though, was the book on the desk. I have to concede it was a handsome volume, with lovely engraving and a formidable look for the library shelf.

"Now, before you say anything," the laird said, "I want to inform you that the subscriptions have been excellent, and the result of your labors has been very well received by the Highland Society. I hear that nearly two hundred have subscribed."

I tried to nod as politely as I could. "But?"

The laird looked as though he was trying to find a delicate way of phrasing something, rubbing his wrinkled hands together, before Young John said bluntly, "But you were right, there are mistakes in the printing."

The laird gave him a withering look.

"What? It's not as though MacKay won't notice them."

"Just have a look," the laird said to me. "I'll give you a few minutes."

I sat down at the desk and began to page through the music. It was riddled with errors, though essentially it was what I had expected. There were countless errors in the scores; no longer was this the precise musical document I had sent away, with every note in exactly the right place, with every part meticulously accounted for. I knew that no published work ever went to press without a blunder here or there – I'd noticed enough of them in my years sitting in libraries – but still, this was beyond any justification. This was a scandal in my eyes. Perhaps the subscribers and gentlemen buyers wouldn't notice if the music was correct, but the pipers I was writing for would know how the tunes were meant to go. I was actually relieved that few pipers would yet be able to read music or afford the book, but it was sickening to me that for those that could and had not studied the tunes before with a master teacher, those printing errors would now be played as though they were the correct notes. And of course, the Society piping judges with no knowledge of pìobaireachd would then insist on the printed versions, and the errors would perpetuate themselves, with the originals lost to history. I was sure I would look like a fool.

I exhaled long and deep. "May I address the errors in the reprints?" I eventually asked.

The laird rubbed at his beard. "I shall see what I can do. But you know, it might not be possible to–"

"I know, sir," I said. My head felt heavy on my shoulders, like gravity was working harder on it than anything else in the room. I had a sudden urge to return to bed, perhaps find a bottle, close my eyes. I stood to bid farewell and swiftly left the room, but when I reached the lawn path and took a deep gulp of the cold air, watching my breath rise above me in a cloud, Young John caught up with me.

"Angus, hold up a minute!" he said, slightly out of breath, his collar ruffled. "You know all the pipers who count, wouldn't you say?"

I nodded. "I'd say so, aye."

"Well, perhaps one remedy is to make copies of some of the tunes most affected, and get them into the right hands. If you needed any resources doing this we'd be glad to provide them. Just make sure the music you intended gets to those who ought to be playing it."

Though this would not erase the failure, the sentiment touched me, and I struggled to master the emotions surging in my chest. They were good people, those on Islay. "I appreciate that, Master Campbell. Tapadh leat."

I turned and walked back to my cottage, spending the following days and weeks getting to grips with what was undeniably a failed first collection, regardless of what the Highland Society or that imbecile Logan believed. It may have been outwith my control, but the fact remained I had not preserved the music I had set out to preserve, at least not with the accuracy it merited.

I wish I could say that the ramifications of this failure were short-lived, but for my entire life I have seen my collection, and more notably Logan's fanciful additions of history, become the source for a lot of misguided writing about pipes and piping. Perhaps it makes good press, but it does not make good history. I saw recently, perhaps a year or so ago, the article named "The History and Antiquity of the Bagpipe" in the *Liverpool Mercury*, which read:

> But in Scotland and the isles, the Piob Mhor is of very remote antiquity, and from time immemorial has been esteemed sacred, and almost deified by means of it being applied to a versatility of

employments speaking, as it does, a language, and exciting emotions, which none but the people themselves can fully appreciate or comprehend.

What drivel! This is the sort of writing that became commonplace after Logan. To suggest that the bagpipe has been "deified" is ridiculous, and every piper who read that article must have had a wry smile. For goodness' sake, Robert Burns, whose work finds so much favor in Edinburgh, had the devil himself playing tunes for dancing! This all goes with the times, however. When lords and queens want pipers, the music and its history must somehow live up to that rank. A mere happy tune will not do.

And I've not even mentioned the hardest part of it all. Undoubtedly, this was having to pretend to be pleased with the book during all of my subsequent dealings with the Society. This was the only way I would ever be able to raise the subscriptions for another, and that was something I fully intended to do, now more than ever. If people knew that the collection was flawed, then it would be much more difficult to get funding for a second volume, and it was blatantly obvious that the Highland Society would not commission an amended edition of this book. To them the whole thing seemed a resounding success. Within a couple of seasons, pipers submitted tunes for the Edinburgh competitions drawn only from my collection; my book increased musical literacy in a way I hadn't imagined. Admittedly, despite the flaws that I and my friends and family could spot with ease, there was some satisfaction drawn from the fact that pipers were using my book as a source. While I was not financially rewarded in any significant way, I was immediately quite famous, and commended for having achieved something that many others would not have dreamed possible by having it published in the first place. Indeed, many true pipers tried to assure me that my collection was unquestionably better than had the tunes not been preserved at all.

But I knew in my heart what the book should have and could have been, if it weren't for Logan's agenda.

Still, I put on a smile as best I could. I would have to play by the Society's rules if I wanted another chance, and I already had my heart set on righting the wrong with a larger collection. And fortunately, there was something else coming to take my mind away from things. Rather, someone. A young woman by the name of Mary. My life was about to change beyond recognition.

Siubhal

Farewell to the Laird of Islay, 1840

Ah, Mary. Perhaps they are difficult to bring to mind these days, but we had some good years and I will gladly recall them. How long was it after we met before we wed? It wasn't long, was it? I remember I wanted to marry you after our first encounter, though I'm not entirely sure you felt the same.

I recall I was trying to make a living by piping in Islay and tutoring in Edinburgh, though without much success; all that traveling back and forth was quite exhausting too. The potato blight had arrived on the island, leading to starving among the people, and so Islay's economic prosperity was in decline. For these reasons, and also on account of his deteriorating health, the old laird Walter Campbell had arranged to move from Islay to France, set to leave his estate in the hands of Young John and MacMhuirich.

All of this meant that my duties as piper on Islay were becoming more infrequent, just as they had at Drummond Castle. I'd been in the position for over three years, so I felt that no matter what was to happen I had made good of it, but I was starting to wonder if my services would be required once the laird had made his move. Young John spent most of his time tending to his father and assuming more of the responsibilities that came with the estate, and he quickly became more serious, even surly on occasion. It seemed that although the Campbells possessed an unrivalled passion when it came to preserving what they loved, this did not translate into any monetary gain, and Young John had discovered that his father was soon to run out. Aye, there were many problems he had to contend with in those days, and finding enough work for a piper was not atop that list. I don't hold this against him.

But I did start to think I should secure myself another position, and when I suggested this to MacMhuirich, he advised me quietly that this would be wise. I knew I would be able to continue with my second book from anywhere – already I had compiled over 180 tunes! – and as I was so thoroughly enjoying my visits to Edinburgh, my first idea was that perhaps I would establish a school of piping in the capital. Tutoring wasn't the most profitable vocation, but if I had enough students, I reckoned I could get by. Yet there was the rub. Piping students were either too few or too poor to pay enough to cover the expenses for opening the school. I was now famous enough for my music, as were my father and brothers for their prominence at competitions and their affiliations with esteemed houses, but we were not wealthy by any stretch of the imagination. Perhaps if I was as well-paid as I was known, I'd still be running that piping school today.

So, I had to look elsewhere for a means of making money, and while little presented itself that spelled any sort of reliable income, I did spend some time working for Lord Ward. He was a decent man, near enough my own age but with vast wealth and holdings, mostly in England. His primary residence was Himley Hall in Staffordshire, and I was often required to go and pipe for him there, getting the coach from my lodgings in Edinburgh, and despite the distance this was no hardship. I enjoyed the traveling, and I was a bit of a standout down there, truth be told, a sort of minor celebrity in the house. They were not used to Scots – certainly not Highlanders with the pìob mhòr – and with Lord Ward's busy social life and innumerable business contacts, there was enough on to just about keep me busy. The thing I remember most from this time is that in the grounds of Himley Hall on spring mornings, not a second would go by without one bird or other singing its song – from over there, and over there, from up there. Strange that any other incessant noise soon gets on one's nerves, yet birdsong relaxes. Perhaps I should have been writing down the notes, learning their music. By the time summer came they had gone quiet; the birds had lost their confidence.

It was while heading back up north from one of these engagements at Himley Hall, heading for a Highland Society event that evening at which I planned to drum up interest for my next volume of pìobaireachd, that I chanced to meet Mary Russell. The coachman had stopped to water the horses at the inn at Biggar, and I had gone to wander by the wee stream at the back of the building, a nondescript little spot that I often passed through. Quite unbelievable that this was the first place Mary and I met, but it's so. I had been on the road for three days by this point. The coachman being the silent type, I don't think I'd said more than a few words to anyone during that whole trip; I'd just been a merry man alone with his thoughts, watching the passing country bask in the summer sun. I stood by the reed-banked water, leaning on a tree just away from the path. A bird was whistling the same few notes over and over above me. I couldn't spy it amongst the leafy branches, though it seemed to be enjoying itself, and I was glad of the performance, gazing at the puddles of sunlight that had formed on the roots.

But this wasn't to be just any old stop. For who was this auburn-haired beauty suddenly appearing along the path, chatting away to an older woman in the shade of the trees? From the tone of her voice it was clear she was jesting, though from the expression of the older woman it wasn't clear if the joke was being taken too well. I found I couldn't take my eyes from the younger's face; she almost didn't look real, like one of those faeries people used to sing about on Raasay. Seeing the briskness of their walk and the baskets in their hands, I gathered the women were on their errands, but when the pair of them slowed a little to inspect the slightly worse-for-wear coach, I took the opportunity to strike up a conversation.

"Good morning, ladies. Lovely day, isn't it?"

The two of them turned and came to a stop, the older remaining stern-faced, the younger continuing to smile, her teeth bright and straight. It was clear the two women were related. Each of them had the same freckled nose, the same soft hazel irises, streaked with specks of green and brown.

It was the older woman who spoke. "Aye, it is indeed, sir. Good morning. Is it just you traveling with that great big coach at the inn?"

"Well, me and those thirsty beasts that pull it, of course," I replied. "I've a lot of equipment I need to take with me."

The faery queen raised her eyebrow curiously. "What is it you do, sir? You look familiar. I feel as though I've seen you passing through here before."

Her lilting accent took me a moment to comprehend, but when I did my face burned at the thought she might have had some prior interest in me. "You're quite right, Miss, I've passed through here a few times. I'm Angus MacKay, and I work for Lord Ward in England."

"And why exactly is a Highlander required by this Lord Ward?" she asked.

"Mary, too many questions," the old woman said, slightly exasperated.

"No, not at all," I said hurriedly, glad now to have caught her name. "I'm a piper, Miss. I play at his Lordship's pleasure, to entertain him and his guests."

"You mean to say that a proper English lord pays a wage for you to play the bagpipes?" Mary laughed, turning to who I now knew must be her mother. "Perhaps Father should take up the pipes. He'll have a much better time of it than he does on the farm."

"Oh, there's no doubt of that," I grinned back. "In his time, my father was both a crofter and a piper, and it's music that's the better deal, mark my words."

"Ach, well, your father enjoys having plenty to gripe about too much," the old woman said, a smile cracking through her tired face at last. "I'm not sure he'd give that up so easily."

We talked a few minutes more, exchanging pleasantries and information about our families, before I heard the coachman reluctantly hollering out for me, letting me know I was holding him up. It was clear I was already smitten, however, and I really didn't want to let Mary go without making firm plans to see her again.

"Well, Mr. MacKay," she said, "I'll look forward to hearing this music you're so fond of one day."

"Perhaps we can arrange that when I'm next traveling through," I suggested.

"Aye, that'd be grand," she said with a nod, before bursting into a small laugh, her teeth shining.

"Brilliant," I beamed. "That's terrific. And it was a pleasure to meet you as well, Mrs. Russell. Do I have your permission to visit to your farm and play you and your daughter a tune at the start of next month?"

"I suppose you could stop by for your dinner," she answered, giving me a knowing look. "I'll start rationing now for a hungry piper."

Eventually, I made it to Edinburgh by early evening, the sky still bright as it turned from faded blue to yellow, wispy white clouds hovering over the Pentlands. Thoughts of Mary Russell were dancing around my head the whole way, distracting me somewhat from my mission. Who cares about a collection of pìobaireachd when you've just met a living, breathing angel? But I strived to refocus. The late summer was when many people came to the Highlands for grouse hunting and other sport, and Edinburgh too became a place of entertainment and social activity.

This wasn't to be a large event I was going to, like one held at the Theatre Royal; instead, it was to be slightly less formal, down the road in the Assembly Rooms on George Street. There were going to be several notable members of the Highland Society present that I wanted to speak to about my next collection, and I had also agreed to perform that evening, thinking that this might help my cause. I had specifically brought with me one of my favorite sets of pipes, won when I bested Donald Cameron the year before at a Society meeting in Inverness. A good conversation starter! Any day you finish ahead of Donald Cameron is a great day, and that one was made even better as I was also awarded first place for the dancing, much to the amusement of the other competitors, given there were better performers on the day.

Despite this mild embarrassment, that first meeting in Inverness was a glorious affair. I was a single man, and I remember well the dresses of the ladies, and at least one lady in particular whom I was able to escort on a lovely walk near the river. Her husband was well-absorbed with political talk and drinking, and though I shan't go into details, she seemed anxious to understand the complexities of Highland dress, and keen to award another prize to the winning piper. She did mention that she liked my dancing better than the piping, because it exposed more of the piper's true self.

John Macbeath's silver dirk for second prize did not come with the same female attachment, and nor did Donald Cameron's third place powder horn, although it was a beautiful piece of work, and well could I see it adorning the wall of some piper a century on. Not every tune at this event met the high standards set by us at the contest, however. There are pipers who lack either the training or the musical gift to really compete for the top prizes, and there are always pipers who just fail to play their best tune on the day. The quality of the performance always depends on the bagpipe and reeds working exactly as hoped. Nevertheless, us pipers competing would not have the press deride one or another of us for a weak tune on any given day, yet this is what happened. What good would come of that? Surely only a mean-spirited man would want to see a fellow competitor written up for a bad tune? That kind of reporting said much more about the writer or his sources than it would about the piper, in my opinion.

But I see I'm off track. I was in Edinburgh, wasn't I?

The Assembly Rooms comprised a series of massive ballrooms, lounges and small performance rooms on the second floor of a well-appointed building. As I carried my bags into the main room, I let the bustle wash over me. The air was hazy with pipe smoke and sweet with wine, and the place was full of different accents from across the country, with the sound of musicians – pipers, fiddlers, singers – wafting through from the adjoining rooms. I managed to put the intoxicating Mary out of my mind for the time being. But as it turned out, she would not be the only beautiful woman I would meet that day. No, there was to be no respite! Next, I was to meet Eliza.

I had time to spare before I was meant to play, and so I wandered from room to room, taking in the sounds of the other performers, until I found myself especially drawn in one direction. It was towards the singing of an island song that seemed to echo deep inside me, rekindling a memory. Listening to the notes, I felt as though when I turned into the next room I might find my mother near a piano, singing a well-loved Raasay song of my early childhood, but instead what I found was a tall, middle-aged woman sitting at the piano, clearly the center of everyone's attention. Her thick, dark curls were streaked with silver, though her sun-kissed skin set against her light green dress made for a truly striking image, and she wore a stunning gold necklace with earrings and bracelets to match. Evidently, she was a woman of some character, and though she was smiling broadly, I couldn't help but notice she was looking at me in a somewhat peculiar way. Perhaps she had seen me play before and was trying to place me, I thought. That was until she spoke.

"Well, here's a Raasay man now," she said, her fingers continuing to fly across the keys, "drawn to hear the songs of his youth."

I was very taken aback, and must have appeared so, because one of the gentlemen standing nearby stepped in quickly to introduce us.

"Lady Elizabeth D'Oyly, I present Mr. Angus MacKay, piper to Lord Ward and a winner of the Highland Society prize pipe."

Lady D'Oyly waved a hand dismissively and looked me up and down, the glint in her eye clearly implying that she was privy to something I was not.

"I know precisely who this is," she announced, at last ending the tune with a mellow chord, "though naturally young Angus may not recall our last encounter. The last we met he was but a few days old, and he was wailing at being carried away from Taigh a' Phìobaire and brought to Raasay House. You had not a hair on your head!"

I blinked in astonishment, wondering if all that time on the road the past few days had put me under some sort of trance. Even hearing the words "Taigh a' Phìobaire" in such an establishment seemed ridiculous to me, never mind that these words were coming from such a well-to-do source! I opened my mouth in an effort to offer some sort of reply but found that I was not quite sure where to begin. I must have looked dumbstruck!

It was plain to see that Lady D'Oyly was relishing the opportunity to intrigue. "But now," she said, framing my face with her hands from where she sat, "yes, the likeness is unmistakable. You are most certainly John MacKay's son."

At last, I managed to speak. "Forgive me, m'lady, I am utterly lost. You know John MacKay?" Glancing around, it seemed the entire group was just as eager to learn the connection as I was.

"I do, indeed. Very well, in fact. Perhaps if I tell you my former name, this might stir something in you. Before my marriage I was Elizabeth Ross. Still nothing? Hm. I moved to Raasay from India following the death of my parents, to live with James MacLeod, my uncle. Him you must know."

I nodded slowly.

"Oh, and they used to refer to me as 'Eliza.' Ah, now I see you are reminded."

"You are Eliza, *the* Eliza!" I spluttered. "You must excuse me, of course I know of you, m'lady! My father speaks of you often, but I had no idea what you might look like now. When John MacKay mentions you, always he refers to a brilliant young girl, and I hadn't … well …"

"Tell me, are you suggesting that I am no longer brilliant or that I am no longer young?" Lady D'Oyly inquired with a flash of her eyes. "I'm only toying. What a delight to meet a Raasay man, born and bred! I can't begin to tell you how much I pine for your little island. I still dream of walking along the beach at Churchton Bay, with those mountains on Skye sitting just across the water."

"Oh, aye, m'lady, the Cuillins," I beamed. "The closest place to heaven on earth. I remember when I was at Drummond Castle, my brothers and I would play the pipes you had made for my father. Sent all the way from India, I believe."

"Indeed, I spent many an afternoon in my youth enjoying your father pipe, and he played me several pìobaireachd so that I might write them out. It seemed only right to offer him something in compensation. I actually tried to teach him to place the notes on the stave but he wasn't having any of that. He was a stickler for the canntaireachd." She gave a small laugh. "I remember he said to me, 'Singing was good enough for MacCrimmon, and it'll aye do MacKay as well.'" My father was well known at the Edinburgh meetings, and this drew a chuckle from a few.

"I left my song collection at Raasay House when I left for India, but I also carry quite a few with me in here," Lady D'Oyly said, touching her temple. "Anyway, let us see what tunes we know before you perform. Come, stand here beside me."

Without warning, she then began to play "Colin's Cattle" and the first words immediately sprang from my mouth. "Gun tugadh crodh, Chailein dhomh bainn' air an fhraoch …"

She was a whirlwind of a woman, and all of my intentions for the evening were happily set aside, until at last I was forced to bid my leave and warm up the pipes for my own performance. But for at least an hour, people listened as Eliza and I sang together and exchanged many happy memories of Raasay. She was curious to hear news of my parents on Skye, and asked many questions about my own life since Raasay days. She was in Scotland visiting from her new home in Italy, where she lived with her husband Sir Charles D'Oyly. The way she described Italy, with its sun and coastal cliffs and sapphire seas, it almost sounded as though it might rival Scotland in beauty. Surely not! We finished by singing the "Salute for Sir James Macdonald of the Isles," and while we didn't fully agree on all the details – I'd thought I was the expert! – she had a musical turn of phrase and a lovely voice. I looked forward to telling my father about this meeting. He would be pleased to hear Eliza was doing so well, and that she remembered his music so fondly. I finally understood why he had been so taken by her.

My own short performance went well, and I did have the briefest of chances to talk about the second collection, but the assurances I got were shifty at best. I was starting to harbor serious doubts that the promises I'd been made after the so-called success of the first collection would be kept. Still, most of this disappointment was completely overshadowed by the experience of meeting first Mary Russell, and then the impassioned Lady D'Oyly – all in one day! I would sleep well that night, certainly.

—

It had been my wish that late summer to pay a visit to Donald MacDonald, whose pipes I had long played, and whose book I had studied in so much detail. I knew that he also had many tunes notated but as yet unpublished, and I hoped to be able to see them. As it turned out, this was not to be. The great man had taken ill, and just a month or two later he died from heart problems. This was a terrible shame, and I had no doubt that there was much musical knowledge that was lost with him.

However, since I had taken lodgings in Mary's village for a couple of days and met her family, I had found myself a new pursuit, and this staved off most of the melancholy I was feeling about MacDonald's death. I was smitten, aye! Soon enough, most of my time between work was spent either with Mary or planning to be with Mary. I did return to Islay to see off the laird before his move, but besides that, my priority was her. I have no idea why I had never felt this way with other women, but immediately there was just something that pulled us towards one another, and made us long for the other's presence at all times.

I got on well enough with her kin, though it took them a while longer to warm to me. Her father, Mason, was a hard-working man of simple tastes, and her mother, Janet, was wise and a bit abrupt, even fierce on occasion. Both were a little skeptical about my employment. The brother Walter was nine and mostly glared at me, but thankfully I was able to win over Mary's sister Maggie without trouble, who was just four and seemed maybe more excited at my arrival than Mary was.

When after a few months the family came to soften, I knew that when I asked Mr. Russell for Mary's hand it would be granted. Being a farm laborer was a well-known and practical employment, and Mr. Russell was respected, but in truth it was no steadier than any other work. A landowner could set you aside because of bad weather, a poor crop, low prices at market, or a physical injury that slowed you down. I think perhaps he realized it wasn't so outrageous for his daughter to marry a poor musician like me, and with his blessing, Mary and I were soon engaged. To her credit, Mary convinced her family that I had possibilities ahead of me, though I suspect neither of us could have imagined quite where those possibilities would lift us.

Before I knew it, the morning of May 26, 1841 had arrived, and when I woke, I swiftly shaved and dressed, before leaving to marry sweet Mary Russell. Because I had little time to spare from my work in Edinburgh, and because as a newly married couple we couldn't afford this in any case, we decided to be married in Edinburgh in the Canongate parish where I had taken rooms. There was little ceremony. Her father had little to give her in the way of a dowry, and I knew that soon I would have to find lodgings more suitable for a bride than my room, just across the road from the pub where I took my meals. But for the time being, that's where Mary and I would stay.

It felt natural to be joining our lives in this way, though in truth I would have preferred to exchange vows in the old Highland manner, with handfasting and a good three-day ceilidh. But that would not do in Edinburgh or for Mary's family. Instead, we were to be married in the Canongate Kirk, standing before a small group assembled, which would include none of my own family, just people who happened to be in the kirk on that Wednesday morning, and Mary's parents.

I was to meet the Russells at the church, and as I made the journey the clouds were thick overhead, but by the time I got from my new lodgings in the Grassmarket down to the Canongate, the bright east coast sun had melted the worst of them away. The sun's rays were beaming through the stained ruby-colored windows inside the cold walls of the kirk. Mary looked a picture of divinity, wearing a new dress of fine wool, sufficiently fine for a wedding, but not so completely a wedding dress that it could not be worn again, with a white bonnet and short veil. Meanwhile, I was standing proud in my kilt, freshly bathed and trimmed and with the ring safely tucked away in my tunic. I checked for the fiftieth time that day. Aye, it was still there!

The service was short and simple, and when it finished I slid the ring onto my new wife's finger.

I breathed a sigh of relief. "Thank the Lord, it fits."

Mary stared at it in wonder. It was the plainest of gold bands, unlike the bejeweled works of art that adorn the fingers of noblewomen, but still, to people of our station it was a rare thing indeed.

"I had it made at Glen's," I told her. I didn't mention that I'd traded one of my prize brooches to afford it, nor that the inside was inscribed "A mo Mhàiri" and the date. There hadn't been room for the verse I'd wanted, but she'd at least see this if she ever took off the ring.

"He said it was not much different than the metalwork they already do."

Mary smiled. "It's beautiful." She looked at it on her finger once more. "Thank you, Angus."

The ceremony complete, we walked out the kirk past a couple of curious onlookers and into the street. No bells, no fanfare, and no well-wishers. But I was overjoyed all the same.

"If only we had a good piper, eh, Angus?" said Mary to me. "Ready to launch into a bouncing reel!"

"What did I do to deserve such a lovely bride?" I looked down at Mary's face in adoration. "That wouldn't be half bad at all, would it?"

Afterwards, we returned to lodgings I had rented for us near the Grassmarket, where we would now be living. They were small and a wee bit musty, with strangers staying in the adjoining rooms, but they were ours. We all had dinner at a local inn – roasted duck and potatoes with bread sauce; I'll never forget it – and afterwards Mary and I shared the marriage bed for the first time. It was as sublime as I had imagined it would be. Never had I felt skin so smooth against mine; never had

I looked so deeply into another person's eyes that I might see my own staring back at me. To be back there, before all this … There was not a real worry in the world back then.

It must be said, though, it was a little awkward, living in lodgings with other people that we did not know particularly well. Like all newlyweds, we made the best of it, and over the next year we settled into a routine that left us happy and fulfilled. Mary was a practical person and enjoyed the daily tasks of living. She took satisfaction in a well-prepared meal, rooms neatly kept, and in the accomplishment of chores and errands in the town. Almost every night we would discuss our money and opportunities; she was undoubtedly wiser than I was in that regard, and I soon heeded her advice more often than not. Mary and I were very eager to source more independent living arrangements, but the tutoring I did and the employment with Lord Ward were never going to be enough.

Of the two of us, it was Mary who was the most determined to get my second collection published, and her encouragement helped me regain some pride in my writing. She had a lot of admiration for the first collection and wouldn't listen if I described any deficiencies. In some ways, she helped me think about that collection as an accomplishment. It was a rare enough thing to have a book published, but books of pìobaireachd were some of the rarest of all. The second manuscript had already been years in the making and was ever growing in size, brimming with music drawn from my father's teaching and many other sources, much more music than could feasibly be put into one collection.

Yet, those with the financial clout at the Highland Society had little interest. I was surprised at this as much as dismayed. The Society considered my first collection a success, and they were quick to boast of its having become the chief source of knowledge on the subject, but apparently this wasn't enough. Apparently – and this was a line I frequently heard attributed to Mr. Logan – it had been such a success that another was really not necessary! This sentiment typified more than anything how little the gentlemen of the Society truly knew about the music they pretended to revere; there was so much more to say, so many more outstanding tunes that deserved to be remembered in print, that they were willing to let pass into oblivion, just as many surely had with Donald MacDonald.

I was at least able to pick up the pen in some capacity, as Alexander Glen, the Edinburgh bagpipe maker who assisted me with Mary's wedding band, approached me to help him edit a second edition of his book, *The Piper's Assistant*. With Glen, agreeing on what to include was utterly painless in comparison to my dealings with Logan, and once we'd done so, my task was to prepare clear, handwritten notes for each tune to go on the plates. This was decent, useful, laborious work; I derived from it an odd mixture of enjoyment and tedium, and would often be working on it for many hours without a wandering thought at all. However, it didn't pay well, and it was clear when it was over I'd need another way to earn my bread.

Evaluating my options, I knew I could make bags and reeds and knew enough about pipes to possibly find a way into making them, or at least work with an established maker like Glen, but playing was my passion. Even if I had to make ends meet as a piper to a lord by doing all manner of dull side jobs on the estate, it would be worth it, and not at all unusual for musicians around the country. My brother Donald had a fine position in London as piper to the Duke of Sussex, and he'd moved his family there. He seemed to be doing well. John was also making his way as a piper, though not in such high company, and he always seemed to be considering what he'd do next. In the meantime, though it meant Mary and I would have to keep counting our coins for the time being, I decided to stick with Lord Ward, as there were vague discussions about his purchasing the Glengarry Estate in Scotland. I thought this might be a more fitting location for Mary and me to live, with more work, and this seemed the only feasible route of advancement for us.

That was the plan, at least. But as happens so often with newlyweds, the marital bliss Mary and I shared soon enough bore fruit, and we found we were to welcome a child into our lives. Gorgeous wee Jessie. She was born in her grandmother's bed in Midlock, while I was in Staffordshire. Bad timing, but I really had no choice. Mrs. Russell was the midwife on the day, and mother and child fared well. By the time I was able to return, Jessie was feeding well and settling into a pattern, and the hardest thing I was asked to do was take her back to Edinburgh and out of her grandmother's arms. Being a father now, the idea of continuing to live so frugally on what I earned in royalties and from Lord Ward became less appealing, and I was ready to make sacrifices to provide more than I was. But, well, sometimes in life a person just needs a bit of luck.

A Queen's Piper, 1843

I suppose I'd better try and explain. How did I go from a penniless musician, scrambling to pay the rent, to Piper to the Sovereign, ruler of the British Empire? It's a reasonable question. To answer it, I must relay some events that were in motion at the same time, far away from me. And pray tell, who were these events concerning? John Ban Mackenzie, of course.

While I was getting settled in our new household – still going through all the joys that come with caring for a first child – John Ban was piper to the Marquis of Breadalbane at Taymouth Castle. How John Ban actually came to that position is where the tale begins.

Before his employment at Taymouth Castle, John Ban was piper to Davidson of Tulloch, a man not exactly beloved around Scotland. I had worked for him briefly after leaving Drummond, in one of those short employments before my time in Islay, and so I knew that he was a fickle master indeed. Perhaps Davidson had an eye for a good piper, but the main thing he was renowned for was his relentless pursuit of women, whomever they happened to be. At the same time his wife was expecting their eighth child, Duncan Davidson was attempting to conduct a clandestine affair with a gorgeous young heiress: Maria MacKenzie of Applecross. The way he was going about this affair was by sending Maria letters – entirely unsolicited – informing her of his dishonorable intentions. Naturally, to deliver such compromising material he had to use one of his most trusted servicemen. He imagined that his tall, strapping piper would be the very man for the job …

After a year or so of this, Davidson sent a letter with John Ban, demanding that Maria elope with him. I'm not sure what he was intending on doing about his current wife, but apparently that was beside the point. Unfortunately for old Davidson, however, something had happened over this past year. John Ban had formed a bond of his own with Maria while delivering these love letters, and each time he called on her they would ride across the hills on Highland ponies, until eventually they were head over heels for one another! John Ban was such a specimen of a man, and with such an engaging character, it seemed almost inevitable that this would come to pass. Needless to say, Maria did not elope with Davidson, but with John Ban. Instead of returning to his employment at Tulloch, John Ban and Maria left on those same Highland ponies, riding to see his relatives, where they quietly exchanged wedding oaths during another relative's marriage. I'd received word from John Ban, telling me of his secret marriage, and explaining that since Davidson was more than a little embarrassed about the whole thing, he had allowed John Ban to leave his station without much fuss.

Shortly afterwards, John Ban was offered the role of piper for the Marquis of Breadalbane at the magnificent Taymouth Castle. He and Maria couldn't really have planned it any better, in all ways but one.

The position at Taymouth was for an unmarried man. Not one to let a good opportunity slip through his fingers, and neither one to do things the simple way, John Ban kept his marriage a secret, making himself out to be a bachelor, while Maria kept house in the nearby village of Kenmore. Apparently this left more than a few young women on the castle staff perplexed at their lack of success whenever they approached this handsome new piper.

As far as I knew, this rather perilous situation was still ongoing by the time John Ban and Maria journeyed from Taymouth Castle to visit Mary and me with our new baby in December 1842. A week or so earlier, John Ban had written saying that he had "an interesting proposition" for me, but before we had got to that, I demanded he and Maria recount the remarkable story of their marriage once more, so that Mary would at last believe me. The four of us were sitting in our lodgings near the Grassmarket, below Edinburgh Castle. We'd had a good meal, and by then a dram or two as well.

"Davidson must have been livid!" Mary exclaimed, with her eyes shining from laughter.

"Oh, he was not a happy man when he learned the truth," John Ban laughed, while Maria shook her head amusedly. "Though I heard that after a week or so he had turned his attentions to some other heiress."

"What do you mean, some other heiress?" Maria arched her eyebrow.

"Some lesser heiress, no doubt," John Ban corrected himself.

"Hm, moderately better, my darling," Maria said. "But honestly, Mary, you should have read what was in some of these letters. Old Davidson coming at me with his wizened, over-used manhood, planning to buy me like a prize beast at the market. It wasn't a difficult choice."

"He should hardly have sent his big, hairy piper as courier," Mary commented. "Didn't he realize that women love musicians?"

"And musicians with bonny legs, even more so," John Ban added, standing to display them for us. "Why do you think I chose a profession that calls for a kilt?"

"Well, I'm glad it worked out," Mary said. "But isn't it just awfully difficult, having to hide your marriage from everyone on the estate?"

Here, John Ban and Maria gave each other a slightly embarrassed smile.

"Well," John Ban said, "that's really why we're here …"

As it turned out, the secret had come to light, all because a couple of months earlier in the autumn of 1842, some very special guests had come to stay at Taymouth Castle: Queen Victoria and Prince Albert, no less. Of course, Mary and I had known of this visit; everyone had known of this visit! It was the royal couple's first tour of Scotland, and the nation was brimming with excitement for it. They made their way to Edinburgh via sea, docking at the private wharf of the Duke of Buccleuch at Granton. Prime Minister Sir Robert Peel worried that such a visit might cause controversy; the papers were filled with conflicting opinions about whether the queen's visit demonstrated support for particular political or religious values. When the time came, though, wherever the Royal party went the Scottish people received them well. The new Conservative government prepared a welcome to match that of the late King George in 1822: streets and buildings were decorated with banners, flags, tartan and garlands. After passing through Aberfeldy, the queen was scheduled to stay in the Highlands, where she was to be entertained by the Marquis of Breadalbane at Taymouth. Given the castle's breathtaking surrounding landscape and its enormous blue-stone, Gothic structure, it seemed a fitting place for Her Majesty to stay. It was here that many Scottish nobles were invited to come visit at the same time, to pay their respects and be introduced to their monarch.

What Mary and I hadn't read, however, and what John Ban and Maria had discovered to their horror, was that one of these noblemen for which John Ban would be performing was none other than Davidson of Tulloch.

"And he knew of your wedding!" I cried.

"He did, indeed," Maria said. "We knew he would surely expose us if only to try and lose John Ban the position and humiliate us in whatever way he could."

"Aye, so I took the only road I thought available to me," John Ban said. "I confessed our marriage to the marquis, fully expecting to be released from my job with a ruined reputation."

Mary and I exchanged looks, each of us confused why neither of our guests seemed particularly unhappy about what sounded like it could only have become a humbling situation.

"Ah, but it did not turn out quite that way," John Ban said, reading our minds, "for to my relief—"

"Our relief," chimed Maria.

"To our relief," John Ban said, "The marquis actually relished Davidson's being outdone, so much so that he was willing to overlook the fact I was married! It seemed that he had heard one of the many yarns regarding Davidson and, well … had drawn the proper conclusions, let's say."

"Riatach sealbach," I found myself muttering.

"Agreed," Mary said, shaking her head.

Such was the mark of John Ban, he was able to steal the love interest of his former employer and lie to his current one, all without consequence. Maria told us that the ladies around Taymouth Castle understood a little better after this confession why their advances on the man had been so roundly rebuked. John Ban was permitted to pipe for the queen and the nobles after all, though the marquis shrewdly ensured that a different piper welcomed Davidson to the grounds!

I have much to thank John Ban for, and perhaps the thing for which I am most grateful is the impression he made on our young queen during this visit, which he told us about over the course of the evening. Though there were a number of pipers on the estate, John Ban was The Piper, and he played for Her Majesty on a number of occasions, including once in a boat while she was being rowed on a glassy Loch Tay. It seemed quite surreal hearing him talk about it: my old friend who used to stay with us on Raasay and get scolded by Father for his timing, playing for Queen Victoria, perhaps the most spoken-of person in the world. John Ban told us that the young queen seemed to be quite taken by him and showed an immense fondness for the sound of the pipes, so much so that on her final evening she asked the marquis if she could arrange to hire John as her own piper. Though this position had never existed before, she was willing to create it just for him.

"But I wasn't interested," John Ban said. "I owed my service to the marquis after what he did for me, and the circumstances Maria and I have at Taymouth are truly all I want from life." He looked at Maria with love in his eyes. "Scotland is the place for us. It's time to settle down, grow old. The queen pressed the marquis on the subject, who asked me to reconsider, but I wouldn't be swayed."

"You would've had a hard time convincing me to accompany you to London, in any circumstance," Maria remarked.

John Ban lit his pipe with a calm look on his face, and wet his lips. "That too. So, when at last the queen accepted that her first choice wouldn't be taking her offer, the marquis then asked me where he might find a piper for Her Majesty as good and handsome as myself. Of course, that search was bound to fail on both counts, I told him. But I did know that from Taymouth, Her Majesty would be traveling to Drummond Castle, where a certain Lady Gwydir had once been the employer of a young, fairly adequate piper. If only I could have remembered this fellow's name …"

Mary and I looked at one another open-mouthed. So this was what his "interesting proposition" was about!

"I recommended you as the most suitable candidate, Angus," John Ban said to me. "That is, unless you've found yourself a better position, mind you! I think you can expect a letter any day."

I can still recall what it said about my appointment in the papers, and it was our habit to keep these scraps when they appeared. This short report originally appeared in the *Inverness Courier.*

HER MAJESTY'S PIPER – *The Queen has just appointed Angus Mackay, brother of the piper of the late Duke of Sussex, to be her Majesty's piper at the palace, so that the Royal ear, and that of various Right Honourables, will be regaled with our mountain music at the Court of England. Highland dresses and ornaments are to be provided for the new functionary, and our townsman, Mr. Macdougall, of the tartan warehouse (who has done so much work to bring the national costume into notice), has been authorised by Lord Jersey and the Honourable Captain Murray to furnish three suits – one for the morning, one for mid-day, and a third for after dinner and state occasions. The equipments will be complete and splendid. We may consider this appointment as indicative of the agreeable recollections still entertained by her Majesty of her Scottish tour, when she was received with a truly Highland welcome by the inmates of cottage and castle, all content to live in peace under a Sovereign so dear to their heart and affection.*

As I said before: sometimes you need a little luck. Though the offer may not have come at the right time for the slightly older John Ban, when it then fell to me, Mary and I didn't need long to consider. With a child to raise and mounting financial pressures as a result, the opportunity seemed perfectly timed for us, and would simultaneously bring me closer to my brother Donald and his family in London. Of course, taking the position would mean we would have to leave Scotland for most of the year, and neither of us had ever been to London; but to be employed by the queen as the very first Piper to the Sovereign, and to be given board and a handsome salary! The status this would provide was greater than even my father or my brother Donald had attained, and it crossed my mind that this would also be of benefit in publishing my next book. It seemed that all Mary and I had been wishing for had come to pass in one fell swoop.

The three of us left Edinburgh for England by carriage on a glorious morning in early June. The royal household had sent a carriage especially, much to the envy of our neighbors. We had little enough to take with us, but I did pack a small trunk of music, pipes, and some of the Highland dress I had acquired. Tools of the trade. Our wee Jessie, despite the hardships of the road, traveled well and caused us few problems. She was a sleepy lass, and seemed to do little but smile and eat, and Mary, she was as brilliant a mother as she was a wife. Though the hours of travel were long, we felt no rush and no impatience, taking each mile as it came.

During the journey, taking well-worn mud roads, watching the scenery grow flatter while the sky grew bigger, it was clear that this would be an enormous change in our lives. If we hadn't reached our lodgings by sunset, link boys were paid to walk in front of the horses and guide way with lanterns so we could travel into the evenings. During these dark hours, Mary and I discussed what life might be like in London, and what our impressions were of my new employer. In their letters, my parents had joked that it was about time I did something remarkable with the gifts they had given me, and noted how strange it was that I would be in the employment of the very woman whose face was on the Penny Red stamp that arrived on my note telling them the news. I'd hardly even considered that this Roman-looking profile on all the stamps and coins was a real-life person before that evening with John Ban, never mind it being the face I'd soon be piping to every morning after breakfast. All of my brothers had been thrilled to hear of my new role as well, with John remarking that he'd be having words with John Ban for not putting both of our names forward! His own employment was in question yet again; he seemed always to be on the hunt for something better.

Soon enough we were over the border and traveling through the north of England, staying in various inns and lodging houses. We passed by the great cities of Manchester and Birmingham and were near enough the estate of Lord Ward at one point, before pressing onwards to London. It helped that I had experience traveling these distances as a single man, though naturally progress was slower with a babe, no matter how well she was holding up. We were willingly aided along the way whenever a local discovered that they could cater for Piper to H.M. Queen Victoria, although we soon learnt to be cautious with that information when the price of a night's lodging was swiftly inflated after an innkeeper sensed there was a profit to be made.

It all felt very new to us, and our imaginations began to run wild as we contemplated what our permanent living situation might be like. We were headed not to London but to Windsor, a lively market town just west of the English capital. Her Majesty was currently staying at her country house, Claremont, and I was not required on her limited staff there, so would be staying near Windsor Castle for a couple of weeks before my first duties at Buckingham Palace. The rural space at Windsor was no doubt an easier landing than had we gone straight to London, meaning we weren't immediately exposed to the infamous noise, smells and filth of London. During the journey, we had also been exposed to the horde of those ready to empty the pockets of any unsuspecting foreigners, and this would undoubtedly be worse in a big city like London. So, aye, we were certainly glad to be beginning our service at Windsor.

Four days after we left, the sun still quite high and warming the early evening, the coach pulled up for the last time, and we stepped outside on to the sandy path of the Lower Ward of Windsor Castle. Mary and I peered about us at our new home. On the way in, Windsor had looked a fairly quaint town, sat by the River Thames and with a decent-sized forest nearby. It all seemed quite green and unassuming, until of course the castle and its various structures came into view. What a sight it all made; the town seemed to almost cower in awe of it. There were the vast wards, the Round Tower, the formal gardens, the never-ending terraces, St. George's Chapel. Our coachman pointed to a window of the chapel and shouted down that Queen Victoria would sit there to watch the services in peace. I wouldn't have said so much to Lady Gwydir, but the place made Drummond Castle look more like a Highland cottage in comparison!

After the coachman had helped us heave our cases off, for a minute or two we just stood there, feeling the weight of such a lengthy journey being gradually lifted from our bones in the slight breeze and the pleasant sunshine. A few seagulls were flying high overhead, seeming barely to move as though suspended on strings. I glanced at Mary, her eyes closed and her chin lifted to the setting sun, Jessie nestled deep in her arms, and I felt another pang of gratitude that I was embarking on this new adventure with them both. I now had all but forgotten how it was the days passed before we were together.

"Angus MacKay?"

Both Mary and I started at this sudden interruption from our daze and turned to see a man of about forty briskly approaching us, with thin black hair and a long beak-like nose, dressed in butler's attire.

"Aye, that'll be me," I said.

A hint of disdain crossed the man's face, before it wrinkled up like a piece of old fruit. "Sounding every bit as Scots as you look."

"Excuse me?"

"Take no offence, MacKay, we see all kinds here, just not so many of yours."

I just stared at him for a moment, finding my reserve of patience normally kept for such arrogance thoroughly depleted following the journey. "And what kind am I?" I asked.

The butler smirked. "As quick to temper as expected."

"Angus," Mary said, shooting a look at me that implored me not to rise to the bait.

I took a moment to compose myself. "You're right, Mary. I'm sure Her Majesty will be better placed to deal with this ungracious welcome party than I. It was her that invited us here, after all."

The butler's Adam's apple bobbed up and down as he swallowed the urge to say anything more. He hadn't so much as glanced at Mary up to this point. "Follow me to the servant's quarters."

With that, the man spun on his heels and started walking away, leaving Mary and myself stunned. I'd been treated in such a way enough times by various lords and ladies who saw no beauty in piping – I was once called a lowly, country simpleton with heather growing out my ears! – but this butler was meant to be of an equal station to me, and so such disrespect astonished us. We struggled to lift as many of our possessions as we could in our arms; clearly the man was not going to wait around. I was about to call after him to help when Mary stopped me.

"Let's not give him the satisfaction," she said. "We probably should have known that not everyone on the royal staff would be so pleased to invite a Gael into their midst."

Such was the unpleasantness of this first interaction at Windsor Castle that we barely took in the magnificence of our new surroundings as we trudged to our quarters, a neat row of houses tucked into the south end of the Lower Ward. An oldish woman with thick hair and bronzed, leathery skin had passed us on the path and addressed the butler as

Stevens, and when she saw how much Mary and I were carrying, to our relief she offered to take one of our cases.

"Haven't you anything better to do, Beatrice?" Stevens scolded, as he stopped by a door and waved a hand for us to go in. I thought how satisfying it would be to slam that door on his arse as he left.

"It won't take a minute," the maid said tiredly. "Now come, open the door for them."

Our rooms weren't nearly so grand as those we had imagined on the journey down; we soon found out that these houses for married staff members were similar wherever we traveled with the royal party. There were milk-colored walls and ceilings, rough and creaky floorboards, a dresser, and a bed that was comfortable but too short. There was a sloping ceiling hanging over it, off which I would crack my forehead more than once. We thanked Beatrice for helping us with the cases. Stevens had already left without another word.

Beatrice allowed herself a smile. "Not a problem, you two," she said. "Pay him no mind. Thinks he's a king himself, so he does. Tell the truth, he might not be the only one you need to watch out for here. But so long as you please Her Majesty, I'm sure you'll survive!"

I hadn't expected that the best I should be aiming for in my new position was merely to survive, but Mary and I chose not dwell on it for much longer that evening. We found basic provisions in the house for cooking our first meal: eggs and bread for toast. It was here we experienced the use of a proper toast fork for the first time, which made it easier to keep the bread from burning. We were a little relieved to have this time to ourselves. Over the next fortnight, though, as we tried to get accustomed to all of the pomp and circumstance of royal life, both the air of competition and the general distrust for Scots on the staff became apparent. Our nations may have now been united under a shared sovereign, but obviously the centuries of conflict were a long way from forgotten. Had I been a mainland Scot, I don't think I'd have been so taken by surprise at this hostility. The Gaelic islanders of the Hebrides, though always aware of the warring and politics on mainland Britain, were often able to survey it from a safe distance, and perhaps I had not understood the full extent of the animosity between the English and the Scots. Before I'd even met the queen, I'd heard us referred to as lazy thieves, inbreds and so on, all from common folk. And it wasn't only Scots that bore the brunt as well; the Irish and Indian staff were mocked and bullied relentlessly in equal measure for their language and appearance. Aye, it wouldn't be fair to say that all the English staff were of that opinion, but kind folk like Beatrice were definitely in the minority.

In any case, even if the welcome had not exactly been as comforting as we'd hoped, we learned a lot in a short time of how to induct ourselves into the staff, and the comforts that were provided for us did not disappoint. Each night Mary and I slept soundly together, still feeling remarkably fortunate to be where we were.

At last, the time came that I was called upon to perform my first real duty as Piper to the Sovereign, and it was to be an interesting duty at that. The royal family had returned from their home at Claremont and were staying at Buckingham Palace, and it was said that the queen was not best pleased about this, much preferring life in the country. The same day that I overheard this tidbit from the cooks at Windsor Castle, a letter arrived for me while I was reading the paper in my room with Mary. The letter said that my services were required on the morning of June 19 – the very next morning – and that I would be piping in front of Buckingham Palace at eight o'clock.

"And we're asked to be discreet on our arrival," I said, handing the letter to Mary as I went to fetch the cases from the closet, "as the performance is to be a surprise to lift the spirits of Her Majesty."

Mary's mouth was agape as she read the letter herself. "There's a room waiting for you at Buckingham Palace tonight, with a coach arriving this afternoon."

"And all of it commanded by none other than Prince Albert himself," I smiled, Mary letting out an audible shriek behind me.

"Ah, I'm just so proud of you, Angus!"

"Thank you, Mary," I said, as I started to rummage in the wardrobe for what I'd need. "I thought you might have heard of him! Now, I'll have to decide what's best to wear until my new service uniforms are complete. I'll only be playing if my wife thinks I look the part."

I felt Mary sneak up behind me and give me a wee peck on the cheek. "I expect you'll be playing, then."

I turned towards her, and took her face in my hands. "I'm sorry we can't go together this first time."

"Well, let's be honest, it's not the first time," Mary said brightly, her eyebrows doing that dance they did, "but we're in a better place now than we were when you were away with Lord Ward. I hated those dark rooms! So don't worry, we'll be fine. Jessie and I will have plenty to explore here while you're in London, doing your duty."

I kissed her then and thanked her once more, before promising that we'd move to a place in London together once we'd found our feet. And in the meantime, I had to prepare myself; I was soon to meet the queen!

Having packed my things and after making sure my pipes were in fine condition, I had to first brave London if I wished to reach the palace. The country roads around this part of the world were better than up north – still with dirt paths but often covered in wooden boards to make for a smoother ride – and it didn't take too long to get to the city from Windsor in the stuffy coach. I might have been on the same rock as Scotland, but as I approached the city, there was a noticeable difference in the climate. The air became rank and heavy, enough to make a person gag on first experiencing it. Tar and excrement and long-butchered carcasses – that's what it smelled like. I held my kerchief over my mouth, positive I'd never grow used to it, no matter how long I was to be in London. The dry and hot June afternoon added to the effect, I'm sure, and I felt my whole body was perspiring.

I'd been to Glasgow, Birmingham, and Edinburgh, so cities were not new to me, but London was a different kettle of fish. As the coach entered the outskirts of the great capital, it seemed we could've been entering any city, but that feeling soon faded. The streets – dusty with dry dirt – just kept coming. Usually when I was in a town or city, I had some notion of where its boundaries were; I'd be able to trace my route of arrival in my mind, or occasionally I'd look down a street or reach the top of a hill and see where the houses came to an end. Not in London. Once you've been swallowed up by London, all you can see is London. Looking down a street, you'll see a street. At the top of a hill or at the edge of a heath or a common, you'll just see bricks and roofs and pavements: the next area of London you're coming to.

The place assaulted all the senses, and none more so than hearing. Every street was alive with the movement of animals and carts, thousands of people, and there was the constant clamor of construction as the city exploded outwards, its borders swelling. On the busiest streets, people were having to lean in close to have a conversation with one another, and every seller shouted to be heard. Some roads we traveled down were being resurfaced with various materials, all requiring loud, physical labor, and all raising significant dust in the air. And of course, we contributed to the din ourselves. Like ours, most wagons and coaches had iron rims on the wheels, and the axles banged and squeaked as they traversed the rough, cobbled streets.

Despite the scale of the place, there didn't seem to be enough houses for the number of people; in the poor neighborhoods that we came to it seemed there was a family staying in each room of every building, all contributing to the noise, with slops getting tossed out on to the road in front of our horses at regular intervals. I was beginning to feel faint following this sustained assault on my senses; how were two million people supposed to live in such close quarters and not expect this amount of filth and poverty? Outside, people yelled to our coach asking for money, and swarms of children ran about between the alleyways, some barely wearing any clothes at all as they chased down a poor wee dog. Hold on, I thought, as I narrowed my gaze. Not a dog, but a rat.

And then, just when it seemed I should demand the coachman turn around and get me out of this hellhole, as though by some trick of the imagination the slums suddenly disappeared, and we were passing through the affluence of the city center.

After what we'd just passed, this part of town seemed positively tranquil. The air wasn't much cleaner, but the noise had faded to a bearable level, and the coach was often cast in a cool shadow on account of the height of the buildings. The coachman called down and asked if I wanted a brief tour of the area, saying he could take me past Trafalgar Square, Kensington Palace, and the new railway stations of Paddington and Euston if I was interested. Euston at this time still had the sheds, not the Great Hall with its ornate ceilings and metalwork that is there today. This was when railways were just beginning to realize their full potential; the previous few years had seen just about every town and city in Great Britain set up their own station, all in a bid to become a part of this new connected world. I wasn't sure I wanted to see railway lines snaking through countless miles of countryside, but it didn't seem people like me got a say in the matter. Even though the worst of our coach trip was behind, I was anxious to get to my quarters and find out what was required of me, so I told him to take me straight there.

"Suit yourself," he replied. "We'll be at the palace in a few minutes."

In truth, we'd have been hard-pressed to miss it. When it came into view, Buckingham Palace seemed to be the only building in London that had suitable space to breathe: an enormous white fortress, with sentinel-like statues perched on the roof and every edge adorned with painstaking masonry. The space around it was made up of a vast cobbled terrace, and beyond that, in front of the palace itself, a huge courtyard separated from the world by formidable iron and stone fencing.

"That there's Marble Arch. You know you're at the right house when you get to that," the coachman hollered as we trundled past a magnificent white archway that led on to the courtyard, complete with four mighty pillars separating intricate depictions of angels and Romans. No doubt they were very significant angels and Romans, though I hadn't a clue who they might be. "We'll be heading round the back."

The coach took us near a sheltered archway round the side of the building, and it was hard not to be impressed. Like Windsor Castle, this was a massive structure, but even more impressive because the stonework and design detail of every piece of the building had a story for the eyes.

After climbing down from the carriage, I was escorted to my room by a silent footman with a brass-buttoned coat. The corridors inside were vast and the floors covered with thick red carpet that muffled all sounds of walking. There was varnished wainscoting along the oak paneled walls like Himley House and Drummond Castle, but I noticed that in some nooks and up on the ceiling there was grime to be found, and the smell that had been ever-present since the city outskirts still reached even these hallowed halls. It was quiet, though, a quiet that was made all the more noticeable by the wordless footman, who seemed to float along in front of me. The silence was perhaps more awkward than our rude greeting at Windsor. When we reached the door, I asked if I might walk about to get my bearings in the area. The footman nodded assent.

"But you mustn't venture anywhere in the palace besides your own room and the servant's hall," he warned, the tone of his voice making it clear he was reluctant to even offer up this morsel of information. I couldn't tell if the nose above his thin moustache was upturned in disdain, or if he merely had an unfortunate face.

"That's no issue," I said. "And in the morning, I'm just to pipe in the main courtyard at eight o'clock?"

"Yes. The prince has requested you play something lively and uplifting to cheer Her Majesty and put her in mind of your country." He paused for a moment, before adding, "But don't worry, I'm sure the novelty will wear off for her in a week or so. Then you'll be shipped right back to where you belong, I expect."

I was thrown by this sudden hostility, and before I had a chance to say anything, he smirked with satisfaction at my surprise, and quickly stepped away from the doorway.

"Someone will come to take you to your position half past seven. Be ready."

Despite the footman, despite the smell, despite the fact I hadn't Mary and Jessie with me, despite all of it, the next morning was everything I'd hoped it would be. I'd decided to play "Johnnie Cope" as my first tune to Her Majesty, as it was in fashion, but with it being a Jacobite air I did feel a smidge apprehensive about playing it for a Hanoverian queen. But my thinking was that if the English staff were right and I wasn't to be here for long, then I had to get a few licks in before they sent me away! And from what I'd heard of her, I was fairly certain the queen would be entertained.

Even at that time in the morning, it was fast becoming another sweltering day, and standing in my full costume, with the buttery clouds being scorched away above me, I could feel the temperature was on the rise. A hardy Raasay man like me would at least expect a fine summer's morning to be broken up with a light breeze, but all was very still in the courtyard, and beads of sweat began forming on my forehead, running down the back of my neck.

I took a sip from the cup of water I'd brought out with me. This really was the easiest kind of piping one could do – a few light airs and lively tunes to entertain – but the piper's mind is always looking for ways to trip the piper, and I had to stay sharp. My sleep had been tormented with nightmares of the tuning going awry halfway through, and when I reached up to correct it, the tops of my drones were rolled up newspapers! I was up well before time to prepare for the humidity. I'd blown the drones without chanter for a few minutes in the apartment, and tuned them to their usual spots, before warming the chanter reed. This was all without sounding it, of course; it was to be a surprise for Her Majesty, after all. I had no clue how far I was from the queen's hearing, though. Knowing the size of the place, I might've had a tune without her knowing.

A few staff members in the know had gathered to hear this first performance, curious to see the queen's reaction as much as hear the music, I'm sure. I was taken to a small courtyard overlooked by a window near the queen's breakfast table, and there I was instructed to begin when directed. At eight o'clock exactly, a footman standing nearby gave me a nod, signaling that the family were just finishing up their breakfast. This was my cue. After a couple of deep breaths, in which the only movement in the world seemed to be a single black pigeon landing on the roof above me, getting the best view, I began to play.

"Johnnie Cope" isn't the most difficult tune in the piper's kit, and I was long bored of playing things the easy way, so I had taken to starting this tune differently each time I played it, the bottom notes echoing off the cobbles beneath me on that day. If I may say so myself, it sounded very good. Despite the stealth and minimal tuning, the reeds vibrated fully in the warm London air, and it was easy to blow them in tune.

By the time I'd been once through the first part, I noticed that more figures had assembled at nearby doors and windows, while the window indicated to me as Her Majesty's was opened fully. There was no mistaking Queen Victoria, more feminine than perhaps she appeared on the stamps and coins, wearing a light dress with ample sleeves. Her eyes were wide, and it looked as though she was holding a child in her pale arms. I made every effort to continue giving the music the attention it required, yet couldn't help but sneak a glance or two towards her. For some reason, I'd thought she would look older; she was only in her mid-twenties, yet her reputation was one that seemed to span a full lifetime already. Still, despite her youthfulness, there was undoubtedly something intimidating about her.

Prince Albert stood to her left. He was an intelligent looking man, and height notwithstanding, not too dissimilar from Her Majesty in their physical characteristics. They were cousins, after all. It was said Prince Albert was almost as involved in the running of government as the queen herself. He wore a neat moustache and was dressed in dark, military clothing, and this was as much as I could see from my vantage point outside in the courtyard. He had an impressive appearance, even at this distance, and he too seemed pleased with this performance.

I played out the remainder of the tune, and followed with several others, piping for about fifteen minutes. Before too long, people began to wander off about their day, and left me to finish the prescribed time. Their Majesties also disappeared from view at the window, and after I was done playing, a footman fetched me to follow him, so that I could at last meet my new employer.

"Wonderful," the prince announced as I was brought into a glorious reception room, clapping his hands together. "Just wonderful. Ma'am," he said, addressing the queen, "allow me to introduce you to Mr. Angus MacKay, the latest addition to the household and your new piper."

"Your Majesty," I said, giving a low bow. "A pleasure to be of service."

"My apologies for keeping you in the dark, ma'am, but I pray that this is a welcome addition to your morning," the prince added to the queen. Beside them stood an excited young lass, whom I took to be the princess royal. I couldn't see Edward anywhere, the younger prince.

"Most welcome, most welcome," the queen replied. This was the first I would hear of that voice: odd and slightly mewing, but composed. "Thank you, Albert, my dear. And it's a pleasure to make your acquaintance, Mr. MacKay. You come highly recommended from the Marquis of Breadalbane, with whom we spent many happy days in Scotland. Your music takes me right back to those blissful times, and I look forward to hearing it each day."

I nodded. "I shall be happy to play whenever called upon, ma'am."

"He'll do admirably well here," the prince concluded, before turning to the queen. "A worthy addition to our household staff, I'd say, as good as any we've heard."

"Yes, Mr. MacKay will do splendidly, won't he?" the queen said, gently rocking the stirring child in her arms. She glanced at the princess. "How did you like it, Puss?"

The girl jumped up and down, clearly delighted to be asked her opinion. "Poor man makes funny music!" she giggled.

I tried my best not to smile too much. But aye, the poor man does, I thought.

Following this day, I was utterly convinced that in becoming piper to Queen Victoria I had secured the most coveted role that a musician could have hoped to secure. This was especially true given that back in Scotland, opportunities for pipers were becoming so limited. The royal family, especially the queen, genuinely enjoyed the music, and like many other Scots, I would now be playing a role at the very heart of this united kingdom.

I was asked to do other tasks as a member of staff, of course, not only pipe. If crowds were so large that decorum fell a little by the wayside then I might be drafted in to serve table and help with various other chores. But even when engaged in this capacity, Prince Albert and the queen both referred to me as "our piper, Mr. MacKay," much to the consternation of the other staff members in attendance. With this honor, and also taking into account the salary, accommodation, and opportunities for publishing and other musical trade, there is no denying that the benefits of the position hugely outweighed the drawbacks.

And so, my royal warrant confirming my duties as piper was officially signed and executed in July. I carried the paper with me wherever I went, and Mary was so excited about it that she transcribed her own copies and sent them to our parents in Scotland. As the weeks went on and my routine began to take shape, I found that I saw much less of Prince Albert than Her Majesty. The queen deferred much government business to him, and he had countless meetings to attend, particularly with Prime Minister Robert Peel, mostly concerning the problems in Ireland. The queen herself still had more than her fair share of religious and political engagements, but with the baby and the other two children so young, much of her time was spent around them. It was while she was with her children that I most often waited on her, and I soon became adjusted to seeing our monarch in an intimate setting each day. I have to say, she didn't much seem enamored with her children, and once or twice I even saw her looking at the crib with disgust if the newborn was wailing. She was not a maternal woman, and strict with their behavior, but nevertheless it seemed as though her family was destined to grow. Evidently, it was Prince Albert that Her Majesty held most dear; she doted on him with a fervor that sometimes bordered on astonishing.

But it wasn't my job to judge any of this. It was my job to pipe.

—

Service Before Family, 1844

We didn't miss Scotland terribly that first year; there wasn't really a moment to think. Always there was so much being introduced to Mary and I that was new and unfamiliar. We stayed at Windsor, and I traveled with the royal household wherever I was required, which was everywhere they went. Her Majesty would not be without pipes in the morning, and I grew accustomed to seeing her slight smile as she listened to me from her various windows, often with her eyes closed. Once or twice after I'd ingratiated myself with the royals, I was even asked to dress the young Prince Edward in his "Scotch costume" for when I was playing. Her Majesty was charmed to see her children attired as such. Later on, I could be expected to perform for evening functions and formal dinners, where I would play around the table after the meal, or possibly reels if a ball was to be part of proceedings.

Given that each of my days was spent piping or preparing to pipe, home always did feel near to me, and I certainly didn't feel out of touch. I would suggest that hearing a tuneful pipe as regularly as I did would keep Scotland well to the fore of anyone's thoughts. But still, when I heard that in September 1844 my position would take me back to Scotland, I felt a jolt of delight. It'd been over a year since I'd set foot there, which I hadn't expected. Her Majesty and Prince Albert had long been eager to experience the charms of the Highlands once again, but it was not until Lord Glenlyon was so kind as to offer Blair Castle for three weeks, that the stars had aligned at last. Fancy being offered lease of a castle for three weeks! For one reason or another, Her Majesty was never short on nobles offering her favors, and it had become quite normal to me that we might travel from one sprawling abode to the next, barely even noticing the grandeur after a while.

One thing I had still not really grown accustomed to, however, was how I was now seen as more than just a piper. Playing in England for a year as a member of the royal staff, I also became viewed as a cultural representative of Scotland, one that would be many people's lasting impression of the country. I felt I often had to play up to this and repeat the same answers to the same questions wherever we went, and I was never entirely satisfied with how these conversations turned out. It's difficult for one man to give an accurate portrayal of an entire nation, especially given that the grandeur of Scotland is something best seen through your own eyes: the mountains of the west and the Highlands, the gnarled trees of the ancient forests, the stark beaches and wild cliffs of the coasts and the islands, the lochs that lie sleeping in the glens. It's a landscape that has a thousand stories of its own, of which Scotland is but one, and I hardly knew where to begin when asked about it. I suppose perhaps I should have said all that, but the pen speaks better than I ever did.

I was very excited to be heading back up north, and from the moment I stepped aboard the royal yacht, named – I thought rather unimaginatively – *HMY Victoria & Albert*, this anticipation only grew stronger.

This would be my first long trip away from Mary and Jessie. I had stayed overnight in London and other places away from Windsor many times, sometimes even absent for a week or so, but it was unclear how long this trip might last for. The queen loved Scotland and wanted the time to get comfortable there, and I knew I was to be an important part of that. It seemed it could easily stretch to a month away from my family.

"A month?" Mary asked, and I could hear a touch of resentment in her voice. We were lying in our bed on the night before I was to leave, exhausted after a day of preparation.

"It depends on events outside my control, my dear," I said, rubbing my forehead and staving off a yawn. "If Her Majesty is able to stay a long time she will, but if the business of the nation pulls her back to London, then we'll return. The only thing I know for certain is that I have no say in any of it."

"I know, I know …" Mary trailed off, turning on her side to face me. "I appreciate all we have, and I know I shouldn't complain, but I came here to be with you and Jessie, and I feel as though I'm seeing less and less of you."

"It won't always be so, Mary. I'll be back just in time for a long winter season in Windsor and London. By the time spring comes next year you'll be sick at the sight of me, I promise, this big piper taking up the whole bed on those icy nights."

"I don't mind that," she said faintly.

I gave her a look as I turned down the lamp.

"Well, maybe the snoring," she admitted with a smile.

"Aye, maybe the snoring. Also, the rest of the staff despise being in Scotland so much that I simply have to go, don't I? I need to report back to you on their expressions when they're met at Blair Castle by a whole troupe of pipers, giving them a proper Highland welcome."

Mary gave a sleepy laugh, burrowing into my chest. "Aye, that's true. I'd like to see that."

I think Mary was comforted by my promises on that evening, and we slept peacefully under that low ceiling in Windsor. When I rose early to get a carriage to Paddington, I felt a little more relaxed about kissing her goodbye. From Paddington, the royal party got a train to Woolwich, where the yacht was docked, and once we were out in the open water, feeling the sway of the sea beneath us, I was actually glad that Mary and Jessie were at home, as I'm not sure how they'd have coped. Most of the servants and maids on the ship had turned a pale green, throwing up at least once every hour or so. As Beatrice put it, they were "hors de combat." That old girl seemed right as rain herself, though. We stood on deck, looking out on the vast expanse of the sea, the sort of sight that cleansed me. It was gray and fairly calm to look at, I thought, but there were a few white horses and eddies here and there that belied the currents beneath.

"The royals are all feeling the effects as well," Beatrice informed me, her silver hair flicking in the breeze, her nose red. "Her Majesty and the princess have spewed thrice apiece now."

"O chan eil," I said. My eyes were half-closed as I relished the salt in the air. "I bet they wished they got the train after all. The prime minister didn't come in the end?"

"Afraid not. His daughter's still unwell, apparently."

"Shame. At least that means we won't be listening to hours of politics, though. It's rare I'm asked to pipe when he's around."

"Yes, I've noticed there's always a bit of peace with him in attendance," Beatrice replied dryly. She often joked about the racket I made with the pipes, claiming it was too much for her old ears.

"Even after a whole year, my music's still not grown on you, then," I chided.

"Perhaps I'm just past the age for new experiences."

We traveled at half-speed that night, and it seemed that everyone on board slept long and soundly following our early morning, as the next day spirits were high. It was another fine, clear day. The royals dined and lunched loudly on the Round Pavilion on deck, seeming to have grown used to the motion of the water, and I noticed that the staff were behaving in a more informal manner than they normally did. Despite the general tone of moral and religious discourse in the royal household, Queen Victoria was always lenient when it came to drink, and folk were being allowed to consume it openly aboard the yacht, which I soon took advantage of.

The sunset that evening was truly breathtaking, with the fiery light dancing across the ocean's ripples seeming to form a shimmering line towards me. I stood watching it for a long time. When it got dark, the lighthouses of Farne Islands with their rotating beams were quite hypnotizing, and the princess royal was very excited by them. She was the only one of the queen's children that had been brought with the couple; I suspected she was Her Majesty's favorite. I made sure to go to bed early once more, as I knew that in just a few hours, my home country would be there before us.

We arrived at about four o'clock in the morning, though you wouldn't have known it judging by the fanfare that greeted us. Dia uile-chumhachdach! I first woke upon hearing the boom of faraway guns, and when I hurried up to the deck, I saw in the half-light that our yacht had rounded the coast to head up the River Tay. We were now in full view of the port of Dundee.

The ships anchored in the harbor were a picture, displaying colored lights and ringing bells. The sound of these grew louder as we approached – I wondered what the royal family would make of it all – but by the time we were moored with them, they had silenced. I knew that it wouldn't be until at least seven o'clock that the family emerged, dressed in all their finery to have their breakfast, but I had a job to do and so I would not be loitering around for that. There was a barge waiting to take me and my pipes across to the shore, and soon enough I was gliding away from the yacht across the cold black water, moving swiftly with the smell of fresh fish in the air, drawing ever nearer to my home soil.

I heard later that when Her Majesty and the prince sailed across to the shore, a huge and adoring crowd had formed, accompanied by a twenty-one-gun salute from nearby Broughty Castle. Barrels of tar were set alight too, to mark the arrival with style. My own reception was not quite so raucous, yet even at that time a few people were beginning to congregate, eager to catch the first glimpse of their monarch. No doubt seeing the familiar sight of a kilted piper in the first barge disappointed them, though when I at last stepped off the boat and on to the red carpet that had been laid down across the stone steps, I did get an ironic cheer from a handful of the locals. I gave them a wave, and as I continued on into the streets, striding with purpose towards the carriage that was awaiting me, I found I couldn't hide the smile that was stretched ear to ear across my face. Every man and woman I passed received a greeting, if only because I wanted to hear their accents in reply. The sleepy folk of Dundee must have thought the queen's piper the most sociable man alive!

I told the driver to hurry on to Blair Atholl, though I knew there was likely no rush; I was simply eager to get on and see the Highlands. On the drive out, I saw that the town of Dundee had gone to some trouble making a fine reception for the queen, erecting arches and welcoming signs. That night I learned from Beatrice that all the most prominent people from the town came to receive the royal party: the Lord Provost, the magistrates, all the nearby earls and lords and sirs. It was a similar story at Dunkeld, apparently, where the papers described a massive crowd cheering and clamoring as Her Majesty's carriage passed through, with the cathedral bells ringing in celebration. You'd be sure to find a Scotsman bitter about bowing to our English queen, but it was clear that in general terms, especially among the poorer folk with more to gain from the union, she really was loved in this part of the world.

I arrived at Blair Atholl a good few hours later: a village situated in the midst of the Grampian mountains. The valley was like something from my father's stories, surrounded by rugged green peaks and waterfalls and the clear, flowing rivers of the Garry and the Tilt, full of trout which soon revealed themselves as both lazy and delicious. All around, most of what could be seen was free of human touch, and there was an old, almost uncanny feeling about the place that was nowhere to be found around London. For my return to Scotland, I'd have been hard-pressed to select a more beautiful place to spend the time, and stepping out of the carriage into what was now a bright late morning, and breathing in that reviving mountain air, so unlike the air down south, I knew that I'd well and truly arrived back where I belonged. The only blemish was that Mary and Jessie weren't here also, but that was not the way of things in royal service, and I at least knew that they were safe and well-provisioned.

I walked the last few minutes to the castle. The architects had taken advantage of all the space available, and its white walls and Georgian towers seemed to go on and on and on. With tall hills directly behind it – in fact there were hills in every direction – the castle was impressive in a different way to the giant dwellings of Windsor and Buckingham Palace, more weaving itself into its landscape than dominating it completely. Some of the surrounding hills had trees creeping up about half their height before giving way to tufts of grass and purple heather, which was everywhere to be seen on the moorland. On that short walk I managed to spot a few hares, some red squirrels and a group of large deer in the distance. Prince Albert would be pleased. I must have been walking with my head turning every which way, because by the time I had reached the castle entrance, I hadn't noticed the men sitting in the shade of a tree by an embankment, until one called over to me.

"Hullo, Mr. MacKay! We're over here!"

"Hullo, gentlemen!" I said, making my way over. These men – there were four of them awaiting me – were the pipers of the Atholl Highlanders. They were the reason I'd been sent ahead of the royal party: I was to prepare them all for Her Majesty's arrival, as they'd not only be playing to receive her but would be her personal guard for the duration of her stay. I'd known that they wouldn't be in need of much additional preparation, as these men were well-drilled by the Duke of Atholl and would be more than competent musicians, but I'd been keen to take the opportunity to travel ahead of the hustle and bustle so as to spend the day with them.

Introductions were quickly made, and immediately I felt right at home amongst them. They were my sort of people. Our company was soon joined by two non-pipers: Sandy McAra and Peter Frazer. Sandy was a funny character I'd met before in Edinburgh, with the thickest Gaelic accent I'd ever heard, and Peter was the Head Keeper, the oldest among the men, renowned for his unwavering loyalty to the duke. All of the men were in full regalia, tartan from head to toe, and quite relaxed as they had lunch before the afternoon's exertions. Those I hadn't met before seemed pleased to make my acquaintance; my name had featured often in the papers over the past year as I played around the country for Her Majesty, and it seemed my reputation had grown accordingly – at least up here!

"A bheil an t-acras ort?" Sandy asked, beckoning to an array of bannocks, cheese and smoked fish they had laid out on a linen sheet. I saw there were also a couple of whisky bottles there as well. It was going to be a braw three weeks! "We're just having lunch before we set to practicing."

"Aye, I'm starving," I said gratefully, and settled myself down amongst them. "Much obliged. And between you and me, lads, we've got a good few hours before they arrive. Late afternoon at best, I reckon."

When we did get around to our preparations, there was much swapping of chanters and reeds to have us sound in unison, and one or two challenges in getting us to play the same notes. It was straightforward enough, but every piper has his own thoughts on tuning, and we had heated debates about nuances that the untrained ear probably wouldn't pick up at all. It felt good to be around people who understood this kind of talk. Once or twice, it looked as though the rain was on its way, but the clouds never did manage to burst over the hills, so besides setting down bags in my room I didn't step foot inside all day. The Duke of Atholl – Lord Glenlyon – and his captains came and listened to our efforts, seeming pleased enough. Yet, despite my announcement that we probably had a while yet before the queen arrived, after a quick inspection of our appearances – and our sobriety – they then had us line up in position. It was a long wait indeed, much longer than was practical. The officer forgets that a great pipe is like a living thing that needs attentive care for it to work when called upon, not to mention that a great piper can cramp up if stationed too early!

It was still bright enough when the royal entourage at last came into view, but it had become quite chilly, and we were all looking forward to a fireside and a dram. When they stepped out of their carriage, the royals looked knackered after such a long day of greeting and traveling. Despite the long wait, the pipes sounded well enough, though I could certainly hear the difference. Fortunately, my opinion was not the one that counted, and I was gratified when Her Majesty – hand-in-hand with the princess royal – took a moment to nod her appreciation of the music. She often said that nowhere did the pipes sound better than in the Highlands, and I was inclined to agree. As the company filed into the castle, with the music of us five pipers still carrying through the glen, I was sure that this was going to be a stay to remember.

Really, every one of the queen's trips was a time to remember, but my first as part of her company is the one that I hold most dear, for many reasons. Sometimes when I'm laid down in bed at night here in the hospital, trying to drift off to sleep – which has become that most elusive of states – through all the guttural shrieks and pained moans from the neighboring cells, or the whistling and banging doors from the attendants, I remember with confusion how easily slumber came at Blair Castle, despite the stags roaring like lions every night.

Recently, though, I've worked out that what keeps me awake here most of all – more than the Bedlam noise, more than the smell, more than anything – are my thoughts. If Hood is right, and I am sick in the mind as well as the body, how can I sleep when I think of this disease ripping through me while I'm unawares? How can I sleep when I think of waking up and finding that it's taken hold of me again, waking up and not remembering having written these pages at all? It's intolerable. At least if I'm awake I can try to fight, to stave it off. Mary was here yesterday, and she mentioned that she is appealing to get me permanently moved to a facility in Scotland, seeing as the northern air seemed to help last time. She is appalled at my new cell in the basement – the cold rock walls, damp, cave-like; the rats scurrying from room to room – where I am locked all day like a dog. To be honest where I am means little to me; it's no less a cage than it was upstairs. They bring me a chair and a desk during the day, and two attendants stand outside to make sure I don't try to fashion a weapon. There is a window, though it's barred and right up in the corner, too high for me to see anything out of it except a small bit of sky, which is hardly enough to convince me that outside the world still turns. I asked for a stool that I could stand on to see out of it, but they said no.

Maybe going up north one last time would be good for me, but I cannot deny that I feel myself flagging, losing the will, losing the ability to remain focused on the tale. If Mary manages to convince the doctors again, then so be it, but I don't think it'll work the way she wants it to. I'm finding it more difficult to pick up the pen each day. But I will write about the stags while I'm able.

I remember those mighty beasts learned to keep a distance between themselves and the castle before too long, courtesy of Prince Albert. He was known to shoot at them from the upper windows of the house if they wandered into range. The locals considered this bad sport. They didn't want the stags to be driven further away from the town than they already were, but who was going to command a ceasefire from a prince? The man was obsessed with hunting, and during the holiday he spent near enough every day roaming around the nearby country, normally going some way along Glen Tilt, accompanied by some of the Atholl Highlanders to guide him. Peter Frazer would be able to deduce exactly where the deer were and when they'd be coming, just by listening and using his nose. The weather was clear – I'd say there were only three or four days of rain the entire trip, which is a grand return for Scotland – so the prince would often head out to hunt in the morning, return to the castle for lunch, and then be out again until just before it got dark.

The prince wasn't a good shot, mind, despite all this practice. The Highlanders leading him would have to carry several loaded rifles for when his first attempt went askew. Still, if you shoot enough times, you will eventually hit your target, and the prince killed a great number of stags during this holiday, perhaps thirty, all in all. It suited me that I didn't see many of these kills, as instead I got to remain side-by-side with the queen. Her Majesty would often accompany the prince on his hunts, but she would follow behind at a distance, advised when to move ahead by myself and Sandy McAra. We were tasked with keeping her entertained while training an eye on the horizon, listening to the shots reporting among the hilltops. Other times, she would take us on her own travels: out to the moors and hills, or possibly a jaunt down to the village just to meet with people. She greatly enjoyed interacting with the local folk, and understandably, the reverse was true as well.

Aye, with the queen I traveled to Glen Tilt, to the Falls of Bruar and Tummel, to the Pass of Killiecrankie where the Jacobites saw their first victory. I remembered the story from my father and repeated it for Her Majesty: the force was led by the infamous Bluidy Clavers, who died for that great triumph. We climbed up hills together where we could see the three counties of Perth, Inverness and Aberdeen. The queen traveled mainly on a pony, for which she seemed to have a greater affection every day, and when she hopped off, she would sit and sketch the landscapes in the serenity of nature, asking Sandy and me the names of plants and landmarks which she wrote down diligently on a separate page. Sometimes if she was taking luncheon at the castle, the princess royal would meet her between her lessons, and Her Majesty would ask me to join them to play a tune. There was one afternoon, as she lunched with the princess by the old stone bridge beside the castle, sitting on the grass – the prince being out on a hunt towards Beinn a' Ghlò – I impressed Her Majesty when improvising a version of "O Du Lieber Augustin."

"I've only heard that played by an orchestra," the queen observed once I'd finished, setting down her cup. "Bravo!"

"Well, ma'am, a full band is still no piper," I said, smiling. I laid down the pipes to take a sip of whisky, listening to the babbling of the water. Perhaps it was all the drink that was giving me the courage to speak so informally, but ever since our arrival the queen had seemed quite unfazed by chatting to the staff. For the most part, due to her abruptness and the seriousness of her responsibilities, I could not quite tell if Her Majesty was in general a happy woman, but here, she truly seemed the merriest I'd ever seen her.

"Ah, of course," she said, nodding with mock sincerity. "My accomplished, modest piper." She held out an arm to the princess, who had returned from trying to catch minnows in the brook. "Isn't Mr. MacKay a silly man, Puss?"

"Silly man," the princess agreed happily, collapsing down beside her.

"Duine gòrach," muttered Sandy from the other side of the shore. He was resting in the sun, while the English servants behind him glared. Evidently, they did not think that he was behaving in the proper fashion for royal company.

"Sandy agrees with you, Your Royal Highness," I said to the princess, before turning to the queen. "It must be nice getting away from all the politics down in London, ma'am."

She squinted at me through the sun's glare, the trace of a smile at the corner of her lips. "You don't know the half of it. I feel as though I'd be quite mad to return every time I get away."

"Particularly mad leaving a place like this, I imagine."

"Mm. There is something rather intoxicating about the country, I must say. Dear Albert thinks so, too. All the green, all the romance. And the attachment between the people as well, quite peculiar."

"You do tend to avoid visiting in winter, Your Majesty. That's normally when things turn sour up here."

"Well, perhaps that is true," she murmured amusedly. "Perhaps I would feel quite differently. But old Mr. Frazer, for instance, nursing poor Lord Glenlyon day and night when he was ill – and that was when His Lordship was unable to accommodate him. I would like to know how many of my staff would do such a thing for me." Her eyes were now closed, but I felt that she was somehow watching the servants across the water.

"I'd be by your side, ma'am, have no fear of that."

"I believe that, Mr. MacKay. You are right, though. The thought of returning to England again this time is a melancholy one. Morocco, France, Ireland … It seems the problems of the world await us in London, consuming all of our time." She took a moment's pause, and thoughtfully stroked the hair of the princess. "And I hate that yacht."

"Ah, it was a rocky journey up, aye," I agreed. "Perhaps you need a bigger boat."

The queen gave a short bark at this, which I knew to be her laugh. "You know, I have been thinking that myself, Mr. MacKay. It's decided. On your advice, I shall commission a larger vessel for our journeys."

"Much appreciated, ma'am. A Scottish residence as well, maybe?"

"Now, Mr. MacKay, the prince consort has the same idea. Some property in the Highlands does sound appealing … Do you know of any available castles in the area?"

"I'm afraid I do not," I said. A crow shrieked somewhere nearby, causing the princess to turn her head suddenly, before lowering it again on the queen's lap. "I'm just a modest, lower-born lad, remember," I went on. "Maybe you could ask the next lord who comes to visit you here."

The queen gave me a shrewd look. "Is today the nineteenth?"

"Aye, ma'am."

"Hm, in that case, there is a guest coming to stay this evening for a couple of nights. I am not sure if I would be able to convince him to give up his home, however." After a pause, she added, "Taymouth is a rather pleasant place to live."

"The marquis is coming today?" I asked with excitement. "Do you know if—"

"Indeed, indeed I do, Mr. MacKay," the queen said, staring absent-mindedly into the water. "I suggested he bring along his big hairy piper, so that he might learn to be as refined as my own. I thought you might approve of that."

I heard John Ban before I saw him; I now realize this was often the case. He was one of those people who don't change at all, depending on whose company they're keeping; he'd be just as likely to bellow with laughter alongside a pauper or a lord.

After lunch by the bridge, the queen's party had joined Prince Albert on his second hunt of the day, following a little behind along Glen Tilt, with several other nobles in attendance. It turned out to be unsuccessful, this being blamed on two local men who had been strolling along the road on which the deer had been driven to, thereby spoiling the hunt. This seemed to me hardly fair, blaming them, given that these men were merely minding their own business, out taking the air in the land around their home, but I knew better than to open my mouth when the prince reprimanded them. What this meant was that some moods in the company were low when we eventually trudged back to the estate, yet about half a mile from the castle, the unmistakable sound of a very fine piper was heard carried on the evening air. This went some way to lifting the collective spirits. And there were only a few pipers in the world who could play like that.

Once the pleasantries between the nobles had been acknowledged and all had stepped inside to prepare for the evening's festivities, John Ban and I embraced, wasting no time in stealing away from the others. I could still scarcely believe he was there, never mind that the queen had specifically asked for him on my behalf. Taking in the sight of him on that mild night, I saw his beard was a little longer and he looked a little older – a little wiser, I should say – but as usual, he was on sparkling form from the off.

"Royal service must suit you, Angus," he commented, looking me up and down as though appraising a horse at the market. "You're keeping in fine shape. You look the spitting image of old John MacKay."

"I appreciate it, a charaid; you're looking alright yourself. It'll be all the hills I've been walking up here, I'm telling you," I said, beckoning around to the surrounding scenery. The eastern peaks were bathed in a ruddy orange as the sun went down behind the distant haze of bluish clouds, the last of the valley not yet in shade. "It's like I'm young again, back on Dùn Cana with John. Remember, the two of us would go prowling around with our pretend rifles, waiting to ambush the enemy!"

"Except your gun now is a great pipe, and the enemy back then was the government, no doubt!"

"Oh, aye. Slight change on that front. The enemy is now whichever sorry stag strays too close."

John Ban snorted, before glancing back towards the castle to make sure we were quite alone. "So, you've been out with the prince, then? Is he really the master marksman the papers claim he is?"

"What do you think?" I grinned. "Let's just say I've heard some grim tales from the cooks about the state of the animals they bring back. But no, you shan't make me speak ill of my employer, you devil you! You never know who might be listening in the household staff. Might be someone eavesdropping in those bushes."

"Of course, mustn't overstep the bounds of good taste," John Ban said, before calling over to the bushes. "He didn't mean it! He was just trying to impress his old friend!"

"His very old friend, aye," I added.

We walked and talked a while longer until we reached the woods, catching each other up on all our family news. An eagle was swooping above the tree line as we stood to take in the scene, and then just as we were about to turn back, I noticed several young roe deer, edging carefully along the boundary of the forest. Some had their noses to the ground while others were eyeing us with suspicion, switching roles between themselves every so often.

"For your own good, come no further," I muttered, giving John Ban a wee nudge with my elbow to point the herd out to him.

"Oh aye, we'd better not get too close in case the prince takes aim."

"Or perhaps it's safest if we go and stand right beside them," I suggested.

John Ban let out a loud laugh, at which point the deer scattered into the growing darkness of the woods. A wind came in, rustling the trees, and as I listened to that calming sound, I wished I'd brought a bottle to warm me.

"And there they go," John Ban said after a moment. "Now, we'd best get back to it. Pipes to get matched for tonight's dancing, and we should play a few tunes ahead just for our own fun, shouldn't we?"

"Some of John MacKay's finest?" I asked.

"You read my mind," John Ban laughed back.

The performance we put together that night was a wild one. After the meal was over, the staff cleared back the carpets and furniture to prepare for the dancing of reels in the big dining room on the ground floor. It was an airy room, walls adorned with detailed plasterwork, though no one could take the time to appreciate it with the ruckus we were making. The men were all up for the dancing, while the drink flowed among the guests and staff alike. To crown it all, the two of us prize pipers received a special mention from the prince and the marquis at the night's conclusion. To share such a moment with such an old friend, one that I'd not seen enough of in recent months as well … Moments like that made me thankful to be alive.

A few days later, the royal party packed up and returned to London. There was no doubt some heartache in leaving Scotland again – if anything I'd been reminded of how it was so much more my home than England – but I was glad to be reuniting with Mary and Jessie, and looking forward to telling them everything about the trip. The two of them were in our cottage when I arrived back at last, quite late into the evening. I left my cases outside on the stones, and stole my way up to the door as quietly as possible. Inside, I could hear Mary singing Jessie a nursery rhyme. She sang slowly, her gentle voice carrying down from the bedroom.

To see my true love in his best array
Or the clothes that he wears everyday
And if his livery I am to wear
And if his bairns I am to bear

Blithe and merry may he be
And may his face be turned to me.

I was a little surprised at Mary's choice of song; I had been away a long time. I tiptoed inside and up the stairs to the bedroom doorway. Mary gently lay Jessie down in the crib, and beamed when she saw me staring at her.

"Angus!"

"Hullo, Mary. I cannot believe how much she's changed in the few weeks away," I whispered, nodding towards the child as Mary approached. "She's not a babe anymore, is she?"

"Oh, trust me, I know. She's her own woman." Mary kissed me before holding me tight. I breathed in the smell of her hair; I can still recall the scent, like sweet tea. She wouldn't let me get that close to her now. "How was Scotland?" she asked.

"It was grand, darling. I'm tired, but I'll tell you all about it in bed. How are you?"

"Well, I've been tending Jessie for weeks and listening to her prattle without break, but I'm fine." She paused, giving a slight shake of her head. "It's just been harder than I thought, doing it alone."

I nodded, and took Mary's face in my hands and looked her in the eyes. "You must be exhausted. I'm sorry this work takes me so far away and for so long. I missed the both of you more than I can say. My face is turned toward you now, I assure you."

"I know, Angus."

"Good. It's just more than we expected, I think that's what it is. But the wage and security this position brings would be impossible to find elsewhere, so there are going to have to be sacrifices."

Mary gave me that direct look I knew so well from her mother. "We've spoken of this already, my dear. I just don't want to be the one making all the sacrifices, while you're up in the Highlands living in castles and swimming in whisky. But let's not talk about it right now. I'm so glad to see you back," she said, kissing me again. "Just promise you'll give me some of the attention that everyone else has been getting these last weeks. You said I'd be sick to death of you, remember?"

"I remember, my dear. High time to fulfil that, I reckon."

But despite this assurance from me, it did not turn out like that, did it mo Mhàiri? I'm afraid I wasn't able to give my family my undivided attention by any stretch, as even at Windsor my life was crammed full of responsibilities. Following her Scottish holiday, the queen had some catching up to do when it came to state business, and though I saw Mary far more in Windsor than I did anywhere else, there were still several important visits and events planned that I had to prepare for. Most notably was the event in early October, where there was a great state ball scheduled to correspond with a visit of King Louis Philippe of France, and following the dinner, I was called upon to play a pìobaireachd round the table. On a great-going pipe and resplendent in my full evening garb, I regaled the table with "Fhuair mi pòg o làimh an Rìgh," and while no kiss of the King's hand was gotten, the music seemed much appreciated by all. I learned later that my performance that night was captured by the painter Joseph Nash, who completed a series of portraits of events at Windsor Castle. I've since seen the artwork, and while his colors may capture the sight, it's a shame they give no indication of the sound, which was lovely in that space, rising to the high ceiling and providing a warm finish to what smelled like an excellent meal.

And that was life, from then on. Over the next couple of years, I was called to Buckingham Palace, Claremont, the newly-constructed Osborne House on the Isle of Wight, all the while leaving my loved ones behind. I wanted to provide the best I could for Mary and Jessie, but in doing so this kept me away from them. Isn't that the way of the world, though? It's said you can have either time or money, and though all around me were stark examples of folk with both, people like Mary and I had long been forced to make do with not enough of either. But the special connection to the monarch that a position in the royal household afforded was a payment in and of itself. It brought stories and status for the rest of the year, and even being around extreme wealth – without ever actually attaining it – had its advantages.

First a Piper, Then a Castle

Reading over yesterday's pages, I see I'm skirting a bit of the story. It's the part that reveals how much I was actually enjoying the work, and even if I wouldn't have admitted so much to myself early on, I likely wouldn't have traded it for anything at the time. It was a conflict in me, undoubtedly. It's easy for me to write that my role kept me away from my family, but once integrated into royal service, I felt I had truly found my calling, serving the monarch and the country. Seeing first-hand the luxury in which the queen and her family lived, and becoming a part of their luxury myself … that was a joyous thing. I felt as though no one else could have done what I was doing, and though I knew there would be future royal pipers in the coming years, I was the first, and that mattered to me.

The work itself presented more than enough opportunities for me to forget about family life. I was not alone in this. Many of the staff and household found themselves whisked away for months, leaving behind all semblance of a normal existence. And normality can be just that – a little too normal. A place in the royal household lifted one from the everyday. Everything was exciting; the world was suddenly more accessible. Instead of having your tea and discussing children, home and relatives, you were on the edge of meetings pivotal for the fates of entire nations, extravagant banquets and balls, with the wealthiest and finest-looking people in Europe. Striking up the pipes in a grand hall for the noble and powerful of the world, versus tidying after dinner and sitting by a wee fire … If the former was available, what man in his prime would volunteer for the latter?

Mary was always eager to know the details of my latest adventure, and as time went on, she more frequently bemoaned her lonely life at Windsor, to deaf ears, for the most part. We still hadn't moved from Windsor, both because of my having so few spare weeks to help with such a relocation and also that in the meantime we'd added to our family, with Margaret in December 1845 and then John in March 1848, the lad named after my father and brother both. They were a delight, but also a terrible amount of work, the three of them. Mary looked out on her feet after John was born, and so we arranged for her sister Maggie, only 15, to come live with us and help with the children. We were comfortable enough by then to pay her a wage that was helpful to her, and she was a godsend to us, both for her help with the children, and for keeping Mary company in the many days and nights that I was away working.

It was a long time before Mary and I had any serious argument about my absences, and even when we did, it was not the sort of aggressive exchange we can have now. But when the time came for the next royal trip to Scotland, Mary voiced her unhappiness about my leaving again, and this was likely the first time we discussed it so frankly.

It came in 1848. Her Majesty had been true to her word: she soon found a residence in Scotland that suited her needs. Ah, Balmoral. Prince Albert negotiated the purchase of the lease, and during a conversation over breakfast at Buckingham Palace, I heard him describe it as a "pretty little castle" on the River Dee, near Aberdeen. I was delighted, but when I arrived back at Windsor that evening and relayed this news to Mary, working to suppress my pleasure at another trip north, she was not fooled in the slightest.

"Of course. There you go, Angus, off on another royal jaunt to the country I'm no longer allowed to see." We were in our bedroom and Mary was by the sideboard, wrestling with buttons on her dress with obvious frustration.

"Here, let me help," I said, reaching forward to assist, but at my touch she recoiled and turned to face me sharply.

"Who do you think helps when you are away weeks on end playing a few tunes, Angus, walking the hills and drinking yourself blind?"

"That's not what happens," I said evenly as I sat on the bed, having rehearsed this answer in my head in the carriage from London. "It's not a sport, it's my duty to Her Majesty and the job we accepted I would do. Not to mention, it's the way we pay for our family to live, Mary."

"That may be. But I don't like the way our family lives anymore. I truly don't. We have three children, my sister, and sometimes even you all crammed in this cottage. It just won't do any longer. If we're going to see more of you, we need to be closer to London, where you work most." She bit her lip, and then said, "And if we're not going to see more of you, then we still need a better house for the family, and it's your responsibility to make that happen."

I knew that Mary was right. Though we had made it our own, the cottage was too small, and it no longer made sense, even if it was good economy. I should have secured a home in London city when it was just Mary and Jessie, a place that they could have really called their own. It stung me that Mary had considered the possibility of my absences being the new norm, but I didn't know what to say, so I rose to close the curtains, despite the blanket of fog that lay over Windsor, obscuring everything outside.

"Angus? Are you listening?"

"I would love nothing better than to be around you and the family more often, Mary, really I would," I said, after taking a moment. I wished the conversation over. "When I return from Scotland, we can start moving closer to the city. That would be better for me, and you know I'd much rather come home to you after a long night in Buckingham Palace than have to sleep clothed on a hard cot in my room there."

"It's not just me, Angus. The bairns need to see their father also. Where would you be if John MacKay had been gone as much from your life as you are from theirs? Would your childhood not have been greatly worsened by that?"

I sighed as I lay back down on the bed, watching her. The lamp was beside my head, casting its yellow light on her body. "This is not a country castle in Perthshire I'm playing at, with a few hunting expeditions and the odd visitor. It's hard work I do. Buckingham Palace sees heads of government and state every day and night, just about. My work is not comparable to my father's."

Mary turned to me. "In more ways than one. I don't remember stories of John MacKay lurching into his house reeking of drink at all hours of the day and night."

I paused, sighing again. "That was once."

"Three times, Angus. And perhaps the drink has something to do with your condition. I really think you should see the doctor about it."

She was referring to the swelling around my genitals and the lesions on my feet, which were becoming increasingly uncomfortable to walk on. "I wish you wouldn't keep bringing this up, Mary. I've been drinking a lot longer than I've had this, and it'll clear up like everything does. And tell me, what if I was told I couldn't pipe any longer? What would we do then? I work for Her Majesty. If I can't pipe, I shall be replaced. It seems like you don't understand the way of things here."

"Perhaps not," she said, her face dark. "But if this is the sort of sinful behavior that goes on in London, I can't imagine the scenes when you go to Scotland."

"What do you want me to say?" I burst out, struggling to keep the fire from my voice. "Aye, there is a lot of drink taken there. But Her Majesty does not mind, and it's more accepted among the gillies and household staff – in fact it's expected. Do you want me to be the only one not doing it?" I could see in Mary's face that my volume had shocked her. "Listen, Mary, I think we do it mainly because the English staff can't stand it," I quipped, trying to force a smile from her.

"Well, they're not the only ones," Mary said quietly. "No one's better for more drink, and I haven't seen it cause anything but strife in the village where I grew up, or in Edinburgh when we were there. It's trouble." She stared at me as she lay down on the bed beside me, looking at me sternly with unflinching eyes.

"I cannot control the actions of those on the staff and those we visit," I said eventually.

She stared at me. "Do you expect me to believe that you're not as bad as the rest of them on those trips, Angus?"

No, I did not. But we did not speak of the topic again before I left for Balmoral. In hindsight, I see that my behavior towards Mary was inconsiderate at best and wretched at worst, but as the journey began, I found myself deeply angry at her, and felt as though she had been the one in the wrong.

I recall the time spent on the yacht was intensely warm, and the clouds following us thunderous at times, so it was a relief when we at last docked at Aberdeen. I had not been lying about the royal trips being hard work, and getting anywhere was a task; no matter the route or destination, the queen was expected to parade through many towns and cities, each one presenting their own challenges. I threw myself into the work and the drink, and as we neared Balmoral, my excitement at the prospect of a permanent royal residence in Scotland was renewed, as it surely spelled more frequent trips up to this part of the world in future.

Neither was I lying when I told Mary that not all of the permanent household staff were as enthusiastic about this prospect as I was. When we reached the glorious Balmoral estate and were in the process of unloading everything that needed unloading into the castle, I heard that bastard Stevens muttering that he felt abused, traveling to the "wilds of Scotland." He was right in saying that the comforts and civilities could not even begin to compare to those of London, but to hell with him, and to hell with those comforts, was my opinion! It was a cool September afternoon, and the place was tranquil and solitary, with huge Scotch firs and hills all around, and birdsong in the air. How could anyone want to be anywhere else? All I cared about was doing my duty as piper to Her Majesty, sovereign of our nation, and I could fathom nothing I'd rather be doing.

That stay at Balmoral was in a number of ways similar to the holiday at Blair Castle, with the difference being that I ingratiated myself even more so with the queen. Both she and the prince adored the company of Highlanders on their northern trips, be it gillies or pipers or foresters; having seen the way that most folk interacted with the royals, I well understood when Her Majesty praised the Highlanders' lack of bluster and flattery in her presence. Our ruler and sovereign she might have been, but she also appreciated being spoken to and cared for as a person. No surprise then that I had become one of the chief names on her staff, and when in my element in Scotland, my company was cemented among her most favored.

Balmoral in those days was still the original building, not large enough to accommodate all the people required to host the sort of gatherings that were part of keeping a royal house, and so events there were held in what they called the Iron House: a new type of construction featuring sheets of corrugated metal fixed to wooden beams that was put up in the grounds. That night there was to be one of those events that in the following years would become tradition at Balmoral: The Gillies' Ball. This was to be an occasion when the household staff could mix socially with the locals who worked on the estate, and I was anticipating it eagerly. The queen saw the ball as her thanks to the local people for their service and hospitality. She enjoyed their rough behavior and watching me interact with them. My only concern was that at mixed events like these, in which the common folk were among those invited, often I was neither fish nor foul. My position as the queen's piper meant I was not quite aligned with the local deerstalkers, drivers and cooks, but neither did I feel I altogether belonged with the rest of the staff who had traveled from down south. I preferred the former, having come from a similar background, but sometimes I suspected they saw me more for my lofty employment than for the Raasay man I was.

The day was to be a good one, though. I had just returned to the house from the breezy sunshine to take direction from Her Majesty for the evening's music, and as I was waiting outside the hall to be invited in, I heard something that I enjoyed enormously. Inside, Her Majesty, in firm voice, was reprimanding Stevens and one or two other Englishmen in the household staff for complaining about the coarse speaking and lack of decorum shown by the Scots of Braemar: the good folk who had been helping with preparations. She lectured a group of them loudly for a few minutes on their arrogance and ill-discipline, and by the time they were expelled, I was having to bite my tongue not to burst out laughing.

"A little quick to temper there, eh, Stevens?" I joked as he came last through the door, not even looking at him, contemplating the state of my fingernails. "I could just about hear you blushing from here."

He gave me a murderous look, and I thought for a moment he might launch himself at me, but his acquaintances ushered him away, visibly cowed by their royal dressing down.

"It's no wonder you feel right at home here," Stevens said over his shoulder, "in a land full of drunks and savages. The MacKays are cut from the same cloth."

"I couldn't agree more," I replied merrily, giving him a wave before being called in. The queen's day room was bright with sunshine, despite the high, wood-paneled walls, the dark and heavy furniture, and the Stewart tartan on nearly every piece of upholstery. There wasn't a room in the house that didn't have a stag's head mounted on the wall, and I saw that further additions were being made all the time. Stag horn chandeliers, cupboard and door handles ... At least Prince Albert's many misfires were of some use in the end!

The queen stood looking out of the window on to the lawn. I could hear the royal children singing in German from the adjoining room. When Her Majesty turned to me, her face was a little flushed after raising her voice, but she gave me a warm smile.

"Is everything in order, Mr. MacKay?"

"Indeed it is, Your Majesty. The Iron House standing tall and ready. I understand you have questions about tonight's music."

"Not so much questions, as a request that the reels be long and lively," she said, smiling and sinking into a large chair. "It's important to us that everybody is of the highest spirits for this occasion."

"We'll do our best, ma'am. I know everyone is looking forward to the evening. They're currently all off to their lodgings to set out their attire." I wouldn't tell the queen as much, but I knew that this was more of a chore than anything else for the family, courtiers and servants who accompanied the queen from London. Many despised wearing Highland dress for these events. Some had the style and income for fashionable garb, but for most it was a matter of finding something that would do to appease the queen's insatiable interest in the "Scotch costume." For others still – like Stevens, for instance – it was an outright embarrassment.

"Superb," the queen said. "I do hope the evening is a success. There seems to be a sense of mischief in the air among the local folk. I've heard plenty of joking and laughing."

"Well, I imagine they are all very excited at the prospect of dancing in your company, ma'am. And they won't be accustomed to all the food and drink that's in store. It'll be a wonderful occasion for them, I'm sure."

"Well, we ought to offer something to our hosts. They've welcomed us so warmly into this place, which before five minutes ago seemed to breathe such peace." She shook her head tiredly.

"It'll be a grand affair, ma'am, you can be sure of that," I hurried to say. "The locals will certainly not forget it. With fuel on board, you'll see them get up a great head of steam. Perhaps more than you bargained for, I reckon."

"Let's hope so. And you are happy to provide the music to accompany such festivities?" the queen nodded, widening her eyes at me.

"My honor as always, ma'am."

I spent the remainder of the day ensuring that everything was as it should be with my pipes, and then at last the event began. The Iron House was a sight to behold. The structure itself was decorated with heather garlands and lengths of tartan and bunting, and the guests were all kitted out as well – more in costume than in dress, it must be said. I much enjoyed the locals delivering their critical and comical commentary of the tartan-clad English members of the household, laughing at the ill-fitted kilts, the unmatched hose without proper garters, the shoes that were so clearly at odds with the rest of the ensemble. These were the days of high interest in tartan, however, and everyone had found enough to get by.

Following a successful few days of hunting from Prince Albert and his companions, deer carcasses were brought down to just outside the Iron House and laid in a circle with an opening on one side. Fir boughs were wrapped tightly together and dipped in resin to make torches, and as the flames leapt about in the dying light, it made for a memorable scene, as people celebrated the successful hunt. Once everyone had eaten and drank for a couple of hours – amid much re-telling of local tales, with levels of detail that to me sounded more real than imagined – I snuck away with the other two pipers for a quick tuning session, before we joined the other musicians assembled in the Iron House for the dancing, where we would take turns with the orchestra in providing music.

The orchestra started sedately enough, with a selection of more refined country dances from England and Scotland. The English guests all knew the steps, having been taught them by the dancing masters in their fine houses, but the locals hadn't a clue what they were doing, much to the queen's amusement. To my side, the orchestra members were drinking at some rate, and before long the tempo built until there was a clamor for the pipers to bring the Highland reels to the party. At a beckoning smile from Her Majesty, I lifted my pipes to begin.

It was my practice to start nights like these with a tune from home, and "Mrs. MacLeod of Raasay" got a good airing for my first dance. It was received well to say the least. I wouldn't be surprised if they heard the commotion going on all the way down in Raasay, and among the first dancers on the floor was the queen herself. Her Majesty was an excellent dancer, and not at all afraid to spin wildly with the largest man in the hall. Seeing the queen dance with such exuberance ignited passion among all the young locals, and soon there was a vivid intensity to the whole place, more than I'd perhaps ever seen on a dance floor before. The energy this provided encouraged me to keep playing long after the song was meant to have finished, and I repeated some parts four or five times over, before continuing on to the next tune with little more than a gulp for air.

Before long, there was barely room to see the floor – hardly a soul was safe from being pulled from their chair into the reels – and when the air grew too stuffy to bear, some of the dancers flooded out of the doors and onto the lawn. I followed behind, leaving the other pipers to carry on the fight inside, all of us struggling to play in unison, and I watched as Her Majesty danced with the prince by the light of the torches, beneath a windy night sky. Clouds seemed to race past the moon, and the flames licked and flickered at the flailing limbs and streaming hair. It was a night of wild abandon, and as the evening wore on, not a few couples began slinking off into the trees nearby, bringing to a close what had started with such promise on the dance floor. I'm sure if I heard my performance sober I'd have grimaced, but at the time, everyone was begging for another tune until the wee hours.

After long sets of jigs, reels, strathspeys, and even the occasional waltz – in which Her Majesty was to the fore for a good portion – the royal party gradually began to withdraw towards the castle. The drink had taken full hold on all by this time, with many of the young locals making too free. Even at a mixed event like The Gillies' Ball, the queen and the prince couldn't be seen stooping to such questionable levels of respectability. When at last I set down the pipes it was a very messy scene. People were slumped against trees, or just fallen on the dance floor where they were. Songs and tears were breaking out in equal measure; people were draining the bottles left strewn around. I watched as a well-oiled gillie attempted to corner one of the last available lassies, running afoul both of his competitor and the poor woman herself.

"But you were dancing with me first!" he cried, looking genuinely hurt as he struggled to walk towards her in a straight line. He had been prancing about so long that his long hair was sticking to his face in comical fashion.

She threw her head to the sky in despair. "I was dancing with everybody, it was a bloody reel, wasn't it?"

"Well, who was the best dancer, me or him?" the gillie slurred, pointing in the general direction of the man beside her.

And so it went on. This was what happened when you mixed unlimited wealth with working folk's appetite for celebration, and I enjoyed it greatly.

I must concede, though I hadn't the intentions to do so, with the amount of drink I'd taken, I did find myself walking back to my lodgings in the company of a young woman myself, one who seemed very anxious to learn about the ins and outs of piping. It's a blurred memory, but I remember assuring her that I would show her everything one could in the time available, with neither of us remembering I'd left my pipes beneath the stage. This was to be the first time I was unfaithful to Mary. As I had predicted, my swelling and blisters had cleared up – I now see it will have been the Highland air restoring me – and I felt no shame at the time in what happened that night. While the royal household carried an air or strict morality, reality could be quite different.

The next day, the scene was like a day-old battlefield. Dawn had long since broken and I hadn't slept, but still, I found myself walking down to the castle to play music for the queen's morning ritual. I picked up a near-full bottle that lay on a wall and took a swig, trying to stave off the headache that was pounding fiercely on my temples. Around me were the remains of carcasses on the grass, half-covered with shredded bunting. The Iron House was a mess of moved tables, overturned chairs, smashed dishes and discarded bottles. Slowly, a few people were moving about, like the ghostly revenants of some bloody massacre, while many others were still sleeping on the grass, unawares of the nausea and regret that was coming to them. Mac an donais!

When I retrieved my pipes, I found they reeked of last night's whisky, and I made sure to keep a wee bit of distance from the queen's window in case she looked down and saw the state I was in. Thankfully, Her Majesty didn't come to her window as she normally did, presumably enjoying the music from the comfort of her bed. My head felt light, and twice I had to stop so as to vomit behind a tree, before beginning again. It was during one of these moments, as I was hunched over and gagging, that Stevens walked by, on his way to oversee the cleanup at the Iron House.

"Ah, so you're alive are you, MacKay?" he said, a wry smile on his lips. "Best get it all out. The smell of you makes me want to spew as well."

Leamluath

Cumha nam Bràithrean, 1848

I had been in London for five years when I heard of my father's death. I had finally secured a home for Mary, Maggie, and the children by this time, at 4 Sussex Street in Pimlico. It was a respectable area of three-story houses a short walk from Buckingham Palace. The area was not much more than twenty years old when we moved in, and the houses had bright fronts and wide streets. The area was built just north of the Thames on a former marsh, and was a very respectable part of the city without being overly expensive.

My £75-per-annum salary was enough to place us at the heart of the expanding empire, and though London was rife with crime, poverty, and disease, it was one of the major capital cities in the world, and the new house was a damn sight better than what we had made do with in Windsor. The final straw leading to the move had come when we had been trying to get a leak in the children's Windsor bedroom repaired, and for weeks on end were not given approval. Those in the royal service – a highly politicized and often incomprehensible bureaucracy, which even the queen herself did not control completely – went out of their way to make things difficult for me. In the end, instead of fighting it any longer, I decided to escape from it. Though the Pimlico house did not go so far as mending the rift that was ever-widening between Mary and me, we were at least able to live comfortably.

It was in this house in April of 1848, sat at the table in the small dining room downstairs, with clanking and chopping in the background as Mary was beginning to fix tea in the kitchen, that I read the letter, just arrived, penned in the small angular handwriting of my mother.

Aohghas daor,

I'm so sorry to write you in such circumstances, but John MacKay has passed on. He went peacefully in our bed. By the time this reaches you, he should already be buried here on Skye. He told me to tell you it would take a lot to make him proud, and you did so. He loved hearing Roderick read out the English papers the past few years, telling of your achievements. Your brother John is coming home for the funeral, and he'll play the lament. Roderick is here with me now, and sends his best.

Mo ghaol uile,

Màthair

I blinked and read it again. John MacKay had passed on. John MacKay – m'athair – had died. My skin felt numb, like I'd slept out in the cold, but inside was an ocean of feeling. Of course, you expect to lose your parents at some point in your life, and at eighty-one my father had made a go of it, but even so, there's no real way to describe the death of the man that raised you, shaped you, sheltered you. So many memories came flooding back to me at that table, a thousand in a matter of seconds. The lessons, the music, the stories, the wisdom. These I would take with me, but he was gone. It had been several years since I'd even seen him. I grimaced. My son John – his namesake – had not even met the man.

I stood to pour myself some wine, before returning to the chair. He had a good life, I reminded myself. More than good, really. From herd boy to MacLeod, to one of the most revered pipers and musicians in the history of Scotland. I read the letter one more time, before folding it, and making my way over to the fire that was struggling to get going in the hearth.

"What did it say?"

I glanced up in surprise. Mary had appeared in the dining room doorway, and she was leaning against the frame, wiping her hands on her apron, alone. Giving birth to three children can take its toll on some women, but not Mary. Even after all these years she had never lost that girlish charm, something her friends were more than a wee bit envious of. But now she looked at me with an almost frightened expression. I could hear the bairns all out playing with the neighbors in the street. It was raining this thin rain outside; Maggie should really have called them in, wherever she was. I tried to explain to Mary what I'd read but my tongue refused to move, so I simply held out the letter instead.

"Oh, Angus," she said, her eyes moving across the page, lips twitching a little as she read. "I'm so sorry."

"He had a good life," I muttered without thinking, before taking the letter from her hands and holding it to the flames. "It was going to happen sometime."

I heard Mary softly crying behind me, and a shudder went through me as I felt myself going as well. "But thank you, Mary. I'll miss the meal tonight, but leave me something and I'll find it when I get back. Just going to go to Donald's now, see if he knows. I'll be back in a few hours."

"Should I tell the children when you're away?"

I thought about it for a moment. "Aye, please. I'll sit with them when I'm back."

With that, I left the house and stumbled out into the chilly evening air. The misty rain and the noise – the noise which would not subside until much later at night – immediately shocked me out of my numbness. At that moment, as I began to weave through the city streets, among the thousands of people beginning to head home from work, I wished to God I wasn't in London. It didn't feel right to feel such grief at such a distance, among so many people to whom John MacKay meant nothing. I should've been in Scotland to see the spring, with a view of the sea.

The walk to Donald's took me through the very fashionable Belgravia area and right into central London past Hyde Park. It took no small amount of effort not to drop into one of the alehouses I passed along the way. Though the rain had stopped, by the time I arrived I was thoroughly sodden, and my boots were squelching in the mud, struggling to keep the wet out. The sky was still gloomy, with dark clouds and a pale sky behind them as the sun set, as it does that wee bit earlier in London than up north. Donald lived in the servants' row of houses attached to Kensington Palace. The dark brown bricks of his house cast a heavy shadow, and a dog was barking angrily somewhere nearby.

I knocked on the door and waited, trying to shake some of the wet from my hair. Normally when I knocked at Donald's house, I would hear his children start to rave about inside like a pack of animals, sprinting to see who had come to the door. Donald's wife Caroline had recently died as well, leaving him broken-hearted and with three bairns who were still in need of a mother. This was especially difficult given that he had to travel with his work, although there was help enough around. Sometimes we sent Maggie to go and help him for a day or so, and to try and allow himself more time at home, Donald had started to invest in the bagpipe trade, whenever his piping duties would allow. My brother had an arrangement with a woodturner who got him started on the lathe, and also did the bulk of the skilled turning work. The first task was assembling the specific tools needed for pipes, and like John Ban's reamer, most had to be made from other things. The pipes were good though. Donald knew what he wanted, and the end product was a combination of turning skill and bagpipe knowledge. Her Majesty, when I made her aware of this, even commissioned him to make a new presentation set for me. However, the eerie silence when I knocked now told me this was a household that had heard the latest news, and when the door opened at last, I could see the features of Donald's squarish face were even darker than usual. His shirt was crumpled, his face lined, and the pain audible in his voice when he finally spoke.

"Good evening, Aonghais," he said, not even trying to smile.

"Good evening, a Dhòmhaill." I stood for a moment, before pulling him into a hug.

"Lord, you're soaking," he cried, and immediately I felt a little ashamed, still easily caught out by the stern tone of my older brother. He stepped aside and I passed through the brightly lit hall, leaving my coat on a hook before heading into the sitting room. The children must have been upstairs as it was empty and clean, but I saw a bottle of whisky was sitting on the table beside the chairs, with two glasses.

"You knew I was coming?"

"Aye, I presumed so. Go on, take a seat."

I did as I was bid and poured us each a healthy dram. Donald stood for a moment, before taking the chair to my left, and raising his glass.

"John MacKay," he said. "Finest man I knew."

"Slàinte mhath," I said. "I'm sure brother John sent him off as he deserves."

After draining our glasses, each of us sat in silence, having so much to say but not knowing where to begin. Between us we had so many years' worth of memories with Father – each of us seeing quite a different man, with Donald so much older than I – that it felt almost unnecessary to say any one thing that came to mind.

Eventually, Donald stood up. "It's good that you're here, Angus. I've been wanting to show you something." He left the room, and when he returned, I saw he was carrying a beautifully mounted set of pipes.

He'd used the darkest wood I'd ever seen, polished to a perfect shine; the ferrules were silver, engraved with delicate floral patterns. The skin was sturdy yet soft, and covered with silky blue velvet, with drone cord and tassel in matching color. They would stand well beside any set I'd seen. My new presentation set. Donald had obviously put a huge amount of work into them.

Donald laid the pipes down on the table, and it was then I noticed that the chanter stock was not yet tied into the bag. He carefully took the drones and blowpipe out of their stocks, removed the cover on the bag, and handed me the stick with the tying cord.

"I had trouble getting this last one tight," he said, "and I could use an extra pair of hands to seal it."

I bowed my head and let out a shaky sort of laugh. "Aye, this seems like the suitable thing to do today."

His face was etched in concentration as he placed the chanter stock in the neck of the bag, arranged the presentation plate on the front and added the packing pieces of extra sheepskin in just the right spots against the stock. As he got things in place and gave me a nod, I backed away and added tension to the cord, while he methodically wrapped the cord around the chanter stock and packing pieces. I saw a great deal of Father in him at that moment. I consoled myself by thinking that perhaps Father's way of looking at the world wasn't entirely gone. He had sons and daughters who would carry on his legacy as best they could in the society they were in, and I knew that I'd be playing and writing the settings of his tunes until I could no longer.

For the first time in a while, I was more determined than ever to find a way to publish the second collection. The Highland Society was not considering it, nor any longer willing to spend time discussing it. They felt that my *Collection of Ancient Piobireachd* was a success, and there was still a demand for copies, and consequently no need of a whole new volume.

For his part, James Logan felt he'd done as much as he wanted on the subject, and that there was no need for further work for the sake of "just more tunes." James Logan convinced them that pìobaireachd was a dying art, and even I had to admit that things had changed in the Highlands. No longer was there the option of training at MacCrimmon's croft or at Taigh a' Phìobaire for six months or a year, singing and learning the tunes by heart. Fewer pipers learned the traditional way. Everything had to be done faster. The written score was dominant at the competitions, and those events were driving the way pipers played the tunes. There was less freedom for pipers to play styles or even variations that weren't reflected in the written score. This also reduced the variety of tunes being played, because pipers weren't submitting tunes for which there was no written score. This in itself was a great reason to publish a second collection: to prevent these tunes from falling from the general knowledge of pipers. How could the Society not see this?

Well, even if those bastards wouldn't publish it, I decided there and then that I was going to copy out portions of my manuscript, and distribute them to my friends who would want and appreciate them, just as I had done with the Campbells on Islay. I wouldn't be able to copy the full body of work, with it now being over two hundred tunes strong, but for my father John MacKay, and for the sake of the music, I was going to make sure there was at least more than one written version of some of my favorite tunes.

"There," Donald smiled, finishing the last knot. "That should be them ready, I reckon. You think the queen will approve?"

"They're magnificent, brother," I said. "She'll be pleased, have no doubt. But we still don't know how they sound, do we? Perhaps we should give them a blow, as our own farewell to John MacKay."

"I'm not too sure the neighbors would be best pleased if we tested them now."

I nodded, disappointed. Donald was straight-laced and always had been. He called his bairns down and I drained one more glass in their company, before I said my goodbyes and went home to my family, after they'd had a good meal. I told our children a few tales of my father, though afterwards in bed, thoughts of how my mother would cope without him kept me awake for a long time.

Summer came to London, and with it a welcome face: my brother John. He had traveled south to seek the fortune that had eluded him in Scotland, and also I suspect to put some distance between himself and our father's death earlier in the year. His absence cast a long shadow, which seemed to weigh upon John more than any of us. Aye, just as I'd felt drawn upwards after the tragedy, John felt the urge to flee the scene. I suppose when something like that befalls a family, there's no right place to be.

It was cloudy and humid on the day John arrived, the sort of day when your shirt sticks to you and it's hard to draw breath. Donald and I had agreed to meet him at his new room in East London, where John had arrived earlier that afternoon. I was a little surprised Donald was attending; he was much less happy than I was that our brother was coming to the city. Donald had high standards, and John was always a problem to be solved in his view, a bent rail to be straightened. Every time the topic of John came up, Donald complained about his drinking habits and friends, and generally found fault with his way of life. John and I had been very close in boyhood, which is perhaps why I often found Donald's criticism tedious; or perhaps it was because some of the complaints were a little close to home. To me, John was an easy companion – a confidant – and the only real difference between us that I could see was that I had experienced more fortune in my line of work.

But Donald had the bit between his teeth that day, "He's not been capable of holding down proper employment in all his life, and now he expects to be able to do so in London! Give me strength. Honestly, what business has he coming down here?"

Usually, I would contribute something in John's defense, but in the muggy heat, I was struggling to engage. My own battles were beginning to catch up with me. In fact, it was taking all of my strength just to put one foot in front of the other.

"Slow down a minute, Donald, please."

I stood to try and catch my breath, and wiped the sweaty film from my forehead with my kerchief. Two weeks before, I had done what Mary had long implored me to do, which was to see a professional about my groin. It hadn't been voluntary. I'd been walking down Belgrave Road on the way to the palace, when suddenly the most tender area of my body, which had been bothersome for a couple of years with itchiness, heaviness and swelling, became downright agony. I hailed a cab to take me the rest of the way, thinking I'd rest when I got there, but when I began climbing the stairs of Buckingham Palace, the pain was so intense that I fell to my knees and cried out. I was escorted by people I did not know to a bed, and Her Majesty's doctor, Sir James Clarke, was summoned. After allowing me a drink to numb the pain, immediately after examination he recommended I begin treatment for the French Pox, or syphilis. It was strange, hearing something I had been living with for so long given a name. Of course, the disease was rife in London and it had crossed my mind that this might have been what was ailing me, but comparing the utter devastation that it had caused throughout the world to my own condition, it just hadn't seemed like the two could possibly be the same. Until now, that was.

Treatment was grim, and though Clarke was one of the most highly regarded physicians in the country, I knew that with syphilis, even the finest doctors didn't really know what was to be done. This is why I do not much regret waiting so long to get diagnosed. Who knows if earlier treatment would have cured me, or just caused me more misery? I was prescribed the blue mass pills, and then on that same day, the so-called hydrocele had to be drained, which involved a needle being inserted into the area of my scrotum containing the fluid. The sensation of the metal breaking through the skin and then into a place that should never be invaded was enough to make me faint. After extraction, this was followed by the insertion of iodine into the area to dry the hydrocele. I can only describe the whole ordeal as a morbid experience; if I hadn't already been swimming in such a sea of pain, I'd have refused it. This was the first of three times I would have to undergo this procedure. I'd assumed that two weeks would be enough time for me to get over the effects, but by the time John arrived I was still keenly suffering. Whisky and brandy did seem to alleviate it somewhat, but after working on the manuscripts all morning, I hadn't yet had any that day.

"What's wrong with you?" he asked impatiently, frowning with his hands in his pockets.

"It's nothing," I said. Mary knew – I suspect she'd long known even before I confirmed it – but I'd decided not to tell my brothers about it, not wanting to tarnish the day of John's arrival. "Too much to drink last night, perhaps."

"Hm. Well, I simply mean, Angus, that without a proper position in London, John'll expect to be looked after by us, and I've bricks enough in my hod. You know that since Caroline died, I can carry no more."

"Aye," I sighed, trying my best to show that I was listening. "Just you leave him to me, brother. I'm glad to have him here, and if he's in need of anything, I'll see to it."

Donald laughed with derision. "When has wee John not been in need of anything?"

I stared at him, and just then something in me flared up, some unfamiliar rage. I wanted to strike him, but I immediately told myself how irrational that would be. Still, I couldn't stop myself from retorting. "If you think like that, why are you even coming to welcome him then? Eh? You should have stayed at home, spared us your sulking."

I stormed onwards, using my anger to ignore the agony, but could feel Donald looking at me dumbstruck. Regret soon flooded in, but I didn't have the energy to apologize. I heard Donald start walking behind me, and he said no more until we reached John's room.

I still hate that John was living in such a place. It was tiny and bare, in a sorry neighborhood in close proximity to the sewers. Donald bristled at the rancid smell as we approached, but I tried to put it out of my mind. I hadn't seen John in years and more than anything, I was just glad he was here. His presence in the city would only be a good thing for me. John came quickly out of the door when we arrived; he must have been watching from a window.

"Three MacKay brothers on one street," he said, narrowly dodging some passers-by, not yet used to the brusqueness of city folk. "London doesn't know what it's bargained for!"

"How are you keeping, John?" I beamed, being sure to shake his hand before he could embrace me, not wanting anything to graze my groin.

"Fantastic, fantastic. And hello to you, Donald."

"Afternoon, John. Shall we see the abode, then?"

"Not much to see, I'm afraid, and I've not yet unpacked." John wrinkled his nose. "Let's just get moving, shall we?"

I couldn't help but notice that despite John's chirpy demeanor, he did not look healthy at all. I suppose I was one to talk, but no, it was true. His face was gaunter than when last I saw him, with skin covered in large liver spots that I couldn't remember being so prominent before. The shape of his skull was more pronounced; his eyes dim; his beard graying and patchy. Being an avid walker and climber his entire life, he'd always been quite skinny, but looking at his hands and wrists now, they were bony and frail.

We stopped at an alehouse for a drink, and afterwards I felt much more like myself, so we happily strolled a couple of hours around London, showing John the impressive architecture and the general lay of the land. Even the lovely Edinburgh – where the three of us had spent considerable time – could not compete with the industry and bustle observed on any day in London. We walked through the fruit and vegetable market at Covent Garden, disoriented by the constant hum of voices and the dizzying movement of people, carts and baskets going in all directions. The market had so many people trying to make a living: flower girls, women selling fruit, legless men flogging kitchen tools, scads of boys searching for used cigar ends, which they'd sell for the tobacco still in them.

Coming out of it, John was delighted to have heard our mother tongue being spoken a few times by those we passed on the street, on account of the recent influx of Gaels. Most had ended up dirty, hungry, cold and despised on the streets. We explained to him that the streets were most pleasant in the early morning, when the smell of coffee and fresh bread was in the air, wafting from the stalls catering to the thousands walking into the city for work. The building work would not have started by that time either, so the noise that to me seemed the main monument of the steam age wasn't so offensive. Still, we advised John to remember fondly those days in the Hebrides when silence was only broken by wind or water, as they were a long way from here and no mistake.

At Trafalgar Square, we passed a crashed carriage – something seen near enough every day in the capital – and Donald then began lecturing John on how to tell the quality of a carriage and horse before stepping into it.

"And even when the equipment is in good shape, there's a good chance the driver won't be," Donald said. We'd stopped at a bench, and with sitting being so uncomfortable for me, I was hovering beside the two of them.

"Aye, drivers work long hours for little pay," I said with a nod, "and they're always trying to exact a higher fare than usual. Full of good stories, though."

John smiled. "That's what really matters, isn't it?"

We waited for some gentlemen to pass us, looking as though they were on the way to the theatre or a club. Donald cleared his throat, and we braced ourselves for whatever argument he was preparing to stoke.

"But remember, John, those cabbies get good stories while making some sort of living."

John looked at me, rolling his eyes. "I wondered how long it would take for this to come up."

"Well?" Donald raised his eyebrows. I could tell from his voice that he wasn't being malicious – perhaps my outburst earlier had tamed him slightly – but still, he was playing the part of overbearing elder brother flawlessly.

"Well," John said, "in actual fact, I'm glad you asked, brother. I've had some ideas of how I might spend my time down here."

I grunted my approval, while Donald looked suspicious.

"Go on. Let's hear it."

Sure enough, John did have a plan. While he didn't have a permanent position secured, he told us he still had a wee bit of money left over from his employment with Leslie of Glengarry, which would see him through a few months' rent. In the meantime, he volunteered to do whatever needed doing with Donald's bagpipe making, which I had also become a bit more involved in. I had started using my reputation among pipers to garner trade, and because of this, there was certainly some work for John to be getting on with, and he wouldn't need to be trained, having learnt everything he needed to know about bags, reeds, and bagpipe assembly back in his youth. John was also interested in writing out the tunes he'd learned from our father, which could be a benefit to me in assembling a wider collection.

"I've started writing some tunes already," he revealed. "Most of them Father's, so they should be of use to you. I must have about forty of them in the works, but there are a lot that are incomplete. Maybe you could have a look and fill in some parts I may have forgotten?"

"Of course, brother. Glad to." I gave Donald a look.

"Hm," he shrugged.

John snorted. "I think that means he's impressed, doesn't it?"

The next few weeks and months were grand ones, among the best I'd spent in London. Autumn came and the trees in the parks began to blush and shed. Though I wasn't in any way clear of the disease, the swelling had temporarily reduced, and I could move about much more freely. It was tempting to hunt for a remedy from one of the many street doctors who plied their trade in the capital, selling pills, potions and miracle cures, but within minutes it was blatant that these were made from nothing more than questionable powders mixed with dirty London water. Hot baths seemed to help, and it was good to lie down a little when I could; I was able to forget the pain almost entirely if I stayed quite still.

Unfortunately, there was not a great deal of time to do so, however. Royal service was as demanding as ever. My name was as renowned as that of any piper alive, perhaps any in history; I was always being welcomed to head up events among the higher classes. This was symbolic of one of the truly amazing changes in British society – one that many were not pleased to entertain – which was the rising prominence of Scots in the business of the nation. Only a hundred years back, Hanoverian solders were destroying the homes and crops on Raasay for our involvement with the Jacobites, and here was a British monarch with a piper to perform for visitors from across the world at the highest occasions of state. I'm certainly glad I was born in this century.

To make their presence felt in social and political life, Scots in London often used tartan and pipes to garner positive attention for our native country, and the question each of them seemed to ask themselves was: who better to assist than Her Majesty's piper? If there was a piping event in London, it seemed my name was always attached. The Scottish Society of London, for example, had become more active in organizing events directed at the welfare of Scots in London, and in June 1849 they held a Grand National Fête under the presidency of the Marquis of Breadalbane at Kensington Park. The fete was really just a games day to raise funds for Scottish charities in the capital. I spent a memorable day with my brothers Donald and John watching the archery and the athletics, before I was to pipe. I also became increasingly involved in arranging pipers and dancers for events which I wouldn't be able to attend. As though I wasn't busy enough!

Whenever I did have that rare night off, it would often be spent with John. We shared many a bottle together, and we occasionally discussed tunes and how they go, but little was done to expand my collection with John's tunes, although I think he did work on them in his room. John visited us at the house from time to time, and the bairns were delighted when he came round. You might not have known it to look at him, but John was still just a big bairn himself. It was not uncommon for the reelpipes to come out and for the dancing to start, John leaping and clowning with the children, until a nasty cough overtook him. Mary, though she disapproved of the drink we got through, loved seeing how happy the bairns were, and enjoyed John's antics in the house.

Ah, how I wish I could say that this is how life continued to progress. But no. What writing it all down is showing me is that nothing lasts, and what's good seems to be most short-lived of all.

In October that year I arrived at my dressing room in Buckingham Palace, scheduled to play at a grand state dinner that evening, which I had been told had over 2000 invitations. The room always reeked of tobacco despite the fact I rarely smoked; I suspect the palace footmen used it for such purposes during the days I was elsewhere. It was a late start that night – I would begin around ten o'clock – and no doubt would continue on to the wee hours, but I was looking forward to it, just applying the finishing touches to my evening dress. Her Majesty had requested I play "Fàilte a' Phrionssa" when the dishes were cleared, which was to be in an hour or so. I think she fancied that "The Prince's Salute" applied as much to her Prince Albert as it ever did to Charles Edward Stuart. Forevermore, that tune will now be tainted for me, as it was the one going through my head when I received the knock on the door that would change my life.

"MacKay, are you in?" said the voice. Before I could answer, a head poked through the door. It was one of the kinder footmen, the silver-haired Arthur Schackle.

"I am, Mr. Schackle. How can I help?"

"I'm afraid a woman called at the gate looking for you with a message about your late brother. She's there waiting right now."

My heart skipped a beat, but immediately I assured myself there had obviously been some mistake made. "My late brother? Are you sure? It's my father who so lately passed up in Skye."

"I'm no seer of what can and can't be, MacKay. I just report the messages as I hear them."

Walking to the gate beneath a starless sky, I remained perplexed, still assuming this was in regard to my father. I wondered how any in London would know who he was, or where I was, but chiefly I was thinking that I hoped this didn't take long. I was telling myself that I had to start warming up in a moment. Didn't this woman know that I was about to perform for the queen? Coming around the corner towards the gate, though, I stopped abruptly. A sickening feeling crawled through my stomach and up my chest. There stood John's housekeeper in some distress, a woman of about fifty. She was accompanied by a London policeman.

Somehow I still managed to complete my duties, though I have no memory of how the tune went. I remained in shock in the cab over to John's rooms. Within minutes of arriving, I was making arrangements for John's remains, and discussing with his landlord the disposition of his limited personal property. I stood in the dingy wee room, filthy without seeming to have anything much in it, ill-lit by a spluttering lamp. The damp in the air mixed with the smell of sewers, slops, and the nauseating, unmistakable aroma of something dead. Rats could be heard beneath the floorboards, and a pile of bottles lay by the door. It was squalor: nothing more, nothing less. The very room felt sick of itself.

Over on the desk there was a practice chanter or two; a little tobacco tin filled with reeds in various states of repair; the remains of at least two meals. In a little space of its own was a folder of manuscripts and blank paper. Here were the most recent tunes he had been writing out.

In spite of the rigor mortis, it was without much difficulty that I lifted John from the floor where the landlord and housekeeper had left him, and placed him on the bed. He was as light as a feather. It had been almost a week since we'd seen one another, and I suspected he'd been dead at least a day. He'd been in decent spirits the week before, I thought. A bit tired. And we'd all grown used to his persistent cough, which sometimes would consume his entire energy to stop it. We'd even laughed about it.

Now, however, he was cold as stone to the touch, and his skin a strange yellowish color. His shirt was on but unbuttoned, exposing his almost child-like frame. From his face, he might have just been in a deep sleep. I was glad I didn't have to close his eyelids.

"Rotten luck, someone dying in a rented room. Twice that's happened here now." The landlord – a fat, bald man with a thick black moustache – was standing behind me, blocking the door with arms folded. "Naturally it's a tragedy for you, sir. It's just the housekeepers charge more for cleaning, and well, it's not exactly clean as it is …"

I wasn't listening. How could this have happened? That was all I could think. How could this have happened, and how do I remedy it? There must be a way for this unbearable thing not to have happened. I stood, rooted to the floorboards, fixed in a daze. The first thoughts that came to mind were selfish ones; I hadn't absorbed what was happening. I thought about how I could possibly write this to Mother and the rest of the family. I thought about how I could go home and break this news to Mary, not to mention Jessie, Margaret, and John.

"… and that's before we even consider re-letting it, sir, you understand, because when people–"

"Stop. I'll pay the next month of his rent if you and the housekeeper keep your silence about his condition and the state of the room."

I realized as soon as I said this that this person had probably never been silent on any subject, but he pretended to consider the proposition thoughtfully, stroking his moustache.

"That'd probably do it, sir. Thanking you kindly."

When the landlord departed with my request to fetch a clergyman, I carefully bundled together the sheets of manuscript John had been working on. Rather, I seemed to observe as my hands and legs set to this task in front of me. I packed up his clothes from the couple of drawers, and took his shaving jar and razor from the wash basin. His worn coat hung on the back of the door. When it was done, the pile was pitiful. I wouldn't have to make a second trip.

I made every effort not to, but couldn't help looking once more towards his face. Move, I willed it. Just a flicker of the eyelids. A twitch of the lips. Something, anything to snap me out of this nightmare I found myself in.

That face was a far cry from the one of my wee brother on Raasay, and that's the face I want to remember here. I want to remember that vibrant, healthy boy: walking the hills, piping, singing, laughing, living, off in his own worlds. But it's difficult to do so, knowing that this sweet young lad did not grow into the man he might have done. And I feel guilty for that, rightly or wrongly. Though we never really said as much, I have no doubt that my own path became a model for John's ambitions, and perhaps it shouldn't have.

I believe that family pressures sometimes work both for and against the tide of a person's life. I often wonder now if John wouldn't have been happier if there wasn't such an expectation in our family to fall into piping. The rest of my brothers, we all seemed suited to it early on, but John was different – quieter, wilder, less methodical – and not necessarily the sort you would expect to excel as a musician, particularly in a landscape governed by the Highland Society. He had time alone with our father that the rest of us might have envied, and moderate success at the competitions; but though he obviously enjoyed the music, he was never really interested in it to the same obsessive degree as Donald and me. He had other interests: perhaps that was the problem. He loved dancing, and always did well at the dancing competitions. He loved reaching the summit of the tallest hills and getting lost in forests and spending time with himself. I think this is why, even when he was in positions of some esteem, serving as piper to Sir Robert Gordon of Balmoral or to Leslie of Glengarry, he so often turned to drink, and his reputation as something of a degenerate began to spread. He just wasn't doing what he loved.

Later, riding back through the streets in the bouncing cab with John's belongings, I wept. Rattling along, I saw and smelled and heard everything that London had to offer: cooking fires; smoking chimneys; alehouses and brothels bustling; carriages and engines and horses; children out playing in the muddy streets. But for the second time in a year, I found myself experiencing it all in a state of disbelief. No one was stopping to recognize that a fine man had just died. A fine man had just died, sad and alone, and yet nothing seemed to have changed.

How could this have happened?

Is fhada mar seo tha sinn

I met with Sir James several times at his office at Buckingham Palace in the months following John's death. The doctor was a tall, well-built man of about sixty, with big bushy sideburns, and an intimate relationship with Her Majesty and Prince Albert. In the beginning, what I appreciated about him was that he spoke plainly, never shying from the truth, and being a Scot himself, he was friendlier and perhaps more understanding of what life in London might be like for me. Now I know the true character of the man, however, I struggle to believe how I was so easily swayed by him.

He asked me a lot of questions early on after my diagnosis. When might I have contracted the disease? When and what were my earliest symptoms? Who might I have infected? I had very little idea of how to answer any of them, in truth. The life of any musician is hardly conducive to a settled family situation, let alone the life of a piper to the most powerful family in the country. Even before all of this fanfare and prestige, I'd never experienced a lack of willingness among the women I met when I was working in the great houses, and I admitted to Sir James that of late, the fact that I was married no longer kept me away from the pleasure ladies of London. I was about to say that even the women of the houses themselves were not always immune to the charms of the piper, but I checked myself when remembering whom I was addressing.

"And did you ever experience any rashes on the skin, Mr. MacKay?"

Rashes? I thought about it for a moment, and it was only then I remembered them, those red blisters on the skin, back around the time I was on Islay. But that was so long ago …

"Perhaps years before, sir, many, many years ago. You don't suspect I've had the disease for all that time, do you?"

Sir James's face was inscrutable, but he made a note on his page. "It's possible," he said. "The symptoms can flare up and then lie dormant for a long time, so indeed, it's possible. Have you noticed any other unusual symptoms? In terms of your behavior?"

"No. Well, I don't believe so."

He nodded. "And you have told your wife, I presume. Mary, is it?"

"Yes."

"Well, you must inform me if you notice any changes. As should she. And you should stop visiting the whores, Mr. MacKay. Do you understand?"

"Yes. Yes, of course."

In these dark months that followed I drank myself blind frequently to numb the pain, and a deep shame about my sickness grew on me like a weight. I was ashamed of bringing the sickness to our marriage bed, and prayed fervently that there would be no problems with Mary's health, or God forbid with Jessie's. Mary had almost entirely stopped speaking to me, unless she was discussing what Sir James had advised.

"Why would you need a doctor to tell you something so obvious?" she asked. "Who knows what you've brought home to us, Angus?"

I don't remember replying. I could hardly object. But it wasn't as though I was in the minority: show me a completely faithful man in London and I'll show you a damned liar. This was a pressure on Mary and me both, and it felt as though there was no needle or iodine that could fix it. She took to spending more time by herself, and the only occasion in her life when she seemed to snap out of this new reverie – at the dining table she would stare into space for minutes at a time without moving a muscle – was for the need of the children. Her parents had been gone a few years now and there was no longer a home in Scotland for her to return to, otherwise I'm quite convinced she'd have taken the children and abandoned me to my fate in London.

Taorluath

In the news, 1850

Losing a father and a brother in the same year is a tough business, and I knew that it wouldn't be too long before my condition flared up again. Rather, Donald was the one to bring my attention to this. I owe him thanks for that; we may not have been as close as I had been with John, but when I needed my elder brother the most, he was there. He told me that drinking would not take my mind off the losses, only rot the mind itself, and that I had better go out into the world and busy myself before I was so debilitated that I'd be confined to bed. Gradually his wisdom dawned on me, and I knew I had better accomplish as much as I could while I was physically able. Who knew how much longer I'd be capable of doing so?

Despite the challenges my health presented, I still piped each morning, and sometimes at night, though in truth I could do it in my sleep by now. I also had many social events to perform for, and often Donald and I were invited to play together, which was always something to look forward to. Many of the things I was involved in brought enjoyment and relief to others, and as a result they were satisfying to me, and helped relieve the melancholy that hung on me.

Donald and I had both been involved in teaching London boys to pipe and dance soon after we arrived in London, and I had long been focused on the boys of the Royal Caledonian Asylum. I cannot praise this institution enough. Here, so much good work was done in raising the orphaned children of Scots who died or were made invalids while serving in the army. Were it not for the dedication of its people to their cause, I dread to think what would have happened to those lads.

When I first began visiting the asylum, just a few years into my employment with the queen, I made sure to get the early lessons right. If the boys' hands started badly or developed unnatural positions on the chanter then the battle would be uphill from there. Initially, I had a little difficulty in getting some of the more troubled lads to concentrate, though this changed quite swiftly as they learnt who it was that paid my salary. From then on, they seemed quite in awe of me, and I had them hanging on my every word. For a long while, repairing the reeds I made for the boys was my main duty: they seemed unable to play a chanter without breaking their reed in some way. But there was talent in the room; I could sense it even then. Eventually, to my great satisfaction, the boys progressed to pipes, and the music started to flow.

In June 1848 we were able to demonstrate the fruits of our labors for the first time, at the 31st anniversary dinner of the Caledonian Asylum, in front of an assembly of London's finest gentlemen. The performance was reported in both London and Scottish papers, including the *Caledonian Mercury*.

The guests were marshalled to their places by six young pipers, headed by Mr. Angus MacKay, whose exertions in training them to the use of "the chanter" deserve every praise. With this rising progeny of musicians, no Highlander need fear that, amidst the gradual decay of the ancient customs and manners of this race, the warlike notes of the bagpipe will no longer be heard among us. In ancient times, had so many pipers met together, it would have been considered the perfection of harmony that they should all play as loudly as they could, each, however, taking care to strike up the gathering or pibroch of his own clan. Last night, in deference to modern tastes, they stuck to the same tune, and it will probably be some time before the ears of the "Sassenachs" present, who for the first time listened to the immense volume of sound, forget the effect produced…

It was heartening to see the boys' first performance reviewed in such glowing terms, but as always, I noticed that the press failed to get their facts right. How could they talk about the decay of ancient customs when piping and dancing were now being taught in London as well as in every village in Scotland? It's true that the old systems and schools were not what they once were – a generation had passed since a MacCrimmon took students on Skye – but the old pipers of my father's era would be amazed to see reports of Highland piping and tartan being so readily accepted in the center of London. And as for the suggestion that pipers would play over one another, that might have held true along the front line at Drumossie Moor, but reporting like this does little to portray the true character of the music these pipers played, and I made sure to tell those six young pipers as much.

By 1850, the lads of the asylum had played for a good few events, and it was in June – a month when glorious blue skies had been general over London – that the welcome distraction I needed presented itself, requiring preparation that I could throw myself into. The Scottish Hospital in London held annual fundraisers to support Scots in the city and raise funds to send them home, and under my tutelage the asylum boys had become so adept that they were among the most hotly anticipated acts scheduled for that evening's entertainment. They would be playing and dancing under my direction, and we had been polishing the performance for several weeks.

"Who's not got a brooch, lads?" I yelled. We were in the chamber that had been set aside for us to get dressed and warmed up: a large but stuffy room with tall windows.

The five boys had all swarmed around me, rummaging in the case I had brought. Their eyes glinted as they picked up the shiniest objects they could lay their hands on.

"Careful lads, one at a time!"

I had brought with me the asylum's bagpipes, some of which were donated by myself and my friends, as well as sporrans, dirks and plaid brooches that I had won in various competitions throughout the years. These sorts of things were lovely to look at, but I think if you were to ask any piper what they'd prefer – a third powder horn or a better cash prize – you'd see few signing up for the horn. All the same, for occasions like these they came in handy, and when I was competing myself, I'd noticed that the better the dirk or the grander the sporran, the better I might fare with certain simple-minded judges.

One wee lad – Fraser, who on account of his complexion, the rest of the boys had affectionately named Freckles – was hanging around at the back of the room. He looked as white as the bedsheet he was nervously picking at with his fingers, and I could practically hear his heart pounding against his ribs. He was only ten and had been taken in by the asylum quite recently, so it was his first time performing to such a crowd. He was ready for it, though. I knew that even if he didn't.

I walked over to him, pretending as though I was just opening the window, looking out at the grounds below, at the leaves of the sycamores rustling. "How are you feeling, Fraser? Ready?"

"Mm. Yes, Mr. MacKay. I'm just … There's just a lot of folk coming."

I nodded. "Well, more than you've played in front of before, that's right. But you know, playing in front of one is really no different to playing in front of a hundred."

Fraser looked at me skeptically. "I don't understand."

"It's true. The difference is all in the mind," I said, tapping my head. "When you think about it, what you actually need to do is the same. You need to stand up, breathe, play the notes. You'd need to do that if you were playing in front of just me, and you'd need to do that if you were playing in front of a thousand people. Ten thousand, even. Just the same as yesterday in rehearsal. How many times have you played the tunes through now without a mistake? A noticeable mistake?"

Fraser's expression screwed up as he thought hard. "A hundred?"

I gave a loud laugh. "Seas you've been practicing! But I'm not surprised. Listening to you yesterday, I'd say a hundred at least. And look, you've got all these boys up there with you, all these pipers, playing to the same tune."

"I suppose. But it's easy for you to say, Mr. MacKay. You're piper to the queen."

"Aye, you're absolutely right. It is easy for me to say. Because I've been in those shoes, believe me. Don't you be telling anyone, but my father had to force me on to stage once or twice when I was about your age."

"Really?"

I nodded.

"And you got through it?" Fraser asked.

"I lived to tell the tale, didn't I?"

He seemed to consider this carefully, before the faintest of smiles appeared on his face, though he tried his utmost to stifle it.

There was more I wanted to say to him, but couldn't find the words that best described what I meant.

"Go on," I said eventually. "Get yourself a brooch. I hid the best one in the side pocket."

As I led them out on to the stage, I was still thinking about Fraser's words, but when the performance began, I was just as transfixed as anyone in that hall. We played a number of well-known airs, most of them from *The Piper's Assistant*, which had become a useful guide for the young learners. "The Highland Laddie," "The Haughs of Cromdale," "The Athole Highlanders," and others had a good airing by the lads. The distinguished faces in the crowd were enraptured, seeing and hearing these young boys echoing the music of their Highland forebears, perfectly in unison. It was satisfying for the students, and I had notions that I'd need to get my son John going on the pipes. Fraser's face had gone red as a berry both from his exertions and from appearing in front of so many people. Following their tunes, the lads set their pipes carefully aside and took up positions for a Highland reel, which I piped. I played the usual tunes and finished with two repeats of "Tail Toddle" which broke the boys into huge grins while they danced, knowing well the bawdy words that can accompany the tune. I'll not forget Fraser's joy that day, right when I needed it. The *Reformers' Gazette* carried an article detailing the reaction of the gentlemen that day.

They appeared much entertained by the performances of Mr. Genge, Mr. Ramsford, and Miss Stuart, the vocalists present, but that which seemed to delight them most was the music of the bagpipes, as played by the boys of the Caledonian Asylum, under direction of Angus MacKay, the Queen's Piper. They were also much attracted by the manner in which the boys danced the Highland reel.

Much attracted, indeed. A good day. And it was made even better when Her Majesty – having heard of the event's success – congratulated me personally for my part. Even if life at home was bleak, and my health in a downward spiral, I reassured myself that Fraser was right: I had got through it quite well.

The Great Exhibition, 1851

The year 1851 in London society was dominated by one thing: the Great Exhibition. This was driven chiefly by Henry Cole and Prince Albert, though it appeared that half of the city was involved in some way. The prince was considered a forward-thinking man, and he wanted to showcase the glories of not only the empire's abundant cultures and industries, but those of the entire world. Almost every country on the globe had been invited to submit products. Britain was held in high esteem at this point in time – possibly borne out of managing to pass through the years of the

1848 revolutions across Europe with relative ease – and seemed a fitting place to host the first of such groundbreaking World Fairs. There had been demonstrations in London and murmurings about revolution and change, but in my opinion, good sense prevailed. Great Britain remained the jewel of modern Europe, and for now, still does.

I feel as though I have often written here that I was a busy man – this is the first time in my life that I can recall having time to reflect – but it truly came to a head starting May of that year. For several years I had the notion at the back of my mind that a break would do me a world of good: a brief holiday to gather my strength and dispel some of the weariness that had gathered in my bones. But it was simply not possible. I had a highly enviable position, and I may have lost everything I had worked so hard to gain if I requested leave. I was not going to allow that to happen.

I will do my utmost to describe the day that the Exhibition opened, but even the finest journalists and writers for the London papers told of their struggles to do it justice. For her part, Her Majesty was unbelievably excited about what was happening – it had taken years of hard labor from the prince in particular to reach this stage – and for weeks the queen had been fraught with a mixture of nervousness and anticipation. This naturally bled through to all of us on the staff.

After my usual piping in the morning, my next task on that bright day at Buckingham Palace was to dress young Prince Albert for the occasion ahead. He was to be attired in proper Highland costume, and the future king of the United Kingdom of Great Britain had grown quite used to getting fitted for his tartan by the likes of me. We were in one of the many rooms off the main hall, and he was gabbling away about the toys his younger brother – Prince Arthur, the queen's third son and seventh child – had received for his birthday that morning.

"And marbles and toy soldiers and a rocking horse and …"

I nodded along politely, thinking how I'd have traded any of them as a lad for a half decent chanter. Just as I opened the door to escort the young prince outside, him still chatting away, I looked up to see the queen walking quickly past the doorway with her maidservants, coming from her breakfast. She wore a pink and silver dress, and a small, diamond-encrusted diadem on her head. It was enchanting. Seeing the wee prince's clothing and hearing him ramble, she smiled and paused.

"Come now, Bertie. Stop boring our dear piper."

I gave a slight bow. "Not at all, ma'am. Might I say, you look exquisite."

The maidservants behind the queen exchanged glances, but she herself took no notice of them. "You're too kind, Mr. MacKay. Enjoy the day."

And enjoy it I did. Nothing could have prepared me for the journey we would soon be making to the Exhibition. I was to travel just behind the nine carriages of the state procession, as we made our way from Buckingham Palace to the brilliant construction that had been built in Hyde Park, what was being called the Crystal Palace. Though it was not a long trip, in that small distance, the number of people there to meet the monarch was unbelievable. There was an endless crowd on the streets, waving and blessing the procession as it passed, but what really took my breath away was the sight that met us when we reached the great expanse of the park itself.

The grass was invisible. For as far as the eye could see, all there was in front of us was a mass of human beings, the likes of which no one on the staff had seen before, even at the coronation. It was a day of proud patriotic celebration: a celebration of love for the queen and for the Empire. The noise of feet pounding on the earth was like an immense drum, and the mood in the air was joyous, almost fanatical. I read the next day an estimate that claimed there were around seven hundred thousand people in the park, and a further twenty thousand or so waiting in the galleries at the Exhibition. Events like this could hardly be expected to happen even once in a lifetime. The mind can barely fathom it.

To crown it all was the building itself. It was the largest, most magnificent glass structure the world had ever seen. It had been designed by a man called Joseph Paxton, whom the queen had once compared to myself, in that he had risen from an ordinary gardener to the lofty circles he now moved in. To put the building in perspective, I saw it reported in *The Times* that it was thrice the size of St. Paul's Cathedral. A building that size, made of glass! I will never forget the effect it had on me until the day I die. Its severe angles, its tiers glinting in the sunlight, its gleaming metal, all of it together seemed like a heavenly beacon. Atop the building were flags of every nation, blowing in unison with the breeze. Raasay seemed a long way from this grandeur, and even my beloved Scotland paled in significance.

When at last the royals entered the palace from the entrance at Rotten Row, trumpets played a fanfare to mark Her Majesty's arrival. I was fortunate enough to be allowed through the doors as part of the queen's essential daily staff, and it was perhaps even more fantastical inside as out.

I'd walked past the building many times in the previous year as it was being developed, but standing in those galleries was something else entirely. The place was illuminated as though we were still outside in the park, and yet being undeniably indoors, a dream-like quality was lent to everything. The queen stood near the Crystal Fountain, in front of a huge elm tree, which the building had enclosed within itself. Leis na h-uile a tha naomh! If that's not the stuff of faery stories then I don't know what is! The faces of everyone there – the ladies in their dresses of all colors, the men in their smart red uniforms, the foreign delegates in their outlandish garb – all of them were giddy. None, even those most privileged, had seen anything of the sort before.

After speeches from the organizers and delegates, followed by the national anthem, we heard music from two hundred instruments and six hundred voices. Many in the crowd had tears in their eyes. Eventually, it was the Marquis of Breadalbane, the very man who had congratulated me and John Ban on our joint performance at Blair Castle, who was to officially open the Exhibition. I glanced around for a moment in case I could spot dear John Ban, but soon realized that if he was in attendance the odds of me finding him were all but none. At a word from his friend Prince Albert, the marquis stood before everyone on the red carpet, and in a booming voice said, "Her Majesty commands me to declare the Exhibition open!"

The applause and trumpets that followed were deafening, and upon hearing it, the crowd amassed outside added its roar. The Frenchman next to me shouted, "Vive la reine!" and many others joined him in their various tongues. I felt tears rolling down my face, yet I couldn't explain why. Still, despite the spectacle, I wasn't sorry that the opening signaled the end of the royal couple's commitments that day, as the few hours it had been since leaving the palace was about the longest I could stand without getting uncomfortable.

I was hardly to have much of a recuperation period, though. There were many esteemed visitors coming to see the Exhibition, and so during the following nights and weeks I played at several enormous events being held at Buckingham Palace. I have the report of one such event from the *The Spectator*, but in truth this description could have been applied to several balls in 1851.

On Wednesday, Her Majesty gave a state ball, to which upwards of two thousand persons were invited. The throne-room was prepared as a second ballroom for the unusual crowd. The Queen opened the dancing with the Prince of Prussia for her partner in a quadrille, Prince Albert and the Princess of Prussia vis-à-vis. After a state supper in the principal dining room, the Queen returned to the ballroom, and the dancing was kept up till two in the morning: Highland reels being performed to the spiriting music of "Mr MacKay, her Majesty's piper."

State balls like these were always tiring work, with the vast and boisterous crowds and the weight of full Highland costume enough to make any piper perspire. The ballroom was always terribly hot with that number of guests as well, so by the end my clothes would be sodden with sweat. The pressure of blowing so long was also often taxing on my groin, and at one such ball – I believe the one described here – I had to stop after the sixth or seventh reel in a set for fear of fainting. Luckily the dancers were so drunk and gay that they hardly noticed, and after a moment outside I managed to return to play "Righ nam Port." The King of Tunes brought me back. It was exciting to see the foreign visitors enchanted by the freewheeling nature of the Highland reels, but having to take a break at all was as sure a sign as any that my usual stamina was waning.

So, I piped at night, and during the days I visited the Exhibition many times, both in service to Her Majesty and for pleasure with family and friends. Where to even begin? I saw jewelry and minerals and perfumes from across the empire; statues and exotic fruits from South America; endless shelves of books full of untold knowledge. I laugh now to think of my being overwhelmed by the wee market in Crieff. There were watches from Geneva; furniture from China; once Donald and I laughed in mild repulsion at the sight of a double piano, on which two pianists were playing simultaneously to horrible effect. The court allotted to Tunis was arranged like a native bazaar; there were artifacts from as far afield as Australia and New Zealand; the Canadian court featured a great snow sledge and a fire engine. I didn't spend much time at this particular court, as the two occasions I went I heard other visitors referencing James

Logan's book detailing his journey through North America. I had half a mind to tell them the true, pigeon-chested nature of the author; how he used to bore me to death with stories of his experiences among the rude colonials there. Mind you, there was something appealing in a land where there was still so much to discover, even in this modern age. For a time, I would have loved to visit, but I imagine I'll not manage it now.

As well as objects there were also famous guests to meet and listen to. I was introduced to the author of *Jane Eyre*, a tiny and ugly woman with bad teeth by the name of Charlotte Brontë, and I attended a lecture by William Makepeace Thackery, whose book *Vanity Fair* was being talked about throughout London. The queen had disapproved of the novel's heavy satire of the upper classes, discouraging people from discussing it around her, and I often wondered how she knew the plot so well without having read it thoroughly herself. The recent losses of my father and brother bade me pay attention to the work of the new poet laureate, Alfred Tennyson, whose work was much loved by the queen. His poem *In Memoriam* was a long and complicated farewell to a friend. We should all be lucky to be so remembered. The philosopher Karl Marx also attended, and after reading his description that the Exhibition was nothing more than the gaudy trappings of capitalist society, I regretted not seeing him with my own eyes. I would have been greatly amused to see the horror on his face when he first walked into that great glass cathedral.

I'm pleased to write that one of the more surprising things to come from the Exhibition was the fact that – for a few months, at least – Mary and I reconciled our differences. The fair brought the city together; it was as though the momentousness of it dwarfed any marital troubles two people could have. The entry fee was modest so there was a refreshing mix of folk being admitted – farm hands and factory workers would be side-by-side in the galleries with government officials – and Mary and I could also bring the bairns. It was no doubt an enriching experience for them. John was a little young, but leaving him with Maggie we managed to take Jessie and Margaret on a couple of occasions. They enjoyed the sculpture court and the medieval room, but most of all they loved the stuffed animal exhibit, where they would just stand and gawp for as long as we'd let them. I'd never even heard of half of the beasts there. In short, there was an endless feast of information and culture, more than any one person could consume, though I tried my very best.

I remember during one of these family visits I was feeling a bit ill-tempered, as for the third time that day Jessie and Margaret demanded to be taken to the Monkey Closets. These were a new form of public conveniences installed for both men and women at the Exhibition. Folk could relieve themselves, use a comb, have a clean towel and a shoeshine, all for the price of a penny! No doubt it was a very useful facility, but the queues were always long and I did not understand my daughters' fascination. I wanted to sneak away to find an ale, but for Mary's sake I resisted the urge.

I'm glad I did, for just afterwards, it was Mary who pointed out the thing which I have to say excited me there more than anything else I saw at the Exhibition. We were walking through the machinery court, when we passed a massive printing press, capable of churning out 5000 copies of the *Illustrated London News* in a single hour.

"I wonder if one day something like that might be used for music," Mary observed. "Seems a waste that such efficiency is put to use printing social gossip and stories about what the nobles wore to that week's ball."

"Especially when you could just ask me," I joked, though my mind was already racing. I'd stopped in my tracks to look at the large wheels and pedal I remembered back to my time with Alexander Glen in Edinburgh, working on *The Piper's Assistant*. It had been such a difficult project: if I made a mistake, or added something I shouldn't, I had to either scrape the surface of the paper away entirely or start over so that the engraver wouldn't misinterpret my marks. Mr. Glen and I then had to pass the samples between us multiple times to ensure nothing was amiss, and when a sample copy was at last prepared by the engraver, making corrections at this stage was time-consuming and expensive. And, after all that work, the actual ink to paper was just as tedious! This would at least solve that problem. Imagine if Mary's prediction was correct, and I could one day typeset one hundred pìobaireachd at such a speed! How different things might have been had this technology been available even twenty years ago.

The Foundation Stone at Balmoral, 1853

With all of the hustle and bustle that came with preparing for the Great Exhibition over, the next momentous project that Her Majesty and Prince Albert decided to undergo – and therefore that the royal staff had to undergo – was the renovation of Balmoral. The previous few years had seen the original house extended, ancillary cottages added, and the surrounding estate generally improved, but as the royal family continued to expand, it became clear that an entirely new construction was required to house them. After purchasing the property in full and also the neighboring estate of Birkhall, 1852 was the year of design and planning before the construction began, and it was to be an eventful if rather showery month we would spend in Scotland that September.

We had raced through the countryside via the railway, going from Reading to Swindon to Gloucester to Derby the first day, and then to Darlington, Newcastle, Berwick and Edinburgh the next, where a great swarm of people were awaiting our arrival on Arthur's Seat. After a night in Edinburgh, we traveled up to Balmoral, and I must say, arriving at the estate on that early autumn evening, it felt blissful to finally be there. The constant travel and taxing hours had long since started to take their toll, and I found I was increasingly exhausted. Despite only having just turned forty, I no longer felt like a young man; my own father had been a similar age when I was born and I'm sure he was in significantly better shape than I. I went straight to the room I had been allocated in one of the cottages and was asleep before my head touched the pillow, not even managing to remove my clothes or unpack, let alone stroll around the grounds as I had planned.

Admittedly, it was a wondrous sleep, and I played "Tullochgorum" well the next morning, but as I trudged back to my room to lie down once again, pipes in hand, my head was filled with apprehension. Over breakfast, I'd overheard Her Majesty discuss the plans for her many excursions to the surrounding hills, perhaps even more than in our prior Scottish holidays together, and I dreaded to think how my body would cope with hiking and standing watch for hours while she sketched and socialized. It was welcome that my doctor Sir James had joined the party for this year's trip; he had informed me that taking the air of my homeland should greatly benefit my condition. But the thought of failing in my duties in front of the queen – particularly if we were miles from anyone else on a remote hilltop – horrified me. So, what happened before I reached my cottage once again ought to have filled me with great relief.

"Mr. MacKay!"

I turned and instinctively smiled. It was John Brown strolling after me, a young and light-hearted Balmoral gillie who had only quite recently joined Her Majesty's staff, but who seemed to be fast becoming one of the queen's favorites. I liked him; he was an easy man to spend time with.

"Hullo there," I said. "Did Her Majesty want another tune?"

"Oh, no, no. It was just to say I've been named leader of the queen's pony, so it looks like I'll be the one traipsing about in the rain this year. Lucky you!"

"Aye, lucky me," I said. I paused, wanting to make sure I understood. "So, I'm to be excused from the outings?"

John Brown nodded. "His Royal Highness thought it would give you more time to prepare for the torchlight ball and the like."

This was an event happening in a week or so, in which I was to lead seven pipers out and play a salute followed by a reel. It was sure to be a lovely event, but I'd hardly paid it any mind up to this point. The guests were only to number about sixty, and the pipers I would be leading were all decent musicians, so I hadn't anticipated needing much preparation.

"Well, congratulations on your new position, Mr. Brown," I said, and not knowing what else to add, I signaled that I would be on my way. Instead of going to the cottage I changed course and headed down through the woods to a secluded spot by the River Dee I remembered from my previous stay here. I laid my pipes down beside me and sat there a long while amongst the tall grass, watching the dark water flowing over the smooth stones, the birds floating in and out of the reeds, the gentle and persistent sound of the river filling my head. Across the water a hawk was resting in the branches of a dead tree, looking at me disinterestedly before turning its head.

But I could not take in the idyllic scene, for it felt as though my world was crashing around me. Why wasn't I delighted by what John Brown had said? Weren't my concerns being solved in one fell swoop? Inside, I felt that same rage brewing, that uncontrollable emotion I had first felt when Donald insulted John that day he moved to London, the rage that seemed to be rising ever closer to the surface in recent times. I pulled out the flask of whisky I now kept on me always and drank. Questions raced through my mind. I realized that this was the first proof I had that my enemies in the household were trying to oust me. Had they sought out John Brown as nothing more than a replacement? And if I was being relieved of some of my most intimate responsibilities, how long would it be before I was let go entirely? I had been around long enough to know that the royal household was a cutthroat environment; any small alteration to your schedule and duties could mean you were soon to become surplus to requirements.

No, you mustn't jump to conclusions, I thought. Just then the hawk flew from its perch and began to hover on the wind, its wings entirely still. I reassured myself that nobody could say my piping had been less than sufficient; Her Majesty would not allow me to be dismissed for that reason alone. Nevertheless, it was terrifying to think that whoever was conspiring against me had the power to strike even here in Scotland. Obviously, this faceless foe was much more capable than Stevens or the other bastards in the household I might have suspected; this was evidently a far greater menace than ever I'd understood. But my mind was such a roiling mess, I couldn't fathom at that moment who it might be. For the time being I simply had to continue to prove my worth, to prove it more so, until the culprit was revealed. This was my test.

"Taing do Dhia airson na pìoba," I muttered, staring at the bird. It looked as though it had spotted something – a mouse or a vole – and was adjusting its position to track it. I turned to look at my instrument: just some silver, some wedder skin, some wood, and some ivory. All together to make the thing by which I lived, by which I'd always lived.

"Now more so than ever."

That whole month I strove to do what I set out on that embankment: to prove my worth. But it was not easy when my only task most days was to pipe a tune or two in the morning.

Still, I made a point of not belying my grievances to anyone. When the gillies would return and tell the staff what had happened on the outings I made sure to ask questions and be light-hearted. When I heard that even the queen – normally ever-doting – was finding the prince's hunting exploits amusing, I laughed and joined in the joke. Apparently, he had missed his mark when a deer had all but wandered into his lap, and after that he only managed to wound a three-legged stag before setting the dogs after it. I could tell that some in the household were enjoying watching me keep up pretenses, knowing that my diminished duties would be an insult to me, and that I wouldn't be able to hide this for long. Really, it was very fortunate for me that news from afar soon took up most of the household's conversation, and as fate would have it, allowed me to connect with the queen.

It became a trip defined by two deaths. The first was good news for Her Majesty, or as good news as a death can be. A few days into our arrival, a series of telegrams arrived specifying that an old miser in London named James Neild, with whom the queen was not even familiar, had died and left the entirety of his estate to Her Majesty. This comprised almost half a million pounds and a number of London properties.

On the morning the news was confirmed – for she didn't believe it at first – I watched as Her Majesty tried to mask her quite understandable joy. After some difficult days of boredom and worry, I had been elated to hear that the queen had called for me so as to enquire about Neild, finding out that I knew much about the man and had actually met him once, with him living in Chelsea, rather close to my own home. The queen was just outside the main entrance to the house on the drive, and she and her party were preparing for an excursion to Invercauld Bridge. The horses were whinnying impatiently, looking magnificent in the morning light. Judging by the clouds brewing in the distance I suspected the fine weather wouldn't last long.

"Quite inexplicable," the queen said again. "Where did you say the man lived again?"

"Cheyne Walk, ma'am," I said. "I once attempted to convince him to donate to the Caledonian Asylum."

"That's the charity with which you are often linked in the papers, is it not?"

I beamed. "Indeed, ma'am."

"And he declined?"

"Oh, aye, he told me where to go, ma'am. I'm sure you'll make a much better suitor for his money."

"Mr. MacKay!" the queen cried, though she couldn't help but let out a small shriek that told me I hadn't entirely crossed the line. Of course, the royals weren't wanting for capital, but all of Prince Albert's meetings with famed architects and landscapers the past few days had surely forecasted hefty costs, and half a million pounds would cover it many times over.

The queen mounted her horse. "It was noted in the latest telegram that Mr. Neild left nothing for his staff at all, so I shall at the very least be ensuring that they are accounted for."

"Most gracious, ma'am," I smiled, clearing the path for the party's departure.

John Brown gave me a slap on the shoulder as he passed, his other hand gripping the reigns. "Fortunate to have such a benevolent monarch, aren't we, Mr. MacKay?"

"Aye, quite so," I said quietly, and waved them off until they were out of sight.

The next death affected the estate far more deeply than the first; in fact, it was one of the blackest days I can remember for Her Majesty. It came only a week or so later. The splendid old Duke of Wellington, who all those years ago had bested Napoleon and won countless victories for the empire, had passed away. He was a good age at eighty-three, but the news still came as an almighty shock for the royals, given that he had been in possession of all his faculties and hadn't exhibited any signs of illness until a matter of hours before his death. Her Majesty in particular was devastated, and when she went out that day, she sent one of her servants all the way back to the estate to ensure the necklace she had received from the duke was still in her room, after having some sort of premonition that she had misplaced it or it was about to get stolen. She and many others were in a state of grief, and the whole of Balmoral remained in mourning for the rest of our stay. Indirectly, the duke's death had a profound effect on me as well.

To mark the final day, the prince and Her Majesty had decided to build a cairn atop Craig Gowan. Initially, this had been to commemorate the royals having at last purchased the property, though it had become understood amongst the staff that it was also in unofficial memory to the duke, at least in part. Getting to the northern summit of Craig Gowan was a far longer walk than I was comfortable with at this point, but the queen had specifically requested I make the journey to play during the party's final portion of the climb, and I would be damned to see another piper sourced for such a meaningful occasion.

Out of fear of slowing everyone down and baring my poorly condition in public, I decided to leave early in the morning and meet with the group at the spot where I was to play. This way I could take many breaks whenever my breathing became too labored, and whenever I felt too downright nauseous to continue. I knew I had better not do it alone, however, so I had asked my friend Arthur Schackle to assist me, the very man who had fetched me the night I learned of brother John's death. He was a man I could rely on to be discreet, and though he was an older man than me – about Donald's age – he was very fit, and had kindly agreed to carry my pipes.

"That's a view you won't forget," he said, some way ahead of me. We had come out of the tree line and on to the rugged slope, and he was standing waiting for me, knee-deep in heather. Above a certain height that's about all that is hardy enough to grow on those bleak mountain slopes. Snow was visible on some of the tallest peaks.

"How are you faring, Angus?"

"I'm faring," I panted. "One more wee stop and then I think I'll make it to the top."

"We've got plenty of time. We can stay here as long as you need."

I reached him and turned, seeing how far we'd come, my hair getting buffeted by the wind. It was a patchy day: looking up it was about even between blue sky and white clouds, casting their shadows over the massive landscape. All I could hear was our breathing and the wind. Schackle and I were the only living souls for as far as the eye could see.

"It's marvelous, isn't it? I'm glad I'm getting to see it."

I could feel Schackle look at me. "All of these deaths making you sentimental, are they?"

"Must be." I took a swig from my flask and Schackle accepted it when I offered.

"You know, I actually worked as footman for the duke," he said.

I glanced at him quizzically. "Really? I don't remember you mentioning that before."

"Yes, for eight years. It was a long time ago, but I knew him well."

"I'm sorry. I didn't know."

"Oh, don't worry. I didn't tell you. But yes, I got a letter this morning from a good friend of mine in the duke's service, his valet. He'd been working for him all this time."

"That sounds a somber read," I said.

"It is. Would you like to hear it?"

"You have it with you?"

Schackle nodded, pulling out a sheet of paper and unfolding it. "I'll read it to you."

Dear Arthur,

Thank you for your words of kindness in your previous letter. There are not many who I believe would be able to comprehend this loss, but you are one of them. Please allow me to confess my sorrow to you, as I might find myself incapable of doing so with my own family. As you know, I was in service to our beloved duke for over 25 years: nearly my entire adult life. I have felt blessed by this service every day, and I must admit I know not what my remaining years hold for me now. That great man, who not only has been my master but has in equal measures been to me a father and a friend, gave me and my family everything. In 25 years, we have never been apart more than a few days, and now we will not spend another together. I wish I had been able to protect him; I and everyone on the staff cannot help but feel that there is something we ought to have done. He had seemed so well. May he rest in heaven, and long live the Queen. Let me write that twice for never have I meant it more than now. May he rest in heaven, and long live the Queen.

With fondest wishes,

James

Schackle let out a long breath, and when he glanced at me, he will have seen me rubbing a tear from my eye.

"You must show that to Her Majesty," I said eventually, taking another dram. "She will appreciate it."

This letter that was read to me in that most beautiful, most remote of places, has since resonated with me deeply and often. I remember scolding myself for being so blind, for thinking that my own reputation, my own well-being, was what was at stake here. No. The ultimate goal of my adversaries was to target my beloved queen. Clearly, the less I was around her, the less I would be able to protect her as she ought to be protected, just as I hadn't with John, just as I hadn't with my father. My enemies had seen this, and were acting on it. I wondered if it was even possible that they had something to do with the old duke's sudden passing ... Well, these devils would be fools to think I could be broken so easily. They had struck the first blow, but now I knew their game, and resolved there and then to be more vigilant.

In silence, Schackle and I continued on to the place we were to meet the party, and I set to warming the pipes. When at last they appeared, I began marching in front and led them the remainder of the way, up to the spot where the cairn was to be built. Stones are rarely in short supply on a Highland hill, and everyone picked up as robust a rock as they could. I blew as hard as possible in my condition, until the pipes sounded just as I intended; I willed the wind to carry the notes far around the hills. This was my statement of intent. If someone wished to harm the queen – my master and my friend – let them hear that they would have to come through me.

Her Majesty was dressed in purple velvet, with a cloak and bonnet resembling the costume of a countrywoman, but far finer, and in that breathtaking environment with "Flora MacDonald's Fancy" playing, never had she looked more worthy of her status. She was the first to place a stone, followed by Prince Albert, and then all of the family and the others of the household who came up the hill. They continued to stack them to a good height, aided by the assembled staff. Her Majesty was quite taken by the whole event, welling up when Prince Albert climbed to place the final stone on top. Afterwards, there was great merriment and dancing, and when the whisky took hold, the reels began. It was the lengthiest session I'd had in a while, but I was not going to stop, no. I piped, that she might dance. And as Her Majesty flew around that hilltop, she seemed to be assuring me that there would be none left standing after her.

The dreams began shortly after I returned to London, on the December night when my fourth bairn – Angus – came into the world. If you asked Mary, I dare say she would tell you that around this time is when my mind started to show signs of corruption, when she could start to tell that my lucid days were distinctly separate from the others. On the contrary, I might just as easily say that this is when I began to notice things for how they truly were.

I now believe that the dreams were God's way of making my mission easier. To me this is the only explanation. Before they began, many times in my lodgings in Windsor or at my house in Pimlico, I would lie awake in torment, knowing that these wee hours were those in which Her Majesty was in the greatest peril. To add to my stress, like Mary, Her Majesty was with child once again, something I thought extremely irresponsible of Prince Albert. Surely it was not the time to burden our blessed queen with another child – an eighth child! – and incapacitate her with all that came with being in such a condition. I lost a great deal of respect for him after this.

Sensing that Mary was any moment now about to go into labor, I convinced a neighbor to take Maggie and our children for the night, before closeting myself in Maggie's room at the back of the house, with all of these thoughts tumbling around my mind. I vaguely wondered why I did not care about this new child that was due to arrive any hour now. I must have been speaking aloud when one of the midwives put her head in the door.

"Are you alright, sir?"

All I could do was stare at her, because I hadn't fully heard the question and I was still inside my own thoughts, and I must have mumbled something back, but I can't quite remember what.

"You should have a bit more warmth there, Mr. MacKay" she was saying as she piled blankets on the bed and lit the lamp. "You don't seem well."

"It's fine," I said. "Fine, fine, fine."

She left, before returning with some warm milk and a bottle of wine.

"Try and get some rest, sir," she said. "I'll come get you to speak with Mrs MacKay in the morning."

I thanked her as she closed the door. Then I took two of my blue pills and drank half of the bottle in one, before turning out the light and lying down on the bed, burying myself under the blankets. The room was cold and dark, save for a meagre glow coming through the window: some neighbor's fireplace, perhaps. I hadn't the strength to rise again and close the shutters. Instead, I resigned myself to staring at the ceiling for hours – there was a brown mark up there that seemed to have no explanation – waiting for the hours to pass. Oddly, however, as my warmth grew, I felt a drowsiness start to take hold that hadn't felt for quite some time.

So began the dreams: God's intervention. I have no idea why they began on this night of all nights, just when my second son was being born, but it's so. Now I will attempt to do the impossible in describing these visions, but if I can hardly understand them having experienced them firsthand, then what hope have I of putting them into words?

Always it would be the queen and I together, and while I know it sounds illogical, I am sure that she was present for these experiences too. We wouldn't be doing anything unusual, at least not in the beginning. It might be as simple as my arriving at Windsor Castle or Buckingham Palace in the morning to play, just as I had been doing for a decade and more. I would see her pale face smile, her eyes close as she let the notes wash over her. Other times we would be wandering around the gardens outside the palazzo-style Osborne House, and the queen would be talking to me of her busy life, or she would turn to me and enquire as to the Gaelic name of a flower or a bird, which I would gladly provide. And the whole time, what was perfect about it was that I could rest soundly, knowing that if we were there together there then she was safe. No evil would come to her.

These visions were so akin to waking life that it now becomes hard to say which were part of the physical world, and which were not. Sometimes I would be surprised to wake up and realize I was lying in bed, other times I was mildly amazed that what was happening appeared to be reality. Dr. Hood says that my not knowing is the very definition of madness, but they were both equally real and given where I had come from, both equally outlandish. All I am sure of is that Her Majesty saw the same. I do not blame her for not saying so; trying to liberate me would hold its own risks, and what with Prince Albert ... But she knows.

Things between Her Majesty and me grew more intimate following the birth of Prince Leopold. This was in April of 1853. For weeks, the only time we had managed to spend in one another's company was in our dreams at night, as she had been in confinement in Buckingham Palace in preparation for the birth. This had been a trial for us, and were it not for these dreams – the night before I dreamed that I was her husband and loving father to her children, sailing on the yacht up to Scotland – I would have battered down the doors of the palace myself to demand proof of her well-being.

I had spent the day drinking alone at the Hoop and Grapes, and had soaked myself into a stupor, dozing in the corner. I vaguely noticed the doors swinging opening and someone walking in, chiefly because a bitter wind accompanied them, but I didn't pay any mind until I heard a voice I recognized. It was one of Stevens's lot, a stout footman called Chester or some such. He was telling the entire tavern that the day had come: the prince was born and the queen was in recovery. He was clearly enjoying the attention he was receiving, and he began to tell everyone that a doctor had given Her Majesty a new drug called chloroform to ease her pain.

"Put her right to sleep, apparently," he bragged, and then pretended to fall asleep where he stood, to guffaws from all.

I stood up and tried to swing for him, but I was so drunk that I fell over without even revealing my intention.

"Easy there, MacKay," the footman smirked, helping me to my feet and pointing me towards the door. "Away and find a nice ditch to sleep in, not in here."

Finding myself suddenly outside, I braced myself against the rain and stumbled on towards the palace without hesitation. From here, my memory fails – I think I argued with a member of staff at the gates about my drunkenness – but somehow, at some point, I found a way inside. After traipsing the corridors for a long time, losing all sense of direction, I somehow made it to the queen's bedchamber. Prince Albert was nowhere to be seen. The queen was standing by the bed, turning towards me in a state of undress.

"Your Majesty," I said. "The baby is fine?"

She nodded. "A little small, I think. But he's healthy."

"Good. And you, ma'am?"

She beckoned me closer. When I came, without another word she eased me on to the bed, before taking hold of me under the kilt. Then she climbed on top of me like St. George over the dragon, while from some unseen set of pipes, music began to play. It was a tune I'd never heard before, singing out louder than sound itself. I couldn't tell if I was horrified or gratified to have Her Majesty lower herself on top of me, but either way, I was in a state of the highest excitement, and our lips were joined together in passion, until suddenly the doors flew open and the music stopped, before Mary shook me awake. We no longer slept in the same room, so she must have come from the children's room across the hall.

"Angus, are you alright?" she was calling, visibly shaken.

"Mary. Of course." I was covered in sweat. "Why did you wake me?"

"You were screaming 'm'eun beag.' Angus, what does that mean?"

Everything was such an unholy mess, and even when I had collected myself, I could make neither heads nor tails of it. But I didn't forget that tune. And before long it was revealed to me what had to be done with it. It came when we went to Balmoral again that year, with the building of the new castle underway. I had been specially commissioned by the queen to write a tune for the occasion of laying the foundation stone. Her Majesty did the honors and placed several small items within the stone, including coins and other mementoes, and while she did, I piped. "The Foundation Stone of Balmoral Castle" is a tune not many will recall, and musically it is not one of my best – people understandably prefer "Balmoral Castle," with its rattling bottom-hand notes – but the gaze that the queen gave me as I played it for her on that day told me she knew its origin as well as I did, and that it was right to play it now. And so it holds a special place in my heart.

Crunluath

Christmas Carousing, 1853

Returning to London late that autumn, it was then that my nameless enemy that had been so long lurking in the shadows at last stepped out into the light. Russia. How could I not have seen it before? This hulking, mysterious country had long been known to me, of course, but then more than ever, the papers were crammed full of news, opinion, and rumor about the conflict between Russia and other states as the Ottoman Empire failed. Russia was making every effort to claim more territory, and as I read more about its vast and deadly and ever-growing power, it became obvious that this was what I had been fighting against. I started to truly comprehend just how enormous a danger this was, for the queen, for the British Empire, for everyone in the country.

I was certain there was Russian interference in the royal household – I felt these forces had already begun trying to separate me from Her Majesty – and I was duty-bound to offer my assistance any way I could. In early December, on a grey and drizzly afternoon in Hyde Park, I took shelter under a tree on the banks of the Serpentine to read the latest news, bringing with me the day's papers. I had discovered that keeping close to the sounds of water acted as a tonic for my racing mind, and walking through an open space like the park made it easier for me to deduce whether or not I was being followed.

I read on, growing more aghast with every column. The Russian navy had just annihilated a large number of Ottoman ships in Sinop, which was causing a flurry of diplomatic activity and public speculation about Britain entering the war. To me, it was plainly a trap: they wanted us to enter the fray before we were prepared. Descriptions of the battle included details about the new Russian Paixhans guns, which were developed by a French officer. These guns used exploding shells rather than cannon balls and metal scraps. It was said that this artillery broke through the wooden ships as easily as a knife through butter, before exploding and setting the hulls ablaze. For the Turks at Sinop it had been a massacre. A Thighearna dèan tròcair, I thought.

The potential of such weapons meant that the Russians could destroy the British fleet in no time at all; that much was clear. And what would the Russians do with Her Majesty if they succeeded in overthrowing the British Empire? It did not bear thinking about. It was then I began to dedicate all of my labors to what kind of weapons of our own we could develop, so as to halt the Russian navy in its tracks. My research had begun.

Staring at the glassy surface of the Serpentine, I soon became convinced that the answer lay in underwater vessels: only through stealth could we manage to defeat such abominable evil. Over the following weeks, I read *Appleton's Mechanic's Magazine* and *Engineer's Journal* whenever I could get my hands on copies. I delved deeply into the work of the American Robert Fulton, who had developed submarines for several nations, including Britain, and who died when I was three. There was an article detailing one of Fulton's demonstrations for Prime Minister Pitt – when Napoleon was still threatening to invade – in which a submarine blew apart a ship on the surface. The war ended soon afterwards and so the research seemed to dwindle, but I became quite certain that therein lay the solution. All I had to do was pick up where Fulton left off, and with technology having advanced at such a breakneck speed – as evidenced in the Great Exhibition – the possibilities were seemingly endless.

While I did not wish to divulge the details of my dreams with the queen to anyone – they were for our eyes and ears only – I knew that my idea for the development of these submarines was something I had to try and convince my allies of, to gain support, or else all would be lost. However, my initial attempts to explain everything to Mary, Schackle, and the rest were fruitless. They did not see my evidence as conclusive, and told me to leave the politics and engineering to those who knew best. Stick to the pipes, they said. I regretted that if John had been alive this is precisely the sort of thing he would have been able to understand, and he would have known what to say to help make my case, but alas.

By Christmastime I had come to the understanding that without models, no one would be able to visualize just how vital these machines were going to be for the war effort. For the first time since I learned how to write, I set aside my music manuscripts in the evenings, and instead set to drawing plans and sketches of these undersea tubes, which I then fashioned out of scraps of wood and metal that were in such abundance at construction sites across London. This was all to Mary's consternation, and she was made livid by the amount of space these prototypes took up both in the house and in my mind. But what choice did I have?

On the night of December 26 I was to attend a Christmas gathering for the staff of the royal household. Despite my growing suspicion of many around me, I still made a point of attending these events whenever I could, to deduce whether there were any new infiltrators or developments to worry about, and to show whoever was watching that I still held a place close to the queen.

Before I left the house, however, at what must have been about six o'clock, I was crouching in our dining room with Jessie and John, showing them my latest submarine model, which was lying on the floor. It had been a good day. I had made progress and in a buoyant mood, I'd called the bairns down to show them what I'd been working on.

"See? And so it really wouldn't matter how powerful these new Russian guns are, as we could just slip right under them and attack them from there."

John clapped excitedly, and made the sound of a musket firing.

"Oh, it'd be much louder than that, lad," I smiled.

"Are you going to save the empire, Papa?" Jessie asked. She was running her hand along the side of the tube, looking into my eyes nervously. "Are the Russians coming for you and mother?"

"They're trying, aye. But Papa's not going to let them get close, don't you worry." I kissed her on the top of the head. "But this is why I've got to keep working so hard on these designs. If I don't succeed, then we might all be in danger."

"Angus!" Mary cried, storming into the room. Her lip was trembling, from fury or fear I could not tell. "What on earth are you doing? Stop filling their heads with such wild rubbish; you'll terrify them!"

I sighed. "It's odd that they seem to be able to understand it better than you, Mary."

"Go to your room," Mary whispered to the bairns, her voice like a razorblade. They flew away without a sound. "And you," she said, "I think it's time you left. You're going to be late."

She motioned for me to make my way to the door.

I stood and shook my head. "You think it sounds like madness, Mary, but I promise, it's the honest truth."

It was then I noticed a bruise on Mary's temple, a faint yellow with a purple line running from its middle. When she saw me looking at it with confusion she turned away in disbelief.

"Just go," she spat, only turning back to me when she was by the door. "And know this: God will turn his back on you, Angus, if you continue down this path. For your sake as much as mine, this talk of conspiracies has to stop now."

This was hard to hear, and the look on her face before she disappeared was one that cut me to my core; she was beyond mere vexation now. Worst of all was I knew that for once I was entirely in the right. Now, aye, there are days when I look back and wonder if somehow, in some way, I was misguided or overreacting; if perhaps it was right what they did to me. But other days, and certainly then, no. I just can't bring myself to believe that at all.

I departed with my fine mood wholly turned to bitterness, darting through the slushy streets. I tried my best to turn my mind to what I might glean from the evening's festivities, but the rage inside me was building and blocking out all rhyme and reason. And, as should have been predicted, it was while I was in this state that my enemies saw fit to come for me once more. If Mary hadn't riled me so before I left, perhaps I could have been able to handle it all so differently. As it was, that night was to be the beginning of the end of my royal employment.

Late in the evening, after the punch bowl had been emptied many times – enough for my physical pain to be brought down to a tolerable level – a heated discussion arose concerning the war in Crimea. Not wanting to betray my knowledge of events to any spies that might be listening, I intentionally steered myself away from the talk, and stood to leave for the water closet. It was at this moment that Stevens spoke up loud enough for all in the room to hear, sitting at the next table with his fellows.

"Ah, so the conversation has grown a little too intellectual for our modest piper, has it?"

The room quietened and stilled. "What did you say?" I asked.

Stevens sneered, encouraged by the laughter around him. "I was just thinking how amusing it was that unless the talk involves sheep or alcohol then you have very little of worth to say, MacKay."

"I see," I said.

What a blasted fool I was. What happened next I am not proud of, for I can now see plainly that a whelp like Stevens was not the true danger at that moment, and drawing such attention to myself provided the perfect excuse for the Russians to set to work at having me removed from service. Over the past ten years, I had actually grown so used to bleating noises and anti-Scottish remarks when I interacted with English members of staff that they no longer had much effect on me. But on this night, I was so thoroughly drunk and already in such a black mood, that I simply could not walk away as I had so many times before. Instead, I rushed at Stevens and kicked him square in the balls where he sat, before cracking him on the nose with my fist.

After that all is a blur, a deafening blur. It took many men to restrain me, but eventually I was tied to a chair with a coarse rope, and a hood was put over my head. They say I was shouting in Gaelic, screaming to the high heavens, impossible to reason with, but however much of this is hearsay I cannot be sure. I remember little beyond the initial comment, the overwhelming fury, and then a few glimpsing images of people staring at me nervously; a glass smashing; someone helping Stevens hobble away with a bloodied face.

Though it was now after midnight, Sir James Clarke was called for. I welcomed this, and said as much to those whispering behind me. When the doctor eventually arrived, it was under his direction that I was fitted into a strait waistcoat so as to keep my fists to myself. I spoke to Sir James as I always did – this man I had trusted through the trials of my illness – and I was sure that I still saw a friend in his eyes. He listened to my testimony and then to that of the other witnesses in the room, before advising that I would be taken, for the very first time, to this fine place in which I now reside. He cited it as a precaution, even apologizing for the inconvenience, and told me he would be sure to discreetly inform Her Majesty that I might be otherwise engaged for a few days.

"On account of your illness," the doctor leaned in to whisper so none could hear, "it's better to be safe than sorry, isn't it?"

Ah, Bedlam. These pages have reached you at last.

That very first stay wasn't to be a long one; if there's any solace to be taken let that be it. I wasn't even put in a cell. By the time of arrival, I was calm enough that the strait waistcoat could be removed, and I was placed in an office close to the entrance. I had sobered a little and regained my composure, reminding myself how paramount it was that I not be imprisoned at this crucial time for my queen and country.

As there was no formal medical certificate to hold me there, after a time of questioning and observation – in which I was sure to insinuate the incident was nothing more than a drunken scrap between two rivals – I was free to go. The hospital staff at the time seemed rightly appalled that a member of Her Majesty's service was being treated that way. I am fairly certain that the younger attendant that still sometimes comes to deliver my food and water was one of those there that day, though he doesn't confirm this when I ask him. As I was being escorted to the carriage, the doctor who assessed me even shook me by the hand and offered his apologies, much to the ire of those household members who assisted Sir James in taking me there, and who tried to insist I be kept there under lock and key until at least the morning.

"That's quite alright, doctor," I said, bowing my head graciously. "Nothing you could have done."

Two of these same household bastards then had to escort me home, and as I was bundled into the carriage, I was sure I heard one of them whispering something in Russian under his breath. A curse on my name, no doubt! No matter. I was given a blanket for the carriage, and wrapped up in it I snugly hummed "The Unjust Incarceration." I'm quite sure my fellow passengers didn't know the name or meaning of the tune, but their obvious annoyance at my good spirits in the face of their failure was a pleasant thing for me.

It was to be a small victory, though. When I arrived home after three o'clock in the morning, Mary was greatly distressed. I had hoped that I wouldn't have had to mention my trip to the hospital, and would have put the bruising on my face down to a tumble with Stevens, but someone had come to tell her of what happened, delighting in sabotaging me at home as well as in service, presumably. Our earlier argument was resumed. We fought until she was hysterical with what seemed to be grief, and we only stopped when we heard the bairns weeping from the other room.

Life was never quite the same after that night. Other members of staff no longer spoke to me. Even the Scots kept their distance. No more casual conversations about weather and politics; no more jokes about sheep or accent or Highland costume. I seemed to be the subject of conversations that ended when I walked into the room. Oddly enough, I did not seem to mind this growing isolation, for it allowed me more time to ponder my designs. One thing I could not get used to, and have not been able to since, was knowing that I was not expected to pipe for Her Majesty that following morning. I hope whoever is queen's piper now is worthy of the name.

After a few weeks, I had collected myself, and though I missed much of the tumultous holiday period, I did pipe in the queen's company one more time. Fittingly, perhaps, this was when I was requested to play at a Burns Dinner at the Duke of Hamilton's London house, in January 1854. I had continued to work religiously on my research in the meantime, but was excited to get back to what I knew best for an evening, and to see Her Majesty again. For me, music and the act of playing the pipes never lost their luster, even in times of such strife, even if playing caused me great pain. Bagpipes were the reason I found myself in such a privileged position in the first place; they were the reason I was in a position to defend my nation and sovereign so effectively. How could I not be thankful for that gift?

Burns's complete works had been published by Adam Scott of London, and excerpts were prepared and delivered at the dinner. There were about a hundred people in the brightly-lit dining room all gossiping and laughing, and the sweet aroma of wine mixed with the salty one of haggis hung in the air. I was waiting to the side of the stage with a dram, charged with rounding off the evening with a tune of my fancy. I'd settled on "Willie brewed a peck o' maut," and was standing quite absent-mindedly, when suddenly I found that the recitation of "Tam o' Shanter" had been interrupted by a gale of laughter, and now all eyes in the room were on me. The old gentleman that was delivering the rendition – a man I didn't know – was pointing directly towards me as he cried theatrically:

> *There sat auld Nick, in shape o' beast;*
> *A towzie tyke, black, grim, and large,*
> *To gie them music was his charge;*
> *He screw'd the pipes and gart them skirl,*
> *Till roof and rafter a' did dirl.*

Though the guests were mostly howling, those on the staff that I could see floating between the tables were exchanging nervous looks, clearly expecting me to react angrily. More than the gentleman, this very expectation of theirs caused my blood to boil. I did my best to laugh and wait with a smile for the focus to shift and the moment to pass, but the longer the laughter persisted, the more I could feel that I was losing this battle with myself, and was about to say something unforgiveable. But just then, another voice cut above the clamor.

"I will happily vouch that our Mr. MacKay has never once 'screwed' his pipes in all his years of service," said Her Majesty, silencing the room in an instant. She was sitting close to me at the head table, and her words were like cold water being poured over the guests. Their faces went dumb with shock. "It is to our great fortune that we have such a patriotic and talented musician in our midst."

I was likely as stunned as most in the room. Though I knew Her Majesty better than anyone by now – better even than Prince Albert, I would say – this was as overt a compliment as I had ever received from her, and as much an admission of our intimate relationship as anyone in London had ever heard.

"Thank you, ma'am," I said quietly.

"Of course, of course, Your Majesty," the old gentleman floundered, and in truth I felt sorry for him, as even though he had thought to slight me, really he had just been offering the crowd the performance they wanted, something I well understood. "Mr. MacKay is rightly renowned throughout London and beyond. A mere jest is all it was. And now, where was I?"

He struggled through the remainder of the poem, but the applause he was given was not nearly so hearty as he must have been expecting when he awoke that morning. I hid my smile as best I could, and when the roof was raised after my tune, I nodded my thanks once more to my queen.

A week or so of intense study later, my designs were ready. At least, they were as ready as I could afford to make them, as according to the latest Russian reports, time was of the essence. Though I wished to go straight to Her Majesty, I was grimly aware that this was not possible. She would support me – there was no doubt of that – but I couldn't bear to put her in the awkward position of trying to convince the government to take the word of her piper: a low-born man with no experience in the field. In hindsight, perhaps I should have tried. But just like all those years before, when I wasn't able to present my work to the Highland Society without the aid of someone from an upper class – in that instance, Logan – now seemed to be the same. I had to present my work to someone who would be able to exert their influence over the esteemed society I was in.

The man I chose was Sir James Clarke. It's easy for me to say I should have known better, but over all those years of treatment he had convinced me of his virtue. Now, I am not saying that I think he is a traitor. I don't believe he is. But gross negligence, and blindly flying in the face of facts, some would say is as good as treachery. At the very least, he should have been more mindful of the company he kept.

Without Mary's knowledge, I wrote to him in early February, requesting a meeting of the utmost urgency, in which I would reveal to him my submarine plans that promised to be the scourge of the Russian fleet. Imminent action had to be taken if the nation was to be saved; I made that clear. He responded soon afterwards, summoning me to his office, where I would be talking with him and another of the queen's physicians: Mr. Gustavus Blanch. Though I was somewhat disappointed that the doctor had not accepted my invitation of coming to my house so as to inspect the larger models, I was greatly encouraged that he was taking my proposal so seriously as to request the presence of a third party.

As I arrived at Sir James's Buckingham Palace office on that day, sure that this would be the beginning of my greatest triumph, I moved with an eagerness that I thought had long forsaken me. Inside and away from the light snow that was falling across London, I took the steps two at a time, a small model in one hand and my best designs in another, outrunning the footman who was escorting me. If I could have seen my foolish face then, I would have seen a face as trusting as a bairn's. Stop, Angus, I would tell him. Na gabh tron doras sin, I beg of you. Now I know, of course. I was running headfirst into a trap.

Entering the room, I ought to have been able to tell immediately that something was wrong. The expressions of the two gentlemen were serious, aye, but not in the way I'd been expecting. They weren't hurried enough. Sir James was sitting down, while his friend Mr. Blanch, a short and mole-like man with round spectacles – who was uncannily familiar – stood on my side of the desk, leaning against it, looking at me intently where I stood.

"How are you, Mr. MacKay?" he said.

"Aye, well, thank you, sir. You must be Mr. Blanch. Forgive me, though, I'm afraid there isn't much time for pleasantries, as you'll have no doubt seen in my letter."

"Indeed, we have each read it over."

"Then you'll know there's no time to waste," I said excitedly, and handing my model to Mr. Blanch I made to spread the designs over the desk. "Please, save all your queries for the end, if you please."

"Hang on, Mr. MacKay," said Sir James, beckoning to the chair. "Before we begin, why don't you take a seat so we can ask you a few questions?"

I was thrown. What possible reason could there be for delaying? I sat slowly, clenching my fists so as not to reveal my trembling, and this was when the two men set to asking me question after question about my own health. At first, I answered as best I could, knowing that I had to remain in good favor if my ambitions were to be realized, but there was only so much I could take before my patience ran dry.

"What has got into you, Sir James?" I demanded, and I could feel the vein in my neck bulge in anger. I began to unfurl my designs without their consent, and launched into the speech I had prepared, telling of the details of my latest model.

"Mr. MacKay, please desist!" Sir James yelled after what might have been a minute or so, slamming his hand on the desk. "These are the ramblings of a lunatic!"

I stared at him in horror. "These are not ramblings, you dunce! By God, on these sheets are the only things standing between this country and eternal damnation!"

"Mr. MacKay, I promise you that you are not speaking sensibly," Mr. Blanch murmured, putting a hand on my shoulder.

Looking from one man to the other, my stomach lurched as I finally understood where I knew Blanch from. He was my neighbor on Stanley Street, less than two minutes from my home. He often walked past my front door. Surveilling me. The blood began ringing in my ears.

"Sir James, what has this man been telling you?" I whispered.

"Pardon me?"

"Him!" I shrieked, before pointing to Blanch's face. "This man is a spy!"

My head swam beneath the scandal of it all. The Russians had agents at the highest level. Blanch had open access to the queen and her children. Our children. I felt the battle had been lost before it had begun.

Sir James was telling me to take a deep breath, to listen to myself. But I would not go quietly. I remember feigning cooperation, before grabbing the model from Mr. Blanch's hand and attempting to bludgeon him with it. Yet within a matter of seconds, a clutch of men had burst through the door to restrain me. They had been lying in wait. For the second time in just three months, I was bound like a butcher's hog, at the mercy of thugs who were happy to kick or strike me whether I resisted or not. The furniture was thrown about the place; a pot of ink was sent crashing to the floor, forming a growing black puddle, some portal into a hell beneath the floorboards.

Eventually, I could barely see for the swelling sustained by my injuries. When I couldn't move, Blanch had the nerve to continue to ask me questions about my own condition, and for this I aimed spit at where I thought his face was, getting a further stamp in the ribs for my troubles.

Turning me so that all I could see were two slits of grimy wall, I was then told they were taking me back to Bedlam, but even then, I was sure this wouldn't happen; they had tried and failed already. The loyal members of staff would not allow it. They would hear my accusations and they would believe them. No matter what happened, I was going to walk away from this place, and get my research into Her Majesty's hands.

I thought all of this until I heard my wife's voice behind me. She had been summoned.

"Mary!" I screamed, my voice little more than a croak by this point. "Mary, come here! Tell them to release me."

But she did not come. And they did not release me. This snub from my wife was the moment I ceased to struggle, feeling the weight of defeat sapping the energy from my limbs. I don't know how long I lay there in that office, but soon they had transported me to Bedlam, and this time it was to be for longer than a few hours. Seeing I had given up, they untied me, putting me in a waiting area where I was briefly questioned again on my health and situation. They wrote my responses in a large book, but I don't remember what I said. It was then I learned that several of my closest acquaintances, including Mary, had spoken against my sanity, and that now there was adequate recourse to confine me to the hospital. The attendants and the doctors weren't nearly so pleasant towards me after hearing that. On the other side of a door, I thought I heard Mary speaking to Blanch in a dull voice. No more tears left. I gently called her again, but the result was the same.

Afterwards, they washed my bloodied face and then took me to my cell on the third floor for the first time. I heard the first lunatics greeting me with their screams and their cackles, and over the following days and nights, the foul place began its work on me. My dreams, from that very first night, ceased to be the sanctuary they had become. I began fighting on the Crimean Peninsula, or if I was with Her Majesty then often there would be Russian agents interrupting us as I tried to show her the designs, assailing us, hunting us down, butchering us.

I no longer think there is much more that Bedlam can take from me, but at that time I felt some part of myself being lost with each passing day. The examining doctors badgered me incessantly. Much was made of my use of alcohol and my disease, and of various matters pertaining to my collections of music. They spoke of my disappointment in my *Collection of Ancient Piobireachd*, and of the further disappointments that came with my failing to publish more of my manuscripts. They spoke of my father's death, then of John's. They spoke as if John had been similarly afflicted, which was untrue. They even tried to convince me that Donald had died some years earlier, but this was patently nonsense: I felt I had seen so much of him recently. They were trying to break my spirit.

Mary's testimony was what truly saddened me. Hearing the troubles of my life so starkly described by her was what removed from me my inclination to fight against the incarceration. She told the doctors of my dreams with Her Majesty, and gave details of their obscene nature, even details I had forgotten. I wondered how she knew. Perhaps I was speaking in my sleep, or perhaps I had simply told her about it one drunken night. She told of my supposed violent outbursts in the house and the destruction I was capable of causing when in one of my rages. I wondered who was telling her to tell these falsehoods. She told of how afraid my own bairns were of me. She said much more than that as well – terrible, abhorrent things – of which I only half-remembered.

But now my hand aches. Not much longer to go. Soon I shall have reached the present day.

The Unjust Incarceration, 1854

Angus MacKay: Patient Record 1

Name: Angus MacKay
Age: 42
Admitted: 4th February
Previous Place of Abode: London & The Highlands of Scotland
Occupation: Musician, as Piper to Her Majesty
Married: Yes
Number of Children: 4
Age of youngest Child: 14 Months
Age of first Attack: 42
Duration of existing Attack: A few days
How many previous attacks: ~
Confined in any Lunatic Asylum: No
Supposed cause of Insanity: Disappointment and Drink, Overstudy of Music
Predisposing: Hereditary predisposition
Whether Suicidal: No
Whether dangerous to Others: Yes
Has the patient been of sober habits: No
Degree of Education: Inferior
State of Bodily Health before Insanity commenced: Able, but suffers from syphilis
Mood at the present time: Indifferent
Religious persuasion: Church of Scotland
Relatives similarly affected: Yes
And the degrees of relationship: Brother

1st Medical Certificate

Facts indicating Insanity observed by myself: His having shown me the model of a tube with which he proposed to destroy the Russian Fleet; his violent and incoherent language and behaviour.
Other facts (if any) indicating Insanity communicated to me by others: From his Wife, to the effect of his great violence; and of his many dreams & revelations of an obscene character.

(Signed) G. Pearl
High Street, Windsor

2nd Medical Certificate

Facts indicating Insanity observed by myself: Exalted notions of himself and various delusions and belief that he possesses great property, absurd schematics for war machines, etc.
Other facts (if any) indicating Insanity communicated to me by others: Various facts from his Wife & friends.
(Signed) Gustavus Wm Blanch, M.R.C.
75 Stanley Street, Clarendon Street, Pimlico

Feb 28th – Since he has been a patient at this Hospital, it has been stated that he is a man of most temperate habits and that he has not indulged at all lately in that respect, but the cause of his illness can be traced to anxiety of mind and overstudy, he having made music his ruling thought lately. Endeavouring to set to written notes music adapted for the pipes. When first brought to the hospital he was restrained in a strait waistcoat, but then he could not be admitted from the medical certificates being informal. He was then feverish and complained much of thirst; when he was brought again he appeared much less excited and no restraint was used but the marks of recent ligatures and abrasions were apparent all over his body. After his admission he became very tractable but assumed much self-importance and occupied the whole of his time writing letters containing charges of ill and cruel treatment, addressed to the superior officers of Her Majesty's Household. He gradually became better, and is now almost well, perhaps a little too much disposed to interfere in the affairs of the Ward, and with other Patients. He works in the Garden and is fond of playing the Pipes. He has a secondary syphilitic eruption on his legs, for which he takes Iodide of Potassium.
April 19th – For the last 3 weeks he has been considered quite convalescent, and before that time in most respects he was well, but there appeared occasional evidences of irritability and unpleasantness of temper that indicated yet some

remains of mental disease, now there is perfect placidity in temper and manner and his nearest relatives consider him quite well.

April 29ᵗʰ – He was to have been discharged yesterday but in the night he was noticed to be talking to himself and in the morning at 6 o'clock he spoke to the attendant in a very strange way about God protecting him from all dangers. He then spoke of his discharge and said he would be removed to the Criminal Wing, and after dressing he became very wild in manner, violent in his behaviour, and either talked incoherently or was obstinately silent. He was placed in a padded room.

May 1ˢᵗ – He continues in a most excited state; for a short time he will appear quieter but the improvement is only temporary. He answers no questions, talks rapidly and with much energy in Gaelic, and only with the greatest difficulty can any food or medicine be given him. His bowels are freely open.

May 4ᵗʰ – No improvement, but even greater excitement has been exhibited. He attempts violence with his attendants and is constantly talking but not intelligibly.

May 6ᵗʰ – No improvement or alteration.

May 8ᵗʰ – There is a slight improvement. He seems to know faces he has seen before, and was rather less noisy last night.

May 11ᵗʰ – He is more himself. Yesterday morning he was very violent, struck an attendant with a broom and cut his own hand in breaking a pane of glass.

May 18ᵗʰ – During the day he is now perfectly quiet, rational and well behaved, but at night there is much excitement still, he laughs and sings and talks irrationally of Christ being with him.

June 10ᵗʰ – He has now again become perfectly convalescent and rational, his health is good and he sleeps quietly at night without an anodyne.

July 13ᵗʰ – He continues well.

August 25ᵗʰ – His wife is very anxious to try a change of air for him and as an opportunity occurs to go now to Scotland she is allowed to remove him though his name is not down in the Convalescent Book.

Oct 27ᵗʰ – He came back to the Hospital with his wife and was discharged; having continued quite well since he left the Hospital.

And there you have it. That's all they wrote for what was eight months of my life. I almost want to sit here and laugh when I read it back and see how close I was to being discharged in April, if it weren't for my talking to myself in the night. But who else was I meant to talk to? Who else would be able to make sense of the news I had just heard that day? I needed answers. And as for that attendant, if he hadn't been taunting me in Russian then he might have been spared his knock to the head. With his own broom, I might add! The doctors tried to tell me he was a farm lad from Surrey. Now I truly am laughing.

The news in question was of course concerning that fateful letter Mary brought to me, explaining my being pensioned from Her Majesty's service. At the time I was convinced it was a forgery designed to antagonize me, but even I must admit that by now, it's been too long since I've been able to play for me to expect to return to my position. The queen cannot be protected properly or piped for at breakfast if I am locked up here. No. I no longer imagine I'll return to my place by her side.

"This will mean a change in circumstances for us all," I remember Mary saying, sitting on the chair while I lay in bed. She had become very practical, very efficient. In my cell, she always appeared somewhat strange, dressed in her normal clothes and with her normal way of talking, as though nothing unusual had happened of late. Her heart has always been too pure for this place.

"I've been looking for less expensive houses in Pimlico," she went on, "but if the search turns out nothing then we must consider returning to–"

"Mary, please," I interrupted her. "You have to warn someone. Schackle, or Donald, maybe. Tell Sir James that Blanch is not the man he thinks he is. Her Majesty will be assassinated if you don't. Please."

"Angus."

"Get Donald to tell the duke, Mary." I looked to the ceiling. "O Dhia, why can she not see it?"

"Because it's not there to see," Mary sighed. It was at that moment that I felt her turn in on herself, as exasperated as I was. "You know you're meant to be released soon, but the doctors won't let you until you come to terms with that, Angus. The children want you back. Think of them. Put everything else aside. You've not been of sound mind."

I bit my lip, feeling my arms shake. "So until I see what everyone else assures me is there, I am a man condemned. My own truths are invalid."

"Yes," she said, before standing and walking towards the door. "Yes, that's exactly it."

Well. No wonder I continued the conversation without her into the night; there was so much left to say. It was at breakfast the next day I was informed that my stay had been extended.

It now doesn't even seem like such a dark time; that's the state of things at present. Time still moved back then, drifting along like a snapped branch on a river. In those days, though water and food ran straight through me to the slops as it does now, my general health was such that I was still able to pipe and work in the garden among the other inmates, using skills I had learned from Drummond Castle. At the time, I was thanked by the staff for my involvement in settling small quarrels and disputes among the other patients; I don't know why they have made out that this was unwelcome. The food was reasonable. I assisted in the bread-making and the beer-brewing. I was still allowed whisky, now and then.

My various requests of paper, pens, and ink were also accepted, and thankfully have not been revoked even now. Seeing no need in sketching more designs if no eyes other than mine would see them, I began writing music again, still capable at that time of keeping my mind straight on one tune. I decided to make copies for my friend and former student, Donald Cameron, Piper to the Earl of Seaforth. I would shuffle the papers with satisfaction; make marks on the stave carefully, artfully; wipe ink from my fingers with a small blotting cloth. The music grounded me. I felt almost as though I could watch from outside myself as I worked on that. It was who I was. It was what I knew.

The certificate is correct in saying that I continued to write letters to other officials at the palace, those in the service I hoped I could trust. I had to. I tried to no longer utter my beliefs aloud, given where they had landed me, but inside I knew that even if my freedom was lost, someone had to warn Her Majesty of the danger she was in. I am sure that none of my letters were delivered, however. There were no replies, and the staff always seemed to know about them.

I remember in the garden, I discreetly asked if Mary would deliver them for me once. She replied that she was not allowed to do so, and neither did she wish to. Then she looked at me with such sorrow in her eyes that my heart broke. She simply could not understand the gravity of the dangers facing the royal family, just how deeply these foreign powers had embedded themselves into our establishment. Nobody could, it seemed. When she then warned that if I persisted in this vein, with these "hare-brained schemes," she would recommend I was moved to the criminal wing, that's when I stopped trying to convince even her. That's when I stopped speaking my mind, and began telling the doctors what I knew they wanted to hear. There was no coming back from the criminal wing.

I can honestly say that I wished I believed what they were telling me. I was wrong; I was mad; I was not lucid. Truly. There were days when perhaps I did believe it. But if I took the time to look, I would always find evidence to the contrary, in some forgotten cellar of my mind. To me it was plain as day.

God was the only one who knew my secrets then. I prayed that this was enough.

—

Beloved Scotland – Home Again

The idea that a change of air was what I required was Mary's. She had not yet given up on me, despite it all. I wonder what I would have had to do for that to happen. I suppose bairns are a binding union. With my newfound silence about the Russians and my abiding by a regular routine, over the months of June and July the doctors thought that I was stable enough that they might entertain the idea of my traveling up to Scotland. My physical health was not worsening but neither was it really improving – I was always tired – and Mary argued that a change in climate might be beneficial. By August, after my continued convalescence, the doctors were convinced, and Mary's wish was granted.

Did I share in this wish? Aye, I suppose I did. The thought of heading up to Scotland was an incentive to conduct myself as people wanted me to. Seeing the same walls; speaking with the same people; eating the same meals … Any break from that would be welcome, and there were places in Scotland from my past I wished to see again, and people whose company I craved. I had also started to miss my children dearly over the summer months; this was not something I'd really experienced before when leaving for piping commitments. Of all the things Mary asked of me, her wish that I could be a better father was the one I could most easily agree with. And yet, I'm ashamed to say that over anything – even then I knew it – the reason I wished to be free was so that I could regroup and one day continue my cause, which I would not be able to if trapped in this place.

"You must keep on with your good habits, Mr. MacKay," Dr. Hood stressed, interviewing me one last time before condoning my release. "Maintaining this schedule is what brought you back from the brink. Exercise, take the air, eat plenty of good food. And sleep."

"Aye, doctor. I'll try."

"Your wife tells me you look so much more like yourself when you've been working in the garden. She says this is when she sees her husband."

"Yes. I've felt that."

"Mm. Well, I'm happy to see you go, meaning no offence. I would say be sure to take some pipes with you, but I know you will. Play outside when you can." Dr. Hood rose to shake my hand. "Good luck to you, Mr. MacKay."

"Thank you for everything, Dr. Hood."

I remember stepping out of the entrance and on to Monks Orchard Road, expecting to feel something momentous, a convict tasting liberty once more. But I didn't. It just felt as though I was stepping into a further part of the hospital, some bit I'd not visited before. The morning air was muggy and foul-smelling. I greeted Mary who was awaiting me with a quick kiss before we stepped into the carriage that was to take us directly to King's Cross Station. Her face was haggard and grey, and I'm sure I looked far worse. We spoke little. As the loud and smoky London streets came flooding back into my life, dark thoughts began to thicken in my mind. I closed my eyes, and felt myself weeping behind my eyelids. I was too exhausted to face these worries now.

The children were brought to us at the station by Maggie and though I was dizzied by the swarms of people milling around, the joy I felt at seeing them again went some way to clearing my head, and told me conclusively that I had returned to the real world. Jessie was adorable with her frizzy red hair and her freckles. Wee Angus was walking, being led by John and Margaret either side. I'd never seen him walk before. John was wary of me at first, perhaps remembering some of the furies I'd had while around him, but after watching me pick each of his siblings up in my arms and holding them close, he softened and held out his hands for his turn. Gathering our luggage, we sought the platform for the Great Northern Railway's Scotch Express for Edinburgh, and I breathed a sigh of relief when we boarded and pulled out of the station.

After the commotion of getting there, I fell into a sort of fugue state as the journey began, watching London slip away like one of my nightmares as forests and fields started to trundle past. However, with all the jostling, I must have been grimacing without my noticing it, as before long I heard Jessie ask if I was uncomfortable. I looked down at her. All of the bairns had a funny sort of accent, what with Scottish parents and English friends and teachers.

"Me? Oh, Jessie." I shook my head and put my arm around her, her body seeming frail as a robin's. "Try not to worry about me. It's meant to be the other way around, remember."

She was smart though. As soon as she said that, I realized that sitting was intolerable. I managed to wait for the children to drift off, before I started pacing, moving forward and back in the carriage to relieve the pressure on my sores. This drew a concerned stare from Mary, but I gave her a nod to assure her it was only to ease the pain of my legs. Only after a couple of hours did she seem to relax.

I saw again how much the country was changing with every place we stopped. Signs of industry were everywhere. We arrived at York after seven and a half hours, and as our carriages were already attached to the Edinburgh-bound train, we didn't have to change seats or move our luggage. In the next leg of the journey, I began to recognize more and more of where I was, passing hills and valleys and rivers I had encountered many times before. With this, my anticipation at last started to mount, and perhaps I didn't altogether feel it, but I at least remembered how glad embarking on journeys like this had once made me.

We were all utterly exhausted when we rolled through Edinburgh and into Waverley Station at last. The children were sound asleep, and we had to rouse each of them separately. Stepping off the train, within a few seconds, Jessie had complained of the chill, and Margaret had commented on how much smaller Waverley was than King's Cross.

"Everything is smaller than in London, darling," I said, before making sure Jessie's coat was fastened properly. "Although if you climb those stairs there, you might see a castle on the hill."

This brought them back to life, and the four of them ran off, as quickly as they could carry young Angus. Mary and I were left with the luggage, and she looked at me with a hopeful smile on her weary face.

"You already seem better, Angus," she said. "You say everything's smaller here. Maybe your reasons for worrying are as well."

"Aye. I'm sure you're right."

Hard to recall now, but there were moments on this holiday when Mary was indeed proved right, when I forgot about it all. Fleeting moments, but more than I'd felt in a long time. Moments in which I might never have been Her Majesty's piper at all. And they were a relief. I cannot deny that. It would happen when I'd pass somewhere I used to know so well, or met with one of my old friends again, someone who either hadn't heard or didn't care what had happened to me. They took my mind off of things.

I couldn't really experience this with Mary's family, who came to see us at our rented lodgings in Edinburgh, though they tried to be as welcoming as possible. My wife was so happy to be back amongst them. Seeing this, I felt guilty at having stolen her away for all those years down south, and awkward knowing that although no one had said as much, Mary would have written everything about the past few years in letters to these people. The subject of my health hung there like a Highland cow in the parlor, of which no person spoke, but all noted with distaste. Many times, I would make excuses to go walking, citing my condition, and take the children out and away from them, to some landmark with memories attached.

When word got out that I was in the city, I remember Alex Glen arranged to see me, the bagpipe maker that I had collaborated with on

The Piper's Assistant. I ended up seeing him a few times, which was a fine thing. He always gave me a warm welcome, and made me feel as though nothing had changed since we last knew each other. It was raining the first time we met – of course it was! – but we still walked the short walk from his shop off St. Andrew's Square to St. Giles' Cathedral. On the way back we stopped at the Scott Monument, which though it was about ten years old was still new to me; I'd never had the chance to stop and look at it when in Edinburgh with the queen. I was extremely impressed by the imposing structure, though already it was somewhat blackened from the coal smoke that settled heavily on the city in most weather. The two of us sat on a bench to take advantage of a brief break in the rain. He had aged much, and his hands were battered from years of hard work turning wood and mounting the ivory.

"And are you still finding the time to play, Angus?" Alex asked me. "'Twould be a bitter shame if an artist such as yourself didn't share their gift with the world."

"Aye, I can get the thing going most days," I replied with a small smile. "Not all the time, mind," I added after a moment.

I was grateful when he changed the subject to what whisky he had waiting for us back at the shop. Ah, I liked that place. He would allow me to stay there awhile as he worked. There was something about being amid the debris of a pipe-maker's shop that was comforting. The steady turning of the lathe mixed with the smell of wood, tanned hides, glue, and tar. The bustle of the shop was punctuated with the raspy sounds of reeds being warmed and tuned; but best of all was the sound of the pipes! It was an oasis away from the world outside, and while the people there were mostly strangers, they were happy to see me, something I'd not experienced in a while. They got a few tunes out of me as I sat on the saddler's bench, with them toiling away. Pipers would come and get me to sign copies of my books for them, naming the dates and places that they'd heard me perform, asking me to play them their favorite tune.

Mary was glad to hear about these afternoons when I got back. She thought that perhaps here lay the future of our life. We could move back to Scotland and I could go into the pipe-making trade, and play and write tunes for smaller, more intimate audiences. A normal life, with no higher ambitions than getting the ferrules to shine. Maybe I believed this could come to pass as well. Someday. Mary explained as gently as possible that there was no longer any post tying us to London, or any family; though I still couldn't fathom that brother Donald was no more and hadn't been for ages, no matter how many times she told me. We no longer spoke of it, as my attempts to convince her that I'd spent many an afternoon in his company before Bedlam brought back that same pained, tense look she would give me back in London.

"All that must be done is to sell the house, and then we could be up here for the rest of our lives, among friends," she said. We had this conversation many times and it would always end the same way, with her asking, "What's stopping us?"

But I never really answered her. It did sound nice; if all she wanted was for me to say that it sounded nice then I would have. But I knew there was more to be done than just selling the house. My mission was not complete. I had to communicate what I knew to the right people. Only then could I look to the future. It was easier to subdue these thoughts and divert mine and Mary's attention up north, but always a part of me knew that I was just biding my time, waiting for my health to get better.

Which it was, in fact. When we left Edinburgh to take that cottage near Crieff, I felt some of my old vitality return. My lungs seemed to take more air; my legs seemed to carry me further with each step. Even my sleep seemed to be less troubled, with fewer dreams, and for the first time in a long time, Mary and I began to share a bed again. We would spend the days walking the hills and valleys around Drummond Castle, where I had spent so many good years. The bairns were in heaven, having been deprived of such opportunities for play by being raised in London. Even the Highlands had felt the pull of the modern world, and there were now trains and larger roads with heavier traffic. But still, it was free of the challenges of the city, and with my young family I visited many places I remembered from my youth. After so long, there were few people there I remembered, but I was able to track down my friend Anna, now the mother of six. She had kept track of my career, she said. She didn't mention if she'd heard the latest, for which I was grateful.

I had grand plans for heading up to Inverness next. Since the days of my winning the prize pipe in Edinburgh, the big events had now moved there and were held regularly as part of the annual Northern Meeting. I wanted very much to attend the next one so as to hear the best pipers of the day. My friend Michael MacCarfrae had won the prize the previous year, and I would have liked to hear him one more time. But I was conflicted, and in the end, after much deliberation, I decided not to go. I could not face the Society members who I was sure would focus on my unfortunate circumstances in London. I did not want to risk tarnishing happy memories with bitter ones. I wish I had been braver.

But those unfortunate circumstances in London had not yet been drawn to a conclusion. Despite the improvements to my health in Scotland, and all the good this trip did me, I longed for Her Majesty. Though she still occasionally appeared to me in dreams, she would always be at a distance, and when the time came to return – all too soon, Mary kept saying – I in fact felt ready to go. I was to check in at Bedlam to show my progress. I was stronger and calmer as we made the journey back. Mary's plan was to sell the house as quickly as possible and tie up our affairs, before returning to Scotland for good, even if we would have to live in reduced circumstances. I agreed. I simply had to tie up some affairs of my own.

Bedlam Again

Even in the cab from King's Cross Station to Pimlico, I could feel in the London fog the Russian agents following our every move. So they have been expecting me, I thought. But I was not worried. I was so much more able to fight them now, and I felt my retreat to my homeland had enabled me to see the landscape more clearly, to understand better how my enemies operated. The prey who knows his hunter will always have the upper hand.

I could not leave the house over the next weeks without my every step being marked, and my dreams soon became as vivid as they were before, with Her Majesty by my side as the mother of my children, and God telling me the secrets of the war. I didn't have anything to do with my time – Mary was dealing with selling the house – so to avoid the Russians I decided to remain indoors, for my own safety. At home, I told Mary I thought it best if we slept in separate beds once again, telling her not to worry, that I was just feeling under the weather. I could not have her spying on me when I was unawares. With fresh eyes, I returned to the plans for my submarines, which now were needed by the empire more than ever before.

What ultimately led to my downfall was that I still required the help of Sir James if I was to get my findings into the right hands. He was a knight of the realm, for heaven's sake! I convinced myself that I could help him remedy his previous error in not listening to me, in having his ear bent by that traitor Blanch. Perhaps this was the reason for my downfall: putting my trust in a man purely out of respect for his high station.

I sent him a note, requesting a meeting to settle things, to allow me to apologize. When after a week I received no response, that's when I began sending him some of the more valuable information I had gleaned about the Russians and the war, and eventually I began sketching out new designs for him. I needed to get him to reply, to comprehend the enormity of things. But no matter what, I heard nothing back.

One evening – I read now in the certificate it was November 20, 1854 – I found myself sitting by the fire, drinking. The children had gone to bed upstairs. It felt as though the chair I was in was sinking beneath my weight. I moved the logs with the poker absent-mindedly, watching the orange sparks flying up before disappearing forever. The fire crackled. I imagined putting my hand in amongst the flames, holding it there.

"Angus. Why are you crying?"

I didn't know who was speaking to me then. I knew it was the queen's voice, but I felt so alone in that room that I was sure it couldn't be. Was this a dream? Did it matter? I took another drink.

"Angus, what is it?"

"He hasn't responded to me," I answered eventually.

"Who?"

"Sir James. You are in grave danger, ma'am. And until he responds there is nothing I can do about it."

"He's not responded because she's been making sure those letters aren't sent, Angus."

I forced myself to look up. Mary was standing there in the flickering light, floating like a wraith, her eyes shining yellow like a cat in the nighttime. But it had been the queen that spoke.

"What do you mean, ma'am?"

From her apron, Mary took out a bundle of papers. My notes for Sir James.

"She's not been sending them, Angus."

I started to panic, and felt screams building in my stomach, the anger coursing through me like the flames. "I don't understand."

Mary was crying now as well. Her voice was changing. "I've not been sending them, Angus. I just want to get you back to Scotland. Once we're out of London, all will be better again."

I rose, a terrible fury willing me to strike her, to grab this imposter by the throat. But my legs could not hold me; they would not move as I willed them. It was as though they belonged to someone else. So it was a dream. My legs began convulsing beneath me. I grabbed the chair for support but it fell to the floor and I with it, smashing my bottle and causing a great commotion. The fire blazed upon my face, though I was shuddering as though trapped beneath ice. I heard feet running down the stairs, oaths being sworn, and I tried to lash out with the poker to impale whoever had laid this curse upon me.

Before a blissful darkness saved me.

Angus MacKay: Patient Record 2

Name: Angus MacKay
Age: 43
Admitted: 20th Nov.
Previous Place of Abode: Sussex Street, Pimlico
Occupation: Musician
Married: Yes
Number of Children: 4
Age of youngest Child: 2 Years
Whether the first Attack: Not
Age of first Attack: 42
Duration of existing Attack: 5 days
How many previous attacks: 1
Confined in any Lunatic Asylum: Yes
Where: Bethlem Hospital
When: 1854
And how long: 8 months
Supposed cause of Insanity: Drink, Overstudy
Predisposing: Previous attacks
Whether Suicidal: No
Whether dangerous to Others: Yes

Has the patient been of sober habits: No
Degree of Education: Inferior
State of Bodily Health before Insanity commenced: Able
At the present time: Good
Religious persuasion: Scotch Church
Relatives similarly affected: Yes
And the degrees of relationship: Brother

1ˢᵗ Medical Certificate

Facts indicating Insanity observed by myself: Delusions regarding plots to destroy the Queen and Royal Family.
Other facts (if any) indicating Insanity communicated to me by others: ~

(Signed) James Clarke, Brook Street, London

2ⁿᵈ Medical Certificate

Facts indicating Insanity observed by myself: Delusions as to his having been born much earlier than I imagined or could conceive from his appearance. That he has some knowledge of the causes of the War in the East not revealed to others which he wished to disclose to Sir J. Clarke.
Other facts (if any) indicating Insanity communicated to me by others: I am informed that he has lately had a precursory symptom before the confusion of mind appeared, trembling of the lower extremities which were so affected as to scarcely support him. Immediately after this temporary fit of Paralysis, the delusions & confusion of mind came on & he feels anxious and concerned for the Queen and her family, who were in danger from a conspiracy.

(Signed) James C. Cumming, M.D.
Cadogan Place

Dec 11ᵗʰ – He had been discharged about a month ago having previously been absent in Scotland for two months with his wife, and during this time had shown no symptoms of insanity but a few days ago he called on Sir J. Clarke and in an excited manner began to disclose to him secrets that had been supernaturally made known to him by which the Russian armies could be destroyed and the Queen preserved from threatened assassination. He was calm and rational on his admission but in a day or two broke out into a state of great excitement declaring that England was ruined and that he must at once leave the Hospital to obviate such a disaster; it was found necessary to place him in seclusion on account of the violence of his conduct; he was also abusive at this time; he again became quiet for a few days and then another relapse occurred. There is no question that the delusion is permanent though expression is only occasionally given to it. but this fact only makes him the more dangerous now if he were at large.

1855 January 17th – The outbreaks of excitement and violence become more frequent and his threats he appears determined to carry out if the least opportunity is given him.

March 5th – He is much less excitable than formerly. After he had heard of the death of the Emperor of Russia he declared that he knew it was about to occur and that the fact made his dreams correct.

April 11th – The irritability has to a great degree subsided and he is well behaved and cheerful but not infrequently at night he talks to himself and is noisy.

May 15th – The same state continues.

June 25th – No change.

August 2nd – During the hot weather he is rather more irritable and more noisy at night.

Sept 12th – No improvement.

Nov 3rd – No improvements. Bowels remain open; patient moved to basement.

Dec 17th – No alteration

1856 Feb 2nd – He has become much quieter and more satisfied with his position here, but still he has numerous & dangerous delusions respecting the Queen & Prince Albert.

Feb 15th – The last week he has been suffering from a severe paroxysm of mania with homicidal tendency and it has been necessary to keep several attendants with him constantly during the day.

I believe it is now the February 23, 1855. I have at long last reached the present day. Looking up at the small corner of sky I can see through the window, it is suitably bleak. There is not the slightest chink of blue to be seen through the thick dark clouds. It is cold in here. Freezing, in fact; my breath hangs around me like a fog. There is a dead rat in the corner, staring at me with dull eyes. I gather the smell in here is appalling, judging by the faces of the attendants when they enter.

Homicidal is a strong word to describe the events of last week. True, I cannot really remember the details. But that doesn't sound like me. Why do they always exaggerate? It happened because I stole the certificate from Hood's office. I needed it for my pages, but he wouldn't let me see it when I asked.

"It's about me!" I argued. "Surely I am entitled to a document that concerns me!"

But no, apparently not. So last week when he summoned me to monitor my progress, when he turned to empty his pipe as he always does when he finishes writing, I snatched it and replaced it with a blank sheet, before copying the original in my room. When they found it next day – it was lying on my table; I'd forgotten to hide it – an argument must have ensued. I didn't think I still had it in me to merit the attention of several attendants, but they say a madman has the strength of five sane ones. And a madman with the power of the Lord God on his side ... There is not a Russian in here who is safe.

I don't remember how I arrived in Bedlam this time. It says that I called on Sir James in person again, but I had thought that was a dream. It has been too long. Over a year, as I mentioned. They have started injecting me with something, leaving me in the isolation room for days. This is good. This is when God speaks to me, and tells me the Truth of the World. He is trying to protect the queen while I'm incarcerated, but He has warned me that He needs my help to deliver us from evil. Mary came to tell me a few days ago that she had arranged for me to be moved to a facility in Scotland that she'd found. Groundbreaking work, she said. We were in my cell, and a pinkish light was coming from the window, an odd light.

"And we needn't worry about the £30 annual expenses for board, as the pension covers it."

But before I could answer, Her Majesty was speaking to me through my wife again. Mary went from wearing her common attire to a regal dress before my eyes, and then she became Victoria, wearing nothing at all. We wildly copulated on the throne of England, with me in my morning attire and the sound of my prize dirk banging the arm of the throne. When I looked into her face, that scolding, imperious face, I saw she had grown antlers several feet wide.

I read back to the first of these pages and I cannot imagine having written them at all. This life I have recounted is not my life. Or rather, it is only one of them. I have just remembered a line from a song: "Tog orm mo phìob 'us thèid mi dhachaigh." I'm singing it aloud now as I write. "I take up my pipe, and homewards I go." Again, I sing it, louder. It's been so long since music came to me.

"Shut up with that gibberish, MacKay!"

And there is the verdict of the attendant outside the door. Very friendly. Not quite the applause I'm used to. Well, in any case. The story seems to have finished.

Crunluath a Mach

No. No, I was wrong. There is a little more. I do not wish to continue writing these pages while my sojourn here goes on; there is too much I must do, and this takes too much time and concentration. I only want to note that I have been moved up to the Crichton Royal Institution in Dumfries, and that I feel much better. Mary, I am talking to you now. Thanks to your efforts in moving me here, my strength is gathering once again. It will, I'm sure, take a long time for me to be as able I must be, but I finally feel that I am in a place where I can properly prepare. Tapadh leat. Because of you I shall succeed in my God-given mission. For that, tha goal agam ort.

I have been here in this excellent place for a few months now – it is so hot on this searing summer's day that I am writing naked at my chair – but I shall only relay the day I arrived, back in March.

Oh, I was in a sorry state then, wasn't I? Though Mary and the doctors had let me know on numerous occasions, I didn't know where I was being taken. I had been given powerful medicine for the journey, and I drifted in and out of sleep the entire way. We traveled by coach, then train, then coach, Mary and others helping to carry me at each transfer. I imagine we looked quite the party. I remember thinking that I saw my mother and father on the platform at the railway station in Carlisle – I saw them as plainly as I see the grain of the wood making up this desk – but Mary assured me I was mistaken. I didn't believe her, but smiled nonetheless. I am now used to being alone in most things I know to be true.

By the time we arrived at Crichton, the effects of the medicine had all but worn off, and I recall gazing at these pleasant surroundings in mild surprise. This was not the sort of institution I had been expecting. The building itself was as vast as a palace in the same way as Bedlam, but being surrounded by countryside it seemed far more welcoming, more like a country estate than a lunatic asylum. It seemed the sort of place I might have piped at in my younger days. We had traveled across a great grassy plateau to reach it, and in the grounds themselves were spacious and open, with elegant birch trees lining the neat frosted paths. It was quiet, save for the sound of our carriage, and though it was still quite early in the day, the sun was already going down.

We were greeted at the great doors by an old bearded man called Alex Bruce, the head attendant. He shook my hand, speaking to me not as though I was an inmate but a new friend. We were then shown into a receiving office, where after a short wait, we met the distinguished-looking Dr. Browne. I thought I had the measure of doctors by now, but from the first moment of that interview, this man seemed to be a medical professional who cared more about his patients than any I'd met before. He told Mary and I that he did not believe in corporal chastisement or in treating his patients like animals; he believed compassion and persuasion were the path to the best results. I agreed vigorously.

I was then shown to my room. This time, I was not to be confined to any basement, no. A normal room. A little drafty perhaps, but I'd lived through far worse. It looked almost exactly like the sort of room I would be put up in if I was piping at a castle in the Highlands: plain, but equipped with everything I needed. A bag of my clothes and personal effects were brought to me, though after a brief glance I enquired with Mary as to the whereabouts of my pipes. She told me they were arriving tomorrow. It's only now I realize that they never did.

But it is better here. The air is clean and there is no sound of heavy construction. When I am hungry, the food is good. There are many interesting characters here as well, very interesting indeed. My fellow lunatics. I enjoy some degree of walking about the gardens when I can; I feel each time I do this that I am experiencing the place all for the first time. It's quite peculiar. The staff try hard to engage us in various ways: art, lectures, music, and work in the garden. It helps, aye. I am getting stronger. There are still times when I wake up with blood on my face and terrible ulcers and bruises on my arms and legs, or in a puddle of what seems to be urine, and I still read in the papers things that terrify me. But God has told me what to do, and God is great. When the time comes, I shall make my escape and put an end to this war for good, restoring the empire to its full glory.

This is how I will do it, Mary. On our accompanied walks, I have seen boats traveling down the river towards the sea. I am telling you so you know where I have gone, when the time comes. By boat I will avoid detection. When it rains, the water gets high and it moves fast. I threw a twig in and it went within in a matter of seconds. I shall make it to London swiftly.

Now, that really is enough. Perhaps when the mission is complete I shall add to these pages once again.

Angus MacKay: Crichton Royal Insitution Case Notes

Admitted 1st March, 1856
I Angus MacKay at 43, married and has children, formerly piper to Her Majesty of a "good" disposition, moderate education and respectful and moral deportment.
II The disease is attributed to excessive exertion aggravated by intemperance.
III Though rarely lucid, when so he can recall almost everything,

IV He suffers from Hydrocele for which he has been operated upon three times.

V The patient is affected with mania with delusions.

VI His bodily health is good.

VII This is declared to be the second attack recurring after a lucid interval of three months but paroxysms of acute and most violent mania occur about every three months. It was persistent; it is now non-remittent.

VIII His most prominent delusion is that Her Majesty is his wife and that Prince Albert has defrauded him of his rights.

IX There exists no disposition to suicide.

X His is described as very dangerous during excitement as encouraging persons to approach him and then attempting to injure them chiefly by kicking in the testicles.

XI His hereditary disposition is not known.

XII He sometimes believes his wife embodies Her Majesty.

XIII With the exception of a lucid interval of three months duration he has passed almost two years in Bethlem Hospital.

1st June 1856

For some days subsequent to admission Mr. M was perfectly rational and tranquil. He read the newspapers with avidity as if to supply the gaps produced in his acquaintance with current affairs by repeated attacks of violence. He accompanied the other patients in their perambulations, he even attended a lecture in the Theatre without betraying vestiges of excitement or extravagance except in describing his treatment inst. Likes, when his conversation became exaggerated and vindictive while thus composed the sinciput was observed to be in a state of ulceration; which appeared to be of the syphilitic origin but which not attributed by him to his practice of standing upon his head. The Gov. Pot has, however, prescribed. Irascibility ushered in a paroxysm of mania which with brief intervals of partial composure but no lucidity of intellect his continued during his res; Whence and almost justified the opinion of Dr. Hood that he was the most violent patient in England. He is destructive, degraded, treacherous, noisy incoherent. All articles of furniture are sacrificed and a mattress is generally torn to pieces in a day. His mild declamations refer to persons of rank and to the transmutations into one or another or into himself. To his marriage with Her Majesty and his repudiation of Prince Albert, to the Royal children and the proceedings in the palace. The spirit which dictates these observations is hostile and ferocious while shouting forth his own greatness or wrongs or the crimes of those who have persecuted or deserted him, he spits, utters a hiss after every word or sentence. His utterances are not however confined to these denunciations. He sings, shrieks, hoots in exact imitation of the owl and howls in every conceivable cadence and manner. He is known to drink urine. Nutritious diet and malt liquor have been allowed throughout his illness: and seclusion has been repeatedly resorted to both for oppression and for the protection of the patient and those around. Upon one occasion when his fury presented the highest degree of intensity and when they were observed indications of febrile exacerbation, Garrentim was prescribed, and purgatives have been constantly required until porridge was recommended as an article of diet. He is somewhat palid: but is a powerful and healthy man.

March 21st 1859
This gentleman attempted to escape and had got down as far as Glencaple. There attempting to cross the river Nith he was drowned. There was no improvement in his mental condition over his years here.

Ùrlar

1859

This final entry is penned by myself, Mary MacKay, widow of Angus. I have found these pages on the 6ᵗʰ June, 1859. Michael MacCarfrae, Angus's friend, last week offered to purchase all of the manuscripts Angus left behind. I accepted gladly. I was sorting through all of the sheets and buried in the middle were these pages. I almost wish I had not found them. They have been a trial to read, the last chapters particularly. I feel as though I know less about him than I did before. But now that I have written out Angus's final medical report, I believe I must add something more. I believe I am owed that: the right to finish these pages as they ought to be.

From the Crichton case notes I have just notated, it is safe to assume by now that I am a widow, though my husband's body was never found. For your own sake I hope you are free of this world, Angus. Despite his last entry in these pages, this life no longer brought him any real joy. Though Crichton was better than that other awful institution, Dr. Browne told me that most days Angus was either despondent or on account of hysteria and violence had to be physically restrained in his room, for the safety of patients and staff alike. He could not control his bodily functions. He was in constant physical pain. That was not the man I met all those years ago. Though by the end I struggled not to hate him, I must say that there was not a kinder, more passionate, more intelligent, more handsome man alive than the Angus MacKay I met at that little inn at Biggar. He was fully alive to every nuance of life. But the disease took that man away from me. His became the sort of life it was better off not living. It became that long ago.

They said he told them he was going for a walk, on that day in March. When he sensed the opportunity, he burst into a run. The attendant who was meant to be watching him was little more than a lad. Angus sprinted down the main path to the gate before vaulting the wall. The other staff members in the yard were delayed from giving chase as they had other patients to attend to. Angus knew that, they said. Eventually, a small party was sent out, all assuming he wouldn't get far given his condition. In fact, he made it a few miles south before he took to the river. I imagine he was looking for a boat to steal, but when he saw the attendants were catching up, he chose to plunge into the Nith and swim. Angus always respected the water. His parents had purposefully instilled a fear of it into him, growing up on that island of theirs. Even having lost his mind, I know he wouldn't have taken the decision to wade in lightly. Years earlier, maybe the year we were married, he had prevented his friend Alastair from leaping off a bridge into the river for a dare, after a night of drinking in Inverness. Quite apart from the drop, Angus had warned that the river was shifty, more perilous than it appeared. Witnesses at the hospital said he swam for a short time and then seemed to just go still, floating on his back. No one was willing to risk their lives going after him. They say he then went under slowly, before being carried out of sight. There had been days of heavy rain. The water was moving quick, just as he'd planned. Over the next week they checked both sides of the river for a body. No one found anything. We assume he was carried out to sea.

The younger bairns ask after him, but Jessie and Margaret seem to understand. They were frightened of him, and cried when I said we were to see him. They never knew their real father.

I had wanted to have a proper burial, when the inevitable happened and Angus met an early death. The fact that I cannot pains me deeply. The papers made little of his passing. He had been out of the public eye a couple of years then. The *Annual Registrar* had the longest piece. Angus seemed to like writing out the articles in these pages. I'll do the same.

Angus Mackay, formerly Piper to Her Majesty, has been accidentally drowned in the river Nith, Dumfriesshire. Mackay was of a race of hereditary pipers, who obtained their instruction at the once-celebrated college of the MacCruimins, in the isle of Skye, which has been swept away in the changes produced by the altered state of Gaelic society. He produced a collection of upwards of sixty of those ancient and peculiar pieces of music called "Piobreach," with historical and biographical letter-press, which is a standard work among the military and private professors of the national instrument. He subsequently published a volume of "Reels and Strathspeys," with their respective names both in Gaelic and English, and had a considerable collection of his own composition. He was besides no contemptible versifier of poems from his native tongue.

No mention of his health, which is welcome because my family back home would have been ashamed. After boasting of Angus's accomplishments for all those years, to see his reputation go up in flames was a humiliation for all of us. His claims to be the father of the queen's children reached many of our friends, and we were shunned in some circles and mocked in others. Only in Dumfries did they seem to look at his illness for what it was: an illness. I hope that more come round to this way of thinking. I hope for my own sake as much as anyone's, as I have been warned somewhere in me might lie the same sickness that took him. I pray, but still, this terrifies me.

Angus left us effects worth over £800, a good sum. But with no income any longer and four bairns to feed and house and clothe, we will need every bit of it. That's why I am not sorry to sell any of the musical things Angus left: his manuscripts, his pipes, his chanters, even his Highland costumes, purchased as such expense. I would sell more if there were more to sell. I want to move us back to Edinburgh, away from this small brick row house in Pimlico we've moved to. Jessie doesn't speak to me when I bring this up, not wanting to leave her friends, but it'll be better for them to up there among relatives. But until that comes to pass, we'll have to use our God-given talents and labor to feed ourselves, and trust that the children's education will serve them well.

It was plain to me that Angus would always go far in life, even though when I met him he was struggling to make ends meet. It was the suddenness of his success that overwhelmed him. Sometimes I tell myself that his misdemeanors and infidelity came purely as a result of his illness, but I know that the heights he achieved in his life continued to thrill him until the sickness truly took hold. Working in the royal service was worth leaving Scotland to him. It excited him to rub shoulders with the mighty at court or in clubs, or to play at the magnificent places his duties demanded. It excited him that the thing he excelled at more than anyone was so well-respected. Perhaps he would have neglected myself and the children even if the disease had never caught him. All I can be sure of is that they worked him too hard. He was a performer to them more than a human being, and if he wasn't entertaining them, if he wasn't doing his job, then he wasn't worth much.

I shall tell the children when they're grown of the old Angus, the man full of song and romance; who loved his wife and children and friends dearly; who treated all with respect; who loved his mother tongue. I won't be able to pass on his love of the pipes, for I never loved them myself. Sometimes I liked to tell him I did, but it was a lie. Before I met him, when I heard that sort of music it was always associated with a military display or perhaps a country wedding. It was not the music I really wanted to hear every day. Give me a tune on the pianoforte over the pibrochs so loved by my husband and his family. And Her Majesty, of course. He would be appalled to hear me say this, I wager.

Wee Angus has started crying once more, away in the next room. John has probably stolen something of his again, his new favorite pastime. I should go through and resolve it. I don't know what else to write anyway. I should go.

Farewell, Angus.

Afterword

One of the things that may trouble the reader of this book is deciding where fact ends and fiction begins. The simple rule I made was that I would write what was likely, based on what is known of life at that time, and on the little that has been written about Angus MacKay and his family. The sections describing the visits of Queen Victoria and Prince Albert to Scotland, for example, contain many details taken from newspaper reports and articles of the time, or from the journals of Queen Victoria, as do mentions of events such as building the cairn at Balmoral Castle. I used those reports to relay the facts, while trying to color them through the eyes of Angus MacKay.

It must be reiterated that while every effort was made to piece the true story together, this is a work of fiction. Even setting aside the inevitable guesswork that comes with looking back so many years, the sheer volume of noteworthy events that Angus packed into his brief life was far more than could be feasibly contained within novel form. Much of the writing process involved selecting what events in his life to include, and ensuring that these events worked within the narrative structure of a novel. For this reason, though I have tried to ensure the chronology of events is accurate and that the original medical documents included remained intact, there were occasionally extremely minor alterations made to avoid discrepancies and, in some instances, to correct for what appeared to be errors in the originals. For those interested I would recommend seeking out the relevant materials listed in the "Further Reading" section.

In addition to the medical documents which revealed so much of Angus' life, relationships, interests and struggles, there were many other sources that aided me in writing the book. I used historical maps of Scotland and excellent suggestions from Professor Hugh Cheape to work out the possible paths that John Mackay and family might have taken from Raasay to Perthshire. They might well have turned south at Glenelg for Kinloch Hourn and Glen Quoich, although the Glen Shiel- Cluanie Inn- Glen Garry route is also a possibility; this route is suggested for the narrative because it is the route experienced by the modern traveler. The descriptions of the crossing from Raasay were taken from my own experiences, crossing from Raasay to Skye, and when describing the later travels undertaken by Angus, I tried to research the most likely routes of the time, and so the descriptions of railways, routes and conditions are based on what actually existed in those days. Writing about the family on Raasay came in part from walking on the island around Taigh a' Phìobaire, getting to know the setting of Angus's early home, while also influenced by a series of articles entitled "The Piper's House" by Hugh Cheape and Decker Forrest in *Piping Today*.

With respect to Angus MacKay's health, I believe "A Diagnosis in Retrospect: The Case of Angus MacKay," makes a lot of sense. This paper reviews and summarizes the patient records, and notes: "[t]he two notable features of Angus Mackay's illness – the relapses and remissions, and the mood-congruent delusions – lead to a diagnosis of manic-depressive illness." The conclusion is that the syphilis was likely contracted as a result of the manic-depressive illness. People with this condition tend to seek thrills, including sex, during a manic phase. They can also be extremely productive and high functioning during these phases. The authors of this diagnosis argue there is little evidence for neurosyphilis, which has been the standard assumption regarding Angus's condition.

Fortunately, Angus lived in London in a time that has been richly documented. There are many sources of information about life in the capital and service at court, and about the Great Exhibition. One of the things I found interesting to speculate about was with what other important historical characters Angus might have crossed paths. He was close to the most powerful reigning monarch in Europe, at the center of an expanding empire, and regularly performed for the most powerful people in the country, yet he has barely a reference in any major biography of Queen Victoria. Dressers, footmen, stable boys, secretaries are named (and sometimes shamed), but hardly a mention of Angus, despite Victoria's well-known love of Scotland and the bagpipes. There will always be an element of mystery about a man whose body was never found ...

Any errors, omissions or faults in this book are entirely mine. Sometimes, a great tune will have a note or two wrong. The performer always hopes the listener will enjoy the music nevertheless.

Acknowledgements

Trying to properly acknowledge all the people who contributed is a daunting task. I have been picking away at this novel for about ten years now, and many people have helped along the way.

I am very indebted to Pipe Major Donald MacLeod, M.B.E., Mrs. Winnie MacLeod and their daughters Susan and Fiona. Piping lessons under the stairs at Grainger & Campbell Bagpipe Makers and later at the MacLeod home in Cardonald set me up with a lifetime love of and enthusiasm for pìobaireachd. Knowledge of Angus MacKay's manuscripts – and the chanter that got me started on this – were part of our lessons. Susan and Fiona have been encouraging of many projects over the years and play a strong role in continuing the legacy of their parents' lives in music.

Professor Hugh Cheape, M.B.E., played a major part in getting me started on this project. His writing and presentations regarding the MacKay family and the piping traditions of Raasay have been both helpful and inspirational, while his friendship and reading suggestions have allowed me to really think about Angus MacKay's life in the context of the times.

The National Piping Centre has been generous and helpful in making available documents and records in their collection.

Jim McGillivray was kind enough to read the manuscript several times and provided many excellent suggestions for its improvement.

Andrew Berthoff took time from a very busy life to read and comment on the manuscript, and he too has provided valuable suggestions and encouragement for the project.

A very old relative told my mother in the 1970s that I was likely the first piper in the family since it left South Uist on the ship *Alexander* in 1772. I have received incredible support from my family over the years: my parents encouraged us all to play music. They spent years taking me to lessons, band practice, competitions, and later helped me sustain myself in Scotland and buy a great set of pipes. Thanks to my brother Dr. Alex MacDonald for early suggestions on direction and process, and to all three of my accomplished siblings and their families for a lifetime of interest and support.

The center of my universe is my wife Barbara, and our three children: Eilidh, Ruaridh, and Duncan. Everything I achieve reflects the support and love I receive from them.

At last, I am very grateful to Blackwater Press for their belief in this book, and for the incredible encouragement and support they have provided. This is not wholly the book I envisioned, and that happy fact is due to the excellent work of John Reid, Elizabeth Ford, and Vivien Williams in helping shape and refine the outcome. If you look intently at Eilidh Muldoon's brilliant cover art, you might just hear the pipes above the waves.

Gaelic Glossary

Gaelic was Angus MacKay's first language, and evidence from his writings from Bedlam show he continued to write and presumably think in Gaelic later in life. I felt this was an important point in understanding the man, especially as a Highlander living and working in London at a time when the Gaelic language was in great decline.

Words and phrases

A bheil an t-acras ort? — Are you hungry?
A chuid de Phàrras dha — May he have his place in Paradise
A Thighearna dèan tròcair — Lord have mercy
Athair — father
Bàn — white, fair
bràthair — brother
ceart — right
dithis — pair
Cèilidh — a dance or party with music and story sharing
Chan eil dragh orm — I don't care
a charaid — Dear
mo chreach — Oh my God
mo chridhe — my heart
Daor — Dear, as in a letter
Dia uile-chumhachdach — God Almighty
Duine gòrach — Silly man
Dùn Cana — Dùn is fort; name of a hill on Raasay
falbh 's tarraing — Fuck you/fuck off
Gun — without
Gun taing — no thanks
Ìlich — People from Islay
Leis na h-uile a tha naomh — With all that is holy
M'athair — my father

Mac an donais — bastard, son of a bitch
màsan — asses
màthair — Mother
m'eun beag — My small bird
mo bhràithrean — my brothers
Mo ghaol uile — All my love
mo ghràidh — my love
mòr — large
m'obair — my work
Na gabh tron doras sin — Don't go through the door
O chan eil — Oh no
O Dhia — Oh God
Oighre — Eyre
Òg — young
pìob mhòr — Great pipe, big pipe
Ratharsair — Raasay
Riatach sealbach — lucky bastard
Seas — Stand up
Sgreamhail — Horrible
mo shlàinte — my health
Slàinte mhath — cheers
An Taigh Mòr — the big house
Taigh a' Phìobaire — House of the piper
Taing do Dhia airson na pìoba — Thank God for the pipes
Tapadh leat — Thank you
Tha gaol agam ort — I love you
Tìoraidh — cheerio

Musical terms and titles

Canntaireachd — syllables used for learning pìobairaechd via singing
Crunluath — variation
Cumha nam Bràithrean — The Brothers' Lament
Deuchainn Ghleus — trying the reed

Fàilte a' Phrionnsa — The Prince's Salute
Feadan — Chanter
Gun tugadh crodh Chailein dhomh bainn' air an fhraoch — May Colin's cattle give me milk on the heather
Is fhada mar seo tha sinn — Too long in this condition
Leamluath — Grip Movement, a variation of a pìobaireachd
Tog orm mo phìob 'us thèid mi dhachaigh. — I take up my pipes and homeward I go
Rìgh nam Port — The King of Tunes
Ruidhle an t-sìthein — The Reel of the Fairy Knoll
Siubhal — Walking movement
Taorluath — Embellishment, a variation of a pìobaireachd
Fhuair mi pòg o làimh an Rìgh. — I had a kiss of the king's hand
Ùrlar — theme

Names

Proper names in Gaelic take the vocative case when someone is addressing another person by name, so Aonghas becomes Aonghais if his parents or siblings are speaking directly to him, and Dòmhnall becomes a Dhòmhnaill.

Aonghas — Angus
Catrìona — Katherine
Ciorstaidh — Cursty
Dòmhnall — Donald
Fionnlagh — Finlay
Iain — John
MacAoidh — MacKay
MacMhuirich — MacMurray (Currie)
Màiri — Mary
Mairearad — Margaret
Ruairidh — Roderick

Song on the Good Points of a Highland cow

Bheir mi ho air m'urrainn ho,
Bheir mi ho air m'urrainn fhèin,
Bheir mi ho air m'urrainn ho,
Thogainn fonn 's gun ceannaichinn sprèidh

I'll make it, ho, on my ability, ho
I'll make it, ho, on my very own ability, ho
I'll make it, ho, on my ability, ho
Would raise a tune and buy cattle

Further Reading

Alderidge, Patricia. *Bethlem and Maudsley Gazette*, Vol. 30, No. 1, 1982. Reprinted in Piping Times, vol. 61, no. 1, 29-37.

Bennett, Margaret. *Scottish Customs from the Cradle to the Grave*. Edinburgh: Polygon, 1992.

Bigelow, Henry. "Notes from Clinical Lectures on Surgery," Boston: David Clapp, 1851. http://resource.nlm.nih.gov/101164373

Braithwaite, W., ed. *The Retrospect of Practical Medicine and Surgery*. New York: Daniel Adee, 1850.Campbell, Archibald. "The History and Art of Angus MacKay," *Piping Times*, vol. 61, no, 10, 8-10; no. 11, 8-19; no. 12, 5-6.

Campsie, Alistair Keith. *The MacCrimmon Legend: The Madness of Angus MacKay*. Edinburgh: Canongate Publishing Limited 1980.

Campbell, Archibald. "The History and Art of Angus MacKay," *Piping Times*, 1954, reprinted vol. 61 (2009), no. 10, 8-10; no. 11, 8-19; no. 12, 5-6.

Campbell, Jeannie. *Highland Bagpipe Makers*. Edinburgh: Magnus Orr Publishing, 2001.

Campbell, Jeannie. "What happened to Angus MacKay's Family?" *Bagpipe News*. June 2020. https://bagpipe.news/2020/06/21/what-happened-to-angus-mackays-family/

Cannon, Roderick. *The Highland Bagpipe and its Music*. Edinburgh: John Donald Publishers, 1988.

Cheape, Hugh. "Song on the Good Points of a Highland Cow," *Review of Scottish Culture*, 23 (2011): 141-144.

Cheape, Hugh. "The Pipe of fluent chanters," *Piping Today*, 63 (April-May 2013): 34-40.

Cheape, Hugh. "The Piping Heritage of John MacKay," Paper presented at The Piobaireachd Society, as part of Piping Live! The Glasgow International Piping Festival, Glasgow, August, 2008.

Cheape, Hugh and Decker Forrest. "The Piper's House," *Piping Today*, 49 (March 2013): 14-19; 50 (June 2013): 14-19; 51 (July 2013): 14-19.

"Competition of Pipers at Inverness." *The Caledonian Mercury*, October 12, 1839.

"Deaths." *The Annual Register or A View of the History and Politics of the Year 1859*, London: J.G. & F. Rivington, 1860, p. 456.

Dickson, John. "The Neglected Teaching Power of Public Lunatic Asylums," *British Medical Journal*, 1, no. 68 (1858): 320-321.

Donaldson, William. *The Highland Pipe and Scottish Society*, 1750-1950. East Linton: Tuckwell Press, 2000.

Donaldson, William. "MacKay, Angus (1813–1859), collector and editor of highland bagpipe music." *Oxford Dictionary of National Biography*. 23 Sep. 2004; Accessed 24 Jun. 2021. https://doi.org/10.1093/ref:odnb/55422

Donaldson, William. *Pipers*. Edinburgh: Birlinn Limited, 2005.

Flanders, Judith. *The Victorian City: Everyday Life in Dickens' London*. London: Atlantic Books, 2012.

Gibson, John. *Old and New World Highland Bagpiping*. Montreal and Kingston: McGill-Queen's University Press, 2002.

Gibson, John. *Traditional Gaelic Bagpiping*, 1745-1945. Montreal and Kingston: McGill-Queen's University Press, 1998.

"Grand National Fete." *Morning Advertiser*, London: June 16, 1849.

Grant, I. F. *Highland Folkways*. London: Routledge, 1961.

Gwynne, Bob. *The Flying Scotsman: The Train, The Locomotive, The Legend*. Oxford: Shire Publications Ltd., 2010.

Haldane, A.R.B. *The Drove Roads of Scotland*. Edinburgh: Birlinn Limited, 2006.

"Her Majesty's Piper." *The Royal Leamington SPA Courier and Warwickshire Standard*. June 24, 1843.

"The History and Antiquity of the Bagpipe." *The Liverpool Mercury*, March 18, 1851.

Hubbard, Kate. *Serving Victoria: Life in the Royal Household*. New York: Harper Collins Books, 2013.

Hudson, Roger. *London: Portrait of a City*. The Folio Society, 1998.

Hudson, Roger. *Travels of a Victorian Photographer*. The Folio Society, 2001.

Johnson, Samuel and James Boswell. *Journey to the Western Islands of Scotland and Journal of a Tour to the Hebrides*. Ed. R. W. Chapman. Oxford: Oxford University Press, 1970.

Lawrence, Mr. "Memorandum on the Sanitary Conditions of Bethlem Hospital and the City House of Occupations." *The Sessional Papers of the House of Lords*, 1854-55, 163-166.

Logan, James. *McIan's Highlanders at Home*. Glasgow: David Bryce and Son, 1843.

Logan, James. *The Scottish Gael*, vol. II. London: Smith, Elder & Co., 1831.

MacDonald, Donald. *A Collection of Ancient Martial Music of Caledonia, Called Piobaireachd*. Edinburgh: Donald MacDonald, 1822.

MacDonald, Joseph. *A Compleat Theory of the Scots Highland Bagpipe*. Edinburgh: Patrick MacDonald, 1803.

MacInnes, Iain I. "The Highland Bagpipe: The Impact of the Highland Societies of London and Scotland, 1781-1844." M.Litt. thesis. University of Edinburgh, 1988.

MacKay, Angus. *A Collection of Ancient Piobaireachd or Highland Pipe Music*. Aberdeen: Logan and Company, 1838.

MacKay, Angus. Manuscripts. National Library of Scotland [NLS], MS 3753-6, 3744.

MacNeill, Seumas. "Angus MacKay," Paper presented at The Piobaireachd Society Conference, The Royal Hotel, Bridge of Allan, 1994.

McWhorter, J.H., E. S. Guy, J. A. Kahn, and H. C. Haynes. "A Diagnosis in Retrospect: The Case of Angus Mackay." *Scottish Medical Journal*, 31, no. 2 (April 1986): 118-119.

Mitchell, Joseph. *Reminiscences of My Life in The Highlands*, vol. 2. London: The author, 1884.

Mitchell, Sally, ed. *Victorian Britain: An Encyclopedia*. New York: Garland Publishing, Inc., 1988.

Moffat, Alistair. *The Highland Clans*. New York: Thames & Hudson, 2010.

Morrison, Ronald. "A Voice from Bedlam: The Secret Diary of Angus MacKay, The Queen's Piper." *Piping Times* 61, no. 9 (June 2009): 13-21.

North, Charles Niven McIntyre. *The Book of the Club of True Highlanders: A Record of the*

Dress, Arms, Customs, Arts and Science of the Highlanders. 1880.
Picard, Liza. "The Great Exhibition." The British Library. October 14, 2009.
http://www.bl.uk/victorian-britain/articles/the-great-exhibition

Rappaport, Helen. *Queen Victoria: A Biographical Companion*. Santa Barbara: ABC-CLIO Inc., 2003.

Ross, Elizabeth Jane. *Original Highland Airs Collected in Raasay in 1812*. Edited by Peter Cooke, Morag MacLeod and Colm Ó Baoill. Glasgow: The Musica Scotica Trust, 2016.

"Royal Caledonian Asylum." *The Caledonian Mercury*, June 22, 1848.

"The Scottish Hospital." *The Reformers' Gazette*, June 15, 1850.

Shaw, Margaret Fay. *Folksongs and Folk Lore of South Uist*. Reprinted 2nd ed. Edinbugh: Birlinn Limited, 2014.

Smith, Mary. "State of Mind," in *Dumfries and Galloway Life*, (February 2010): 22-25, 27, 29.

Syme, James. "On Hydrocele and Spermatocele." *The Retrospect of Practical Medicine & Surgery*, edited by W. Braithwaite. Vol. XX1. New York: Daniel Adde Publishers, 1850.

Tyrrell, Alex, "The Queen's 'Little Trip': The Royal Visit to Scotland in 1842." *The Scottish Historical Review*, LXXXII, no. 213 (April 2003): 47-73.

Wallace, Robert. "Specialist Treatment at Crichton Royal Hospital." *Piping Times* 62, no. 1 (October 2009):37-40.

Ward Lock, *Ward Lock's Complete Guide to Scotland*. London: Ward Lock and Co., [1950].

Werner, Alex and Tony Williams. *Dickens's Victorian London*. London: Ebury Press, 2011.

Winchester, Simon. *The Professor and the Madman*. New York: HarperCollins Publishers, 1998.

Online databases:

Alt Pibroch Club: Musical Materials. www.altpibroch.com/sources/

Queen Victoria's Journals. The Royal Archives. http://queenvictoriasjournals.org

Records of Crichton Royal Hospital. The Wellcome Library. www.wellcomelibrary.org